RUN FOR YOUR LIES

by A.A. Abbott

Copyright © 2024 A.A. Abbott

This novel is entirely a work of fiction. All persons and incidents portrayed in the book are a product of the author's imagination. Some locations in the book exist but the homes and workplaces described are fictional. Any resemblance to actual persons, living or dead, or real events, is entirely coincidental.

A.A. Abbott asserts the moral right to be identified as the author of this work.

Edited by Katharine D'Souza Editorial Services.

Cover design by The Cover Collection.

Published by Perfect City Press.

This book was written by a British writer in British English.

PAPERBACK EDITION

ISBN 978-1-913395-15-5

A FEW WORDS OF THANKS

Thanks to my editor, Katharine D'Souza, and everyone else who helped make this book great, especially Alice Dent, Andrea Neal, Callie Hill, Colin Ward, David Wake, David Ward, Elizabeth Hill, Jill Griffin, Jo Ullah, Katherine Evans, Marie Wright, Nicki Collins, Nigel Howl, Nigel Messenger, Rod Griffiths Suzanne H Ferris, Suzanne McConaghy and Tom Blenkinsop.

A.A. Abbott
England, November 2024

Contents

Chapter 1

June 1992

He struggled to lift the body. That surprised him. The boy had looked all skin and bone. Strong for a thirteen-year-old, though. Quite a scrapper. He hadn't expected that either, and it had led to this mess. Who, outside the military, ever plans to kill someone? If only the kid hadn't fought back.

That shouldn't have happened. The lad had smoked an entire joint, inhaling greedily, on top of three cans of Breaker. It had been enough to secure compliance from the others. Perhaps this one was already addicted to drink and drugs. They would have bounced off him.

He should have listened to the silly cow. Hadn't she said the kid had a flaky home life, a father in and out of prison? Why, the youth would have grown up to become a petty criminal. Not now: a ton of misery and government money saved in the space of five minutes.

He'd done the world a favour.

Good luck explaining that to the police.

Dropping the corpse with a thud, he sighed. Should he chop it up? He had to get it into his car, parked on the street outside, and a few bags wouldn't attract attention. Then again, however carefully he cleaned (and cleaning was not his forte; he paid Cynthia for that), traces of blood would remain in the apartment. If the boys in blue came sniffing, their forensic guys would hit the jackpot. Besides, he wasn't a butcher. He had no idea of the best ways to cut bone and sinew. And he had a work deadline to meet. He should focus on that.

It made sense to wait for darkness, anyway. Past sundown, it would be quieter. Easier to hide. Cooler. He'd worked up enough of a sweat in this June heat.

Tonight, he'd do it. Late, after the witching hour, at dead of night. He chuckled at his wit. A strategy formed: he'd go out this evening to one of the DIY places and buy a trolley or wheelbarrow. Then, in the slow hours of morning, he'd cover the stiff with plastic sheeting and trundle it out to his car. He'd take a short trip to the centre of Bristol. To the harbour.

The Canon's Marsh car park lay right at the water's edge. But wasn't it too near the cinema? When the screens dimmed, folk still hung around:

drunks, lovers, rough sleepers. No, he'd stop further out, by one of the derelict wharves. Only rats for company. No human eyes to spy on him.

A quick push.

Job done.

Tenderly, he touched a mottled cheek. Already cooling, it remained soft and downy. Closing his eyes, he caressed the peachy skin and tried to imagine that the last hour had never happened. Because it was such a shame that throttling a person spoiled their looks. The boy had been so pretty.

Chapter 2

September 2023

Juliet

A loud crash woke her. A dead weight trapped her lower legs. A scream choked in her throat.

She heard ragged rasps of breath.

They were her own.

Juliet's eyes adjusted slowly to the dim light. She remembered. This wasn't the dormitory at the farmhouse, that spartan place where she was never alone. The bed was in Greg's flat, where she'd arrived late last night.

She saw faded wallpaper, piles of boxes and clothes. Something had slipped off a heap and pinned her to the bed. She wriggled free. It fell to the floor with a dull thud.

Her tension eased when she saw it was only her suitcase. Maybe she shouldn't have balanced it on a tower of objects, but there was no space elsewhere. Now she'd have to climb over it to get to the door.

She hadn't known her brother was a hoarder. She hadn't known he'd been divorced. She hadn't known he was dead.

A fuzzy image of a young man remained frozen in her mind. Older than Juliet by a year, Greg shared the same thick dark hair, clear blue eyes and sense of ambition. While she'd been a teacher, he'd just started a job in IT when the family cut her off. That had been over thirty years ago. His life since was a mystery. And now she'd inherited his heavily mortgaged flat.

The call from his solicitor took her unawares. When Sister Anya summoned her to the phone, Juliet had been picking strawberries in a hot polytunnel. Sweating, fifty-six-year-old back aching, she'd expected another translation project. They still brought in money for the cult, although less since potential clients began consulting Google instead.

Hugh Wimbush had blindsided her. He was sorry for her loss. However, he hoped the modest estate might soften the blow.

"What loss…?" she'd asked.

She learned Greg had died suddenly of a heart attack. His will left everything to his wife, but the bequest failed because the couple had divorced. The law placed Juliet next in line.

Hugh hadn't lied about the modesty of the estate. Greg's apartment was basic: a lounge, bedroom, bathroom and kitchen, and his in name only. He'd borrowed heavily to buy it, and the bank expected to be repaid.

Unnervingly, a sweet, rotten stench permeated the property. It must be the drains. She noticed the odour peaked near the sage-green bath. Up close, everything else smelled of dust. The flat's contents had lain untouched for months. They were mostly junk, perhaps items Greg had salvaged from the marriage. Marie must have cleaned him out of valuables in the divorce. Hugh volunteered nothing about the split, and Juliet didn't ask.

Was she sorry for her loss, even? Greg had been dead to her for a long time.

Through the fog of sleep, Juliet tried to think fondly of him. Happy memories must have drawn him here. Once, a sweetshop had occupied the ground floor of this apartment block in Bristol. Although no trace remained, she was sure their grandmother had brought them along as children. They'd bought penny chews and blackjacks, treats they didn't disclose to their parents. She supposed lack of money had caused them to be so strict. It had been a happy childhood, though, unlike the tsunami of pain that followed.

No point dwelling on that. Joints aching, she shifted in the bed. The soft mattress wobbled. It was difficult to get comfortable. Still, snuggling under the duvet, she willed herself back to sleep.

The buzz of a drill brought her to the brink of wakefulness again. A whiff of fried bacon hit her nostrils. Juliet sniffed the air. After so long on a vegetarian diet, it triggered a wave of nostalgia.

The aroma lingered. She savoured it. Dust caught in her nose, and she sneezed, eyes snapping open.

Wincing at her creaking knees, she crouched on the bed to peer out of the window. While the cityscape was magnificent, a sweep of rooftops down the Avon Gorge and beyond to south Bristol, she focused on the car park immediately below. Two workmen lounged against a van, munching doorstep sandwiches and smoking. It was a feat of multi-tasking she had only previously observed in prison.

One of them glowered under his hard hat. "Where's Brooklyn?" he demanded, his angry voice clearly audible.

The other shrugged. "He's late. Apprentices, ennit?"

So Brooklyn was a person rather than a place. The first man muttered a string of curses before disappearing from view, his colleague following him inside. They must be working in the former sweetshop. It had been converted into the flat below this one.

The delicious smell faded. She'd been right about its source: the draughty, ill-fitting windows. The apartments had been built in the middle of the last century, when the Victorian houses of Aldworth Terrace were thought no better than slums. A couple at the end of the row had been pulled down and replaced with these flats. It would have been seen as progress. Yet this property was hardly an improvement, with its thin internal walls and shoddy finish. Sounds would carry through the building. She must be careful.

At least no-one would spy on her innermost thoughts.

They couldn't earlier either, not in the cult where she'd spent decades, nor the two years in prison which preceded it. She'd told them she believed in God. They'd taken her at her word until Anya arrived from the mother house in Germany, a new broom sweeping clean.

Perhaps it had been true when she'd been released from jail into a hostile world. The cult offered a safe space where she wouldn't be judged. While it took only twelve people on a jury to find her guilty, millions more agreed with them. Lurid newspaper headlines had seen to that.

If God really existed, he wouldn't have let it happen. He wouldn't have turned her loved ones against her. He wouldn't have taken the baby away.

Chapter 3

September 2023

Brooklyn

It had rained overnight, heavy drops drumming on the metal roof. Brooklyn loved that small silver van. It told the world he was a professional. He not only had a driver's licence, but he was a workman. Yet he wouldn't have expected a dog to sleep in the vehicle, much less Vix and himself. She claimed she hadn't dozed at all. He knew different. As he lay awake in the small hours, he'd heard her snore.

Brooklyn glanced across at her, tiny and blonde, scrunched up in his passenger seat. With her eyes closed and face at rest, his sister seemed younger than her fourteen years. She'd drifted off again. Lucky her.

He would have welcomed oblivion. No matter how his brain churned, it wouldn't give him a solution. But he must find one. He was nineteen and an adult, the head of the family now. His parents had checked out years ago and his foster carer was gone. Whether he felt ready or not, the responsibility was his.

At least he had a plan for the next ten hours. He would go to work as usual and Vix would attend school. He must take her there, crawling along rain-slick roads. His brain barely functioned, unable to process the events of the night before. He watched, gritty-eyed and slack-jawed, as the cars ahead of him all indicated left. Only at the last moment did Brooklyn realise why. The main road had flooded. He followed the impromptu diversion, his van bucking as it swerved.

Vix woke up. "What was that?" Her teeth chattered.

"I'm taking you to school. That's why you're wearing a uniform, remember?"

She began to cry. "Do I have to? I'm so tired. It was cold. I swear a bag of spanners dug into my back."

It might have. He didn't keep the van especially tidy, although he could always find his tools.

"Where else would you go?" he asked. "Unless you'd rather I took you home."

Her face, already pale, lost all its colour. "No."

Brooklyn doubted she'd ever go back. But where would they sleep instead? Along with what happened last night, he tried to forget it for now. They'd have to deal with the problem this evening.

He drove into the car park of the flats across the road from the school, its low rise brick campus reminding him of happy times. Brooklyn had enjoyed his five years there, despite failing to get more than a couple of low grade GCSEs. Vix would do much better. One day, way into the future, she would have a nursing degree. It was what she dreamed of. Nanna Lizzie said Vix was a brainbox and could do anything she set her mind to.

Nanna Lizzie approved of Brooklyn's career choice too. If carpentry was good enough for Jesus, it was good enough for him, she said.

He missed her already.

"You'd better go," he said to Vix. "I'll pick you up tonight."

She nodded. They'd talked about it. She couldn't take the bus with her friends anymore, seeing them alight at the same stops and walk along the same streets to the same families they'd left this morning. Everything had changed.

She wiped her tears on the sleeve of her blazer, then left the van without saying more. Before crossing the road, she looked back, features pinched and eyes red. He hoped the teachers wouldn't notice. They didn't need awkward questions.

When she joined the melee at the school gate, Brooklyn fired up the engine. He punched the words 'Aldworth Terrace' into his phone. It turned out to be a road near the centre of Bristol, in Clifton, where the millionaires lived. Businessmen, lottery winners, drug dealers. It was typical of Simon Heath to be working on a project there. Brooklyn's boss always followed the money.

He was late. With no time to stop for food, Brooklyn had to ignore his hunger pangs. To his relief, the route avoided the city's clean air zone. His van was too old to be exempt, and Simon wouldn't pay the charge if you were just commuting to work. He wouldn't pay parking fines either. Brooklyn's delight at finding a space in Aldworth Terrace turned to alarm when he saw it was for residents only. Luckily, a lane beside the flats led to a car park at the back. Simon's Mercedes and one of his Transits were already there. Brooklyn left his Astra van next to them.

Clover House was a square brown brick block of flats, four storeys high and newer than the properties Simon usually renovated. It loomed over the terraced houses nearby. Brooklyn walked to the front of the building, where he saw a lobby behind a glass door. It was locked. He squinted at the keypad beside it, making out the numbers 1 to 12 on a column of buttons. A glass circle above was probably a camera. There was no Flat A, the address he'd been given.

He pressed the button marked 1.

Nothing happened.

A twenty-something man in a suit approached the lobby door from the other side, pressing something on the wall to open it and dashing past Brooklyn.

"Hang on," Brooklyn said.

The man, briefcase in hand, stopped. "What's up, mate?"

"Um, do you know where Flat A is?" Brooklyn asked.

"There. The old shop."

Brooklyn followed the line of his finger. Flat A, it turned out, had its own door onto the street. There was a bell too. As his index finger reached for it, his phone rang. Simon Heath's name flashed on the screen.

"Where are you?" his boss asked.

"Um, at the front?"

"Come round the back."

As Brooklyn returned via the lane, Simon emerged from a door at the rear. A whiff of expensive aftershave clung to him. The personalised Merc, designer clothes and huge house in Westbury-on-Trym: Brooklyn's gaffer had it all, and he believed in flaunting it. Today, he wore one of the tailored suits he donned for meetings with clients. Incongruously, a hard hat hid his greying hair.

Simon tapped his smartwatch. "What time do you call this?"

Brooklyn couldn't help himself. "Why the hat, boss? I thought we were just finishing off."

The older man scowled. "You'll see. I asked you a question, lad."

Brooklyn shifted from foot to foot. "Nine o'clock?" he hazarded.

"Right. And we start at eight." Simon sniffed. "You smell ripe, too. Suppose we'd had a client onsite? It's not good enough. I installed a shower for your foster carer, and you should use it."

"You put in Nanna Lizzie's shower?" Brooklyn coughed, guilt choking him as he spoke her name.

"Twenty years ago, when I did smaller jobs." A grin briefly cheered up Simon's face. "A Mira. Should still be doing Liz proud. Anyway, no excuses. I'm telling the office to dock an hour's wages, and you're lucky I'm not making it two."

"Okay." Brooklyn couldn't afford to lose the money, but it didn't pay to argue.

"Well, come on then, let's get down to work." Simon barged back through the door, letting it swing so that Brooklyn caught it just in time.

He followed Simon into a kitchen smelling of paint and wood shavings, footsteps echoing on the herringbone tiles. Everything screamed of newness: the black gloss units, polished granite worktops and island in the centre.

"Looks nice, boss," he said.

Simon's expression grew darker. "You think so, lad? The wall units are upside down. You and Ricky are going to rip out and replace."

As if he didn't have enough problems. Ricky Tamm was easily his least favourite colleague, the laziest member of Simon's team. Unfortunately, he was also Simon's cousin. Brooklyn covered his discomfort with a whistle. "That's a big job."

"You're telling me." Simon's lips met in a grim line. "And there's more."

He led Brooklyn through to a lounge dominated by French doors to a garden, thick with weeds. Beyond its walls, it was just possible to make out Bristol City's floodlights in the distance.

Brooklyn gagged. A mouldy odour dominated over the fresh paint in this room.

"Don't like the view?" Simon asked. "Can't say I blame you, with the Robins in sight. Clock the ceiling, though. Or lack of it."

"Oh." Brooklyn's gaze flicked to the gaping hole in the ceiling and a pile of rubble on the laminate floor.

"Yeah, a leak from the flat upstairs," Simon said. "Must have happened over the weekend. Ricky checked the place over on Friday."

As if on cue, a door slammed. They were joined by a short, baby-faced man in paint-stained overalls.

Ricky pointed to his yellow plastic hat. "Get yours on too, Brook. 'Er bath'll crash through any minute." He grinned at Simon. "Nice avocado suite, she has. Older'n you, even."

"It's a she, is it?" Simon asked. "What does she say?"

Ricky pulled a face. "Denies responsibility. Happy to chat, though. Just got out the shower." He licked his lips. "Nice legs for an old bird. Catch 'er now, you might be in there."

"I don't have time for this."

"I thought you always had time…" Ricky backtracked. "Sorry, I forgot you likes 'em young."

15

"I'll see her later. She needs to fix it. May be some work for us there, depending on her insurer." Simon glanced across at two alcoves at the back of the room. "Make yourself useful, Ricky. You and Brooklyn can fit oak bookshelves over there. Start on that, then the kitchen."

"Where's the wood?"

"You'll have to buy it. Dark oak, mind. Stick it on the account and make sure the Binkster doesn't rip me off. That's all for now. I'm putting off the rest until the ceiling's repaired."

"What do you want us to do about that?" Ricky asked.

"Leave it. I'll call the client." Simon's watch buzzed. "Look, I've got a meeting to go to. See you later, yeah?"

"Keys," Ricky said.

Simon reached into his pocket for the biggest key ring Brooklyn had ever seen, festooned with twenty or thirty slivers of jingling metal. He peeled off three for Ricky. "I want them back tonight," he warned.

Ricky didn't complain, simply making a rude gesture towards Simon's back as the gaffer returned outside. He relaxed once Simon had left. "Make some tea, will you," he commanded.

Brooklyn returned to the car park and rummaged in the works van, one of Simon's white Transits. On its back and sides, the business name HEATH HOUSE RESTORATION was picked out in black letters, along with Simon's phone number and website. Like all his vans, it contained a beverage kit in a cardboard box. Brooklyn brought this into the pristine kitchen, unpacking an electric kettle, melamine mugs, teaspoons, tea bags, instant coffee, a bag of sugar and sachets of UHT milk. It turned out that he didn't need the kettle. A sleek chrome kitchen tap produced boiling water at the touch of a button. Although they didn't have a fancy one like that at home, Simon frequently installed them for clients. You want the kitchen to have the wow factor, Simon would say.

He tipped five sugars into his own mug, grateful for the first calories of the day. Ricky had two spoonfuls, an extra tea bag and a mere splash of milk. They'd worked together often enough for Brooklyn to make it on autopilot.

"Perfect," Ricky announced, taking a swig. "How about a guided tour?"

The apartment was U-shaped, filling all the ground floor except the lobby and central stairwell. Bedrooms and bathrooms ran down one side, the kitchen and lounge sat at the back, and another large living room fronted onto Aldworth Terrace.

16

"Look at this." Ricky pointed to the whirlpool bath in the master bedroom's ensuite. "I fitted that. Cutting the marble tiles was a game. Solid as a rock, they were."

Simon wouldn't trust an apprentice with tiles, especially marble. Ricky was showing off again. He liked to boast about his certificates too, because he had them all: building, plumbing and electrics as well as carpentry. Ricky never admitted where he'd studied, though. Nanna Lizzie said it was in prison, and Ricky only had a job with Simon because his wife had begged for it.

Nevertheless, the older man's workmanship was superb. "Looks amazing," Brooklyn acknowledged. "But why a Jacuzzi? A shower isn't good enough?"

"Yeah, right. Client insisted. It's all high end. Can you believe what the paint was called? Magic Mushroom." Ricky sniggered.

Magic mushrooms meant something else to Brooklyn, and evidently to Ricky as well.

"Sludge colour," Brooklyn said. He pictured Nanna Lizzie's bungalow, a jumble of gaudy flower prints which matched neither each other nor the artwork on the walls. Pictures he and Vix had drawn at primary school were still pinned up. A lump lodged in his throat, and he choked on a mouthful of tea.

Ricky misunderstood. "I can't stand it either, but it's trendy. Leanne designed it."

"Simon's wife?"

"Yeah, that's 'er," Ricky said. "A property presentation consultant, she calls 'erself. Posh title, big bills. Even so, Simon reckons the guy will make a fortune. Bought it cheap at auction, dinnee? It was an old shop with half a dozen students packed in. He tried to get planning for a wine bar."

"Here?" Brooklyn gestured towards the road outside. "It's residential." Even as a small cog in the big wheel that was Simon's money-making machine, he was aware of urban planning zones.

"Right," Ricky said. "The guy's in Hong Kong, and I bet 'ee hasn't even been to England. 'Ee'd have seen this place on the map, just downhill from Clifton Village, with all the posh pubs and stuff. You can't do what you like in this country, though." He drained his tea. "'Specially not in Bristol."

"So he's selling it?"

"Who knows? Might be starting a high class knocking shop. Bring a babe or two over from the old country." He leered. "Simon will be round like a shot."

Brooklyn didn't react. It was fine for Ricky, who was family, to jeer at Simon's failings. An apprentice would be crazy to copy him. He imagined Ricky telling his cousin, 'You wanna watch that Brooklyn. Guess what he said?'

Ricky drained the mug. "Wash up, mate, then let's get that wood."

They took Simon's Transit rather than Brooklyn's van. Ricky drove, of course. He had the vehicle on semi-permanent loan. They headed downhill, towards the Hotwells Road.

"Hey," Brooklyn said. "You don't want to go through the clean air zone. Simon never pays."

"News to me, Brook. Guess 'ee won't pay yours, but it's his van, so 'ee 'as to."

"And why are we going over the river? Binks is Filton way, up north."

Ricky pretended to mop his brow. "You ask too many questions. I'll tell you. Old Binks will rip you off soon as look at you. You 'eard what Simon said. Well, I'm saving us the bother. We'll buy it from my friend in Bemmy."

They plunged into the urban sprawl of south Bristol, past the old bonded warehouses hugging the River Avon, newbuilds sprouting by the roadside and the Bristol City football ground. Ricky visibly cheered at the sight of the huge red stadium. Unasked for, he gave a rundown of the game he'd watched there at the weekend.

Brooklyn might have welcomed the diversion from his problems if he'd supported the team. As a Rovers fan, born and bred north of the Avon, he found Ricky's chatter irritating. Best to say nothing.

He stayed silent as football news was exchanged at the wood merchant in Bedminster. The hangar-like building smelled of resin. Ricky's negotiations were conducted against a backdrop of Radio 1 and the whine of saws. The oak they bought was of excellent quality and value, but Brooklyn suffered misgivings when Ricky didn't pay. Instead, his friend handed him a fistful of notes. Ricky pocketed them, asking for an invoice to be sent to Simon.

"Help Simon, help yourself. Win win," Ricky said as they jumped back in the Transit. He gave Brooklyn a tenner.

Brooklyn took it. While the scam made him uneasy, he daren't offend Ricky. Simon's cousin was supervising him on this job, and would do so again in future; he could make life difficult for Brooklyn in a hundred ways. Anyway, he needed the cash.

They navigated the narrow roads up the side of the Avon Gorge without difficulty until they arrived at Aldworth Terrace. A large lorry blocked the passage to the Clover House car park. Ricky swore and sounded the horn.

The lorry driver hopped out of his cab. A burly, balding man, he frowned at them, suddenly rearranging his features into a smile as Ricky wound down his window. "You here to help me unload?" he asked.

"Dunno what you mean mate," Ricky said. "Can you move your truck please, I've got to take my van round."

A muscle twitched in the man's neck. "You're Simon Heath, right? It says so on your van. Your missus told me you'd have fellows here."

"I'm not 'emm. 'Ee's the gaffer."

"Should we ring Simon?" Brooklyn ventured.

Ricky shook his head. "No. If Leanne sent stuff over, it's part of the finishing."

The truck driver folded his arms. "I wouldn't know. All I know is, I'm delivering furniture and I've waited twenty minutes on double yellows. If my buddy wasn't off sick, we'd have dumped it all on the pavement. Or in there." His face reddening, he pointed to the lobby door, which somebody had propped open with a wine crate.

"Brook, get out and assist the gentleman," Ricky said. After giving Brooklyn the flat keys, he remained in the Transit, smoking.

Brooklyn struggled at first to work out which keys to use. For the main door, he needed both a Yale and a mortice shaped like a clover. He took most of the weight as sofas, beds, tables, lamps and rugs were brought into the front room. All the items were new, swathed in polythene or cardboard; some were flat-packed and would need constructing. Finishing off seemed never-ending. He had no idea where he was supposed to position the furniture. Keeping it away from the leak would be a good start.

The truck driver didn't chat much, but he'd calmed down by the time he left. He made a point of thanking Brooklyn while ignoring Ricky.

"Grumpy old git," Ricky observed once he'd moved the Transit and instructed Brooklyn to make tea. "Let's take a look at Leanne's goodies." He whistled. "That rug's just like one our Karen has been pestering me for. I wonder…"

19

"Don't even think about it." Despite his fear of upsetting Ricky, this was a battle Brooklyn felt obliged to fight. Simon would never discover the truth about the oak, but he'd notice a missing rug. And then who would get the blame?

Chapter 4

September 2023

Juliet

Ignoring the bashing and crashing of the builders in the flat below, Juliet began translating a legal document from German into English. Her surroundings were less than ideal, but a deadline was a deadline. She perched on the sofa with her laptop, having painstakingly cleared enough space. After a loud thump that rattled the floorboards and the heaps of junk piled on them, she hooked up to Greg's wi-fi and found a radio station playing eighties music. Cheesy pop had always been a guilty pleasure. It helped her concentrate.

A tinny doorbell rang. The apartment block had an entryphone system with a camera at the front entrance, but there was an old bell just outside the flat too. It would be that builder again. She made a mental note to check Greg's insurance arrangements. Her brother hadn't left enough money for repairs, and she was almost broke. Shoulders tensing, she stared at her screen, hoping the visitor would leave.

No chance. The bell sounded again, followed by a smart rap or two. Juliet stepped over the piles on the floor, and opened the door.

George stood outside.

She gasped. How was it possible to travel more than thirty years back to the past? She stared at the man she recalled so well, but had tried to forget. The man who had fallen in love with Jules, and with whom she'd been obsessed: preppy clothes, blond hair swept back from his broad forehead, blue eyes, strong jaw. And that smile…

Juliet staggered back. She was no longer Jules, a young woman with a dazzling future. That person had vanished when she went to the police and her world came crashing down. And however much it appeared she'd met George fresh from a time machine, it couldn't be true. Time travel didn't happen outside books and films.

"I say, are you all right?" George's voice, mellow and well educated, betrayed no hint that he recognised her.

She should be pleased. Surely it was liberating? If even her ex failed to identify her, it was proof she could pass through the world unchallenged. Anonymous. How lucky that her brunette locks had turned grey and been chopped short, her face settling into lines and folds. Age changed everyone, but not George, it seemed.

As she clutched the door frame, chest heaving for breath, a look of concern replaced his smile.

"I can come back another day, if it's more convenient?" he said. "Here's a leaflet about me. I just wanted to introduce myself. I'm James Sharples…"

"James Sharples, did you say?" Her eyes swam, unable to read the flyer he tried to press into her hand.

"Your local Conservative candidate." The smile returned. "There are council elections next year, and, well, I'd like to say hello. I'm one of your neighbours, actually, just two streets away. You've seen the Passivhaus building on Aldworth Road, with the living roof?"

Juliet hardly took in a word. "You're George Sharples' son?"

"That's right. Do you know Dad?" His eyes narrowed just a fraction. George was the kind of man to make enemies as well as friends. James probably wondered where he stood with her.

"We've met. Years ago." That didn't begin to describe it. Still, if James was unaware of her identity, she wasn't going to tell him. She straightened up, letting go of the doorframe as her dizziness eased.

"Have you considered how you might vote?" James's eyes sought out hers, laying on the charm.

"I'm not registered. It's my late brother's flat. I'm clearing it out to sell it." She added a white lie to soften the blow, "Sorry I can't help you, but I hope you win."

"That's the nicest thing anyone has said all day," James replied.

"But you stand a good chance here, don't you? They usually vote Conservative in Cliftonwood." She racked her brains. "Or are you worried about the Lib Dems?"

James's brow furrowed like George's used to when he was puzzled. "Not so much the Lib Dems. It's the Greens who hold the seat at the moment."

"Oh." She shouldn't imagine Bristol was the same city she'd left in a prison van.

"Are you sure you're all right?" James asked. "Should I come in and help you make a cup of tea?"

Sitting down with George's son for a cuppa was not high on Juliet's bucket list. Then there were the boxes and books and newspapers and broken toasters and other random objects piled high in the flat. "No, I'll be okay, but thank you for making sure. It's good of you, especially as I can't vote for you."

"But of course," James said. "You sound out of sorts, and it's the least anyone can do. Well, it's been nice to meet you, Miss—?"

"Price. I'm Juliet Price."

James saluted her and walked across the landing to the flat opposite.

Juliet slammed the door and slumped on the sofa. How on earth had a political canvasser got into the apartment block? She would have words with that builder, Heath.

James's visit was a sour reminder of everything she'd lost.

And everything Penny had gained.

Chapter 5

November 1991

Jules

"Mr Purslow?" Exhausted, Jules pasted on a smile for her last appointment. She'd given feedback on twenty-two children during this parents' evening. It had reached the point where she hardly remembered if she'd taught them French or German.

Little Steve was different. He worried her. Thank goodness Mr Purslow had turned up. She'd insisted that Steve booked a slot for his parents, and been grateful when he didn't argue. It had made her suspect he wouldn't actually tell them. Well, she'd been wrong to doubt him.

"I'm afraid not." The man standing in the doorway ran a hand through sun-streaked hair. "Our child is called Jenks-Robinson."

"Of course. Rebecca." The class swot. How odd that her father hadn't mentioned her first name. Jules mentally filed away her list of Steve Purslow's aggressive behaviours. She glanced at her watch. "I'm afraid the children are supposed to sign up for a particular time for you, Mr Jenks-Robinson. It's the end of the evening and we're already late—"

"It's Jenks. Malcolm Jenks." Rebecca's father flashed a smile, transforming his face.

He was rather attractive if you liked men rocking the Wall Street look. The red braces were a bit 1980s yuppie, surely? Her husband wouldn't be seen dead in them anymore.

"I won't take up much of your time, I promise, but Toni — that's my wife — was keen for me to speak to Mrs Sharples. I say, you're not related to George Sharples, are you?"

Strangers frequently asked, as the surname was unusual. Malcolm's intense gaze suggested a real interest in the answer, though.

"He's my husband."

"I've done business with him. He may have mentioned it. I produce educational CDs and workbooks."

"We don't talk much about work." George wasn't interested in the finer points of teaching. She didn't understand the world of high finance, either.

Malcolm's eyes appraised her. "I'd guess he's much older than you."

Men always did this. They looked at the trendy raven bubble cut, the long legs and stilettos under the Lycra skirt, and they saw a bimbo. Well, it wasn't her fault that the school's dress code forbade trousers for female teachers. She didn't have to spend money on a perm, of course, but why shouldn't she make the most of herself? Everyone said curls flattered her. Still, she must stay professional in front of a parent. There would be no sassy put-down. She'd gently tell him she was twenty-five and the deputy head of department.

He saved her the bother by apologising.

"I'm so sorry," he said. "I didn't mean to be patronising, but I hardly know which way is up. Toni is in the maternity hospital – you know, St Michael's. I'd been for a visit and she told me, we mustn't forget the parents' evening and Mrs Sharples. That was news to me, but it's been rather hectic. It's our eighth…"

"Congratulations."

Jules almost choked. How wonderful it would be to stay in St Michael's, emerging with a brand new baby. Eight children, though? Perhaps that was why he couldn't remember their names.

"I tell you what. You're right, it's late, and, er, Rebecca didn't sign up. I should get back and relieve the au pair. Let me buy you a drink after work tomorrow. You can tell me about Rebecca then. I'd be terribly grateful to hear your thoughts on our latest German workbook. May I leave it with you?"

He handed over a brightly decorated plastic folder. "Snap it open, and you'll see the CD and booklet. Plus a little something for your trouble. But I'll thank you properly with a drink. Let's say the bar at the Swallow Hotel, six o'clock tomorrow."

Before she could reply, he turned and was out of sight.

"Be seeing you," he yelled, feet clattering down the corridor.

He was the kind of brash individual who wouldn't take no for an answer, Jules suspected. Tempted to stand him up, her annoyance faded when she opened the folder. The workbook, aimed at beginners, looked excellent. She found herself eager to listen to the CD later. The 'little something' was a book token, which she would definitely use.

After filing her paperwork, she desperately needed to unwind. George would have willingly helped her relax. Alas, he was away in London all week. That meant she could meet Malcolm, so why not? Even better, she'd made plans to see her best friend tonight. She looked forward to catching up on Penny's gossip.

Jules parked her red XR3i in front of the wine bar. Soft rain fell from a dark, moonless sky. She hurried inside. The atmosphere was cosy, dimly lit by lamps shining through displays of fake plants. She chose a table where a candle flickered from an empty Mateus Rosé bottle. Jules ordered a full one, pouring herself a large measure from the bulbous flask.

Penny was late. Perhaps her date with Rufus had gone better than expected. Jules grinned. Finally, she'd fixed up her best friend with a decent guy.

Still, if Penny didn't show up, that left Jules with a whole bottle to herself. She'd take a cab home, she decided, replenishing her glass. It would help her forget about the boring parents' evening.

She was halfway through the bottle when Penny arrived.

"What have you got – Mateus? Gosh, I so need it." Penny draped her raincoat on a spare chair. Her mousy bob was damp and starting to curl. She flicked the fringe out of her eyes. "Ugh. It needs cutting."

Jules filled an empty glass almost to the brim. "Get this down you. How did it go?"

"Don't ask," Penny said, lighting a cigarette. "Rufus is so not my type."

"You have a type?"

Jules regretted her words at once. Penny had a soft spot for George, everyone knew that, but George was way out of her league. Jules herself hardly believed her luck in finding such a handsome, generous husband. Whatever Malcolm implied, there wasn't a big age gap either.

"You never told me Rufus was ginger," Penny complained.

"There's a clue in the name. Also, I didn't think you'd mind."

Penny huffed. "I'm not desperate. Anyway, talk about boring. He wanted to discuss my work all the time. What was teaching like, were the kids nice, what ages were they, did I run after school clubs? As if. I flipping hate my job. You won't catch me wasting my spare time on it."

"Maybe he thought his own work was dull. He's a computer scientist."

"Oh yes, I heard all about it. He designs video games. Looking for someone to test them."

"Heck, he asked me about that too. I told him I'd think about it."

"That means you won't, will you? I don't blame you. It's not my thing either." Penny took a long swig of the pink liquid. "This is lovely.

26

Thanks. Jeepers, a date with a geek after seven hours of classes. That school is a zoo. Did I tell you, one of the little devils stole my handbag last week?"

"We've got a maternity cover coming up, and it's your language, French. Barbara." Jules winced. How come Barbara had fallen pregnant so quickly, when she couldn't? "She's already on sick leave and I've covered her classes. They're well-behaved. Want me to give you a mention?"

"I'd love that, thanks. It's not what you know, is it? It's who you know." Penny stubbed out her cigarette and started another. She glanced meaningfully at her empty wine glass.

"I'll get another bottle. Same again?" Jules expected to pick up the tab. Once she'd married up and left their shared flat, the difference in income between the two friends was embarrassing. George had helped in other ways, too. He pulled strings. Thanks to him, Jules had walked into a plum job after her teacher training course.

"Can we have Frascati, please? Like last week."

"Of course." She preferred a sweeter wine, but poor Penny needed cheering up. It would be charged to George's credit card, obviously.

Jules ordered sparkling water and a jug of ice too. "I'm having a spritzer," she explained when she returned to the table. If you chilled a drink enough, it tasted of nothing at all.

"So," Penny waved her cigarette, sending a shower of sparks over the marble-topped table, "What's new with you?"

"Nothing much. Parents' evening tonight. Uneventful apart from my father-in-law turning up." A book token and the promise of a drink from Malcolm hardly counted as news.

Penny's eyes widened. "Jeff Sharples went to your parents' evening? Oh, I get it. You teach George's little brother — Aidan, isn't it?"

"Damien. He's a nice kid. Bright. Always in the top three, but that's not good enough for his dad. He wants us to push Damien harder. That's me and every other teacher."

Penny tutted. "What a shame. Jeff should meet the little devils in my classroom. Then he'd see how lucky he is. Can't George talk to his father?"

If only it were that simple. "He won't," Jules said. "George has this ridiculous idea that Damien is spoiled because he's the baby of the family. Jeff gave him a hard time too. George thinks it made a man of him."

27

"What did Philip Larkin say about parents?" Penny asked. "Oh fudge, I'm sorry. I forgot you're trying for a baby. Dare I ask?"

"Still no." Jules sniffed. How had the conversation ended up here? She wanted to stay light and bright for Penny; she mustn't cry.

Penny passed her a tissue and poured wine into both glasses. "Oh sugar. I've done it now. Come on, Jules, have another drink. You'll feel so much better."

Jules blew her nose and gulped the wine straight, without adding ice and water. It was too sharp for her taste, but the alcohol took effect. She relaxed again. "Three years," she muttered. "We could have had a five-a-side football team in our house by now, if... if everything was working."

"Have you had tests?" Penny asked.

"All clear." Jules wiped her eyes. "I even gave up smoking."

"What about George?"

"Fine too," Jules lied. Because that was the problem. She didn't really know, as George refused to go for tests.

"There's this new IVF, isn't there?" Penny burbled. "How about trying that? My cousin had twins with it. They used a sperm donor, though, when it turned out that Gary was infertile. You can't tell from looking at the kids—" She hiccupped and giggled. The wine had gone to her head.

Jules frowned. "George would never do that."

But Penny was right. It was no use just hoping for the best. Jeff and Sarah constantly nagged her about grandchildren. Her biological clock was ticking. When she walked past a pram, she welled up.

She needed a baby. So how could she get one?

Chapter 6

November 1991

Jules

The Swallow boasted the priciest bar in Bristol, a place where George took people he wanted to impress. Jules made her way to it through the hotel's lobby. There was nothing understated about the decor, all dark wood, marble and chandeliers. It screamed of opulence.

Malcolm waved. He'd already bagged a table, and sat in a plush velvet chair, a pint of beer in front of him.

He stood up and air-kissed her. "What would you like?"

"Mateus, please."

"Not sure they do it. How about chardonnay? The girls in the office are mad about that."

"I'll give it a try."

He went to order, waving a twenty pound note at the smartly jacketed staff. It certainly commanded their attention. Jules had hardly made herself comfortable by the time he returned.

He sat down, leaning forward. "Cheers. What do you think of the CD?"

She clinked glasses, retrieving the colourful folder and placing it on the table. "What I've heard sounds good, but I haven't listened to it all. I like the workbook."

"Take your time." Malcolm stretched out like a cat. He smiled. "If you're interested, I'll do a deal for you. It's Rebecca's school, after all."

"That's very kind of you. As the deputy head of department—," there, she'd said it, "—it's not my decision, but do give me a quote. I'll obviously put in a good word. Now, about Rebecca. She's well beyond the workbook's level. Top of her year, in fact."

"We road-test the materials on her," Malcolm said.

"I should have known. She has an excellent grasp of the subject. I wish more of my pupils were like her. Rebecca gets on well with other children, and works hard."

Jules struggled to think of anything else to say about his daughter. Yet Malcolm crooked an eyebrow, as if expecting more.

"Do you have any concerns about Rebecca?" she asked.

He shrugged. "Only that she doesn't get much individual attention at home. That's to be expected, with so many kids around. Do you have any? I recall George saying a while ago that he hoped to start a family."

The chatter around them seemed to still.

"No." Jules squinted, her eyes hot and heavy. A drop of moisture escaped.

Malcolm winced. "I've put my foot in it, haven't I?"

He reached over and squeezed her hand. "Be careful what you wish for. You can have too much of a good thing. Frankly, I go out to work to escape the madhouse."

His pity was more than she could bear. Tears began in earnest.

"I'd be happy with one baby. Just one."

Malcolm shifted in his chair. Despite his sympathetic gaze, she realised she'd made him uncomfortable. He hadn't stopped holding her hand, though.

Jules withdrew it, found a tissue and dabbed at her face. What was the matter with her, losing her self-control in front of a parent?

She picked up her bag, rising to her feet and pulling on her coat.

"I'm sorry," she said. "I should leave."

"No apology necessary. I obviously hit a nerve," Malcolm said ruefully. "Can we meet again when you've spoken to your boss?"

It was the following month when she next saw him, a chance encounter as she looked for a cab. The language teachers had been for a Christmas drink in Bristol city centre. Heading for the taxi rank outside the Swallow, umbrella fending off snow, she felt a hand on her shoulder.

"Mrs Sharples, I presume?"

Jules jerked around. Malcolm, wearing the ubiquitous black wool overcoat — George had one the same — smiled at her.

"Fancy a nightcap?" he asked. "You can't get a car for love nor money at the moment. All these festive parties."

"I've just been to one."

"Me too. Listen, it's freezing. Join me in the Swallow for a swift pint, and I'll ask them to phone for cabs."

"Good idea."

A welcome blast of warmth hit Jules as she entered the hotel's revolving doors. Inside, the lobby sparkled with swags of tinsel. A massive Christmas tree stretched to the high ceiling. The atmosphere was cosy and comfortable, a pleasant contrast to the blizzard brewing outside.

Malcolm spoke to the man at the concierge desk. "An hour," he reported back. "Plenty of time to chat. Shall we see if they have mulled cider?"

He placed a hand on the small of her back, guiding her to the bar. Although busy, several patrons were leaving, and they found a table.

"Did the school secretary fax you?" Jules asked. "We didn't have a budget for your CDs, it turned out, so I spoke to the head of the PTA. They want to place an order as soon as poss, then the kids can learn in the Christmas holidays. If you've got a more advanced version, I'll buy one for my brother-in-law."

Malcolm cocked his head. "Brother-in-law?"

"George's brother is one of my pupils. And before you ask, George is three years older than me. Damien is definitely the baby of the family."

Malcolm laughed. "Well, a big order calls for a celebration. Forget the cider. And yes, I have a package for next stage learners. I'll make sure you get one."

When he came back with a bottle of Moët et Chandon champagne, Jules wondered how good a deal he'd offer the PTA. He obviously expected a healthy profit from it. She banished the thought as she sipped the heady fizz.

"This is the best bubbly, isn't it?" Malcolm said. "You deserve it, Jules. Bottoms up."

"Merry Christmas."

Malcolm chuckled. "Here's hoping Father Christmas brings you everything you want."

"A baby, you mean?" She was a cheerful drunk tonight rather than a maudlin one. Thank goodness she wasn't blubbing all over him again.

"A baby if that's what will make you happy," Malcolm said. "Why the rush, though? You're young. Enjoy yourself."

"George wants a family. And my mother-in-law. She's only got George and Damien…" Jules stopped suddenly. She'd been so used to Sarah's constant nagging for grandchildren that she hadn't considered why her mother-in-law was so keen. Perhaps Sarah herself hadn't found it easy to conceive.

"Don't do anything for them. Do it for you." Malcolm split the remainder of the champagne between them. "I'm getting another one."

Jules checked her watch. "But our taxis—"

"I'll put them off. You need more fun in your life."

He was right about that but wrong about her motives for wanting a child. She should have explained better. It was an unaccountable yearning, an instinct to nurture. When he returned with more Moët, she'd tell him, she decided. Jules yawned, senses pleasantly hazy.

But when Malcolm topped up their glasses again, somehow he was sitting right next to her. His hand fondled her knee and slid up her thigh.

"Stop it." She dragged his hand away from her leg.

"I thought you liked it."

She did — he wasn't unattractive, after all — but she'd never intended to flirt with him.

"I'm not looking for this."

"Sure?" His lips brushed hers.

Suddenly, she wasn't so sure. Because Malcolm had eight children. Just an hour in one of the Swallow's luxurious bedrooms upstairs, and she could get pregnant.

And no-one needed to know how.

Chapter 7

January 1992

Jules

The bell rang incessantly to signal the lesson's end, time for a break. With a hubbub of chatter and chairs scraping across the floor, thirty pupils dashed from the classroom. Young Damien was telling Jules the headmaster had summoned her. Yet her feet wouldn't move, as if stuck in treacle.

"Hell's teeth, it's a fire alarm."

Malcolm's voice. What was he doing here?

She felt someone shake her shoulders.

"Jules, wake up," Malcolm yelled. "We've got to get out."

She stirred, opened her eyes and looked into his anxious face.

"Come on, hurry up." He threw on clothes, clipping the red braces to his trousers.

Jules staggered out of the comfortable bed, head still muzzy from the Moët she'd drunk the night before. How many empty bottles had they left outside the room?

She pulled on a dress and heels, searching for her bags.

"There's no time for that." Malcolm flung the door open and hustled her into the corridor.

"Where are we going?" she mumbled.

"The car park. Follow them." He pointed to the guests streaming past them. The hallway was still lit, illuminating startled features. Malcolm elbowed his way into the line.

"We should keep apart from each other," he hissed.

They'd chosen a luxurious country house hotel, less reliant on the business market than the Swallow. The clientele were older. Jules ended up behind an elderly couple shuffling along with walking sticks. Once they'd made it through the exit, they stared in dread at the fire escape. The metal staircase zigzagged down three floors.

Jules helped them to the bottom, standing on tiptoe throughout. The steps, perforated with small holes, seemed designed to catch stiletto heels.

Stark sodium lamps illuminated the car park and a freezing wind cut through her flimsy garments. Clouds loured overhead. They threatened snow, which Jules prayed would be slow to arrive. The Mendips would be impassable.

Her feet slipped on frosty ground. Looking around, she spotted no flames. The chilly gusts of wind contained no hint of smoke either. Guests in varying stages of undress huddled together. Jules stayed with the old couple. She didn't recognise a soul, which was the point of staying an hour out of Bristol. Malcolm had suggested this place after their first drunken coupling.

He was more than keen to continue seeing her. She'd agreed, because she wasn't pregnant yet. Once that happened, she'd stop, despite enjoying her time with him.

That had come as a surprise. When Malcolm had splashed out on a suite at the Swallow, Jules had closed her eyes, pretending it was George's blond hair she stroked, his lips kissing hers. Yet her brain refused to be deceived. While George focused only on his pleasure in the bedroom, Malcolm considered hers.

As she watched, a number of vehicles switched on their headlights. Malcolm's, a Volvo estate, pulled away. Where was he going, and should she care? She wasn't in love with him. They both had marriages to protect. She had no idea what lies he'd told his wife. George imagined Jules was visiting her parents in Somerset.

They'd be horrified if they knew. To them, making a good marriage was the pinnacle of Jules's achievements, outweighing a first-class degree and her teaching qualification. Rich, successful and handsome, George could do no wrong.

She agreed, really. What she and Malcolm did must remain a secret. It would hurt George so much if he found out, and George was everything she needed in a man.

Except he fired blanks. The desire for a child nibbled at Jules's awareness from dawn until bedtime. Perhaps this had been her lucky night.

A lad in the staff uniform, a black waistcoat and trousers stiff with nylon, came around with a clipboard. "So sorry for the inconvenience, madam. We're just taking a roll call, but I think we can let everyone back inside soon—"

"Where's the fire?" a grey-bearded man asked him.

"A bin in one of the smoking rooms. We've put it out. Um, the manager and his team will serve refreshments in the lounge shortly—"

"Well, I'm going back to bed," the questioner announced.

"Wait, if I can just take your name and room number?"

34

"I'm Mrs Smith, Room Fifteen," Jules said, making sure her voice carried. It might help the youth out. Like a teacher, he needed to establish his authority. "Mr Smith left early," she added.

The grey-bearded gent leered at her. "Mr and Mrs Smith? Nudge, nudge, wink, wink."

He turned to the youth. "Percival. Room Twenty-Three. May I go back in now?"

"If you must, sir, but would you be discreet about it, please?"

"My watchword," the old man said, without a hint of irony.

The lad moved on to another group, smokers who coughed and spluttered their details for him. Jules hobbled after Mr Percival, who headed for the main entrance. Her shoes crunched on the gravel drive, a spray of stones hitting her feet and working their way underneath them.

Inside the lobby, plates of pastries and thermos flasks of coffee had been laid out on a long white-clad table. A guest stood nearby, louche in a flowing white shirt and jeans, light catching the medallion at his throat and haloing his red curls. Taking a sip of coffee, he nodded to Jules.

Her heart missed a beat. She wasn't safely anonymous at all.

Chapter 8

January 1992

Jules

"Ah," Rufus said, "fancy bumping into you. So George was right."

"What do you mean?" Jules gawped at him. Play the innocent, she told herself. Rufus might be suspicious, but he knew nothing.

"Take a coffee and sit down." Rufus gestured to one of the groups of armchairs invitingly clustered around small tables. He poured his own while she did so, seating himself across from her.

"Want something stronger in it?" He removed a monogrammed silver hipflask from a pocket. "Armagnac. The best brandy, I'm told."

"No thanks." The cup and saucer wobbled in her hands. She set them down on the table.

Rufus added a slug of the amber spirit to his coffee. He took a sip and tutted, his expression rueful. "You know, I didn't expect to find anything when George asked me—"

"Hang on," Jules interrupted, her neck prickling as a chill ran down it. "George asked you to spy on me? And you agreed?"

"As I just said, I didn't think I'd find anything," Rufus replied smoothly.

"What kind of friend are you?"

"I'd like to think I'm a good one to both of you. True, George has invested in my games business—"

She hadn't known that.

"—but we go back, you and I. Remember rolling back the carpet to dance?"

"And sleeping on it afterwards. Crazy student days. You were wild then."

"You too. All of us."

That wasn't true. Rufus had done every drug ever invented, and probably baking powder too. Jules was too focused on her degree to join in. Anyway, he'd calmed down in his twenties. Now, he complained that he wanted to get married like everyone else their age. No longer would he chase unattainable ice maidens. Did Jules know any nice teachers, he'd asked. She'd sent him on a date with Penny. It was hardly Jules's fault that Penny didn't see past his ginger hair.

Was Rufus annoyed because Penny had snubbed him? Was it peevishness that persuaded him to snoop for George?

She daren't ask, at least not until she found out how much he'd seen.

"I've got photos," he said, his voice casual. "I took shots earlier in the bar. And later, when the pair of you left Room Fifteen."

"How?" Her jaw dropped in horror.

"You weren't looking." To his credit, he didn't gloat, his tone remaining matter of fact. "I started the fire. It was the only way to get proof."

"And now," she decided to appeal to his better nature, "you're going to break George's heart?"

He grimaced. "Honestly, I don't want to do that. I feel terribly conflicted. Believe me, I set out to prove your innocence. I was wrong about that, wasn't I?"

"It's not how it seems." Jules cast about for an excuse. "We were writing German workbooks."

She was aware it sounded lame, and it was clear she hadn't fooled Rufus at all.

"I bet you were," he scoffed. "In a double bed, with Moët on tap. But look, you've left me in a bind. Of course, I owe George a favour. Thanks to his support, my business is going to make the big time."

She grasped at straws. "As long as he doesn't shoot the messenger," she said.

"Perhaps he won't need to." Rufus scrutinised her intently, like a snake sizing up a mouse.

Jules took a deep breath. Blackmail started like this. How much did he want?

"I've got a couple of computer games in the final stages of development," Rufus said. "Like I told you before, they need beta testing. That's where you can help."

She'd forgotten all about it. "Heck, I've never been near a computer. Why, I can't even switch one on." She almost giggled, her astonishment obvious.

Rufus smirked. "You're not my target market. But you know the guys who are."

Chapter 9

January 1992

Jules

Young Damien's expression was sombre. It signalled, 'Life is hard, but I can be stoic'. Head down, hands in his pockets, he trudged out of the classroom.

Jules suppressed a smile. She remembered how terribly serious life seemed at the age of thirteen. Carefree childhood days lay behind you, the excitement of leaving home ahead. In between sat a hinterland of seething hormones and an uncertain destiny. She didn't miss adolescence.

"Want a lift home later, Damien?"

The other pupils had already exited, or she wouldn't have asked. It was hard enough on Damien being the teacher's brother-in-law; he didn't need reminding in public.

He glanced up, his face a softer, rounder version of George's. One day, he would be tall and handsome like his brother. Right now, he was still a cute child.

"Yes, please, a lift would be nice," he said, adding, "As long as it isn't out of your way," Jeff and Sarah having drummed politeness into him.

"It's no trouble," she said. "I drive past your road."

She paused, an idea taking shape. She could help Damien, help Rufus, and help herself.

"You look like you need cheering up. You play video games, don't you?"

Damien shook his head. "Not for a month. I'm grounded for listening to music too loud."

"The Smiths?" She caught his eye.

"How did you know?"

"They're your favourite band, aren't they? I used to like them too, when I was your age. Funny, I thought you'd be more into the latest trends. The Smiths don't get played on Radio 1 anymore."

"Their songs speak to me."

He stared at her, gaze intense and lips puckering, yet didn't say more.

Jeff and Sarah were too strict, but it would take a braver woman than Jules to tell them. When she finally managed to start a family, she'd think twice about letting her in-laws babysit. Meanwhile, where was George's old Discman? He'd upgraded last year to a newer one.

If Damien listened through headphones, that wouldn't annoy his parents. Even better, Jules could offer him another treat to look forward to.

"Damien, one of my friends has new games that need beta testing. Are you interested? Maybe once you're no longer grounded."

Jules expected him to ask what sort of games. Then she'd be floundering. Rufus had mentioned a shoot-em up and a platformer, whatever that was. But Damien simply said he didn't think his mum would agree, as he had so much schoolwork.

"I tell you what," she suggested. "Let's pretend you're going to German Club. We'll say it's an hour after school on a Wednesday. That gives you time to see Rufus and test his games. He lives near the school, so you can go round, do what you need to do, and go home as usual. How about that?"

"Brill." Damien's cheeks dimpled as he smiled. "You'd lie for me?" he asked.

"It's only a little white lie. Do you think you can work a tiny bit harder at German, though? If you came top of the class, your parents wouldn't ask questions."

"I already try," Damien said ruefully. "But it's impossible. Becky Heath Robinson is way ahead of the rest of us."

"Becky Jenks-Rob…" The words died as Jules realised he was joking. He had a point, though. Malcolm's daughter was that unusual breed, rarer than a unicorn: a pupil who adored studying. You didn't read her homework, you weighed it. "Well, just do your best," she said.

"You bet, Jules."

Her heart lightened. It felt good to bring joy to poor Damien's world. And to keep Rufus on her side.

Chapter 10

April 1992

Jules

Jeff's black BMW 525 and Sarah's smaller white BMW 318 sat side by side on their driveway in Stoke Bishop. George and Jules didn't live far from his parents in this exclusive enclave of Bristol, but he preferred to take the car when he visited for Sunday lunch. Jules knew the score: she would get behind the steering wheel on the way back. George liked a drink. He'd already had one driving ban, despite pulling strings through the Freemasons.

There was plenty of space to park George's vehicle, a twin to his father's. The prettily gabled house sat in half an acre of land. Shrubs and spring flowers edged the block-paved drive. Jules admired the heady scent of narcissi as she rang the doorbell.

Jeff welcomed them in. "A small sherry?" he suggested. "Come through to the lounge."

They sat in the large, bay-windowed room, a vision in pink with chintzy furniture and swagged curtains. Jules preferred the cleaner lines of Scandinavian brands, or Habitat. The drinks cupboard, with its dark wood and leaded lights, struck her as old-fashioned. No doubt it suited tweed-jacketed Jeff, though. He kept it well-stocked; a dozen or so bottles were on display, with hand-cut lead crystal glasses.

Jeff poured them each a measure of Bristol Cream, and took a schooner to Sarah in the kitchen. They returned together. Sarah, as usual, looked as if she'd been nowhere near a cooker. Her short grey hair was neat, her make-up perfect and her white dress spotless.

"Lunch will be twenty minutes," she said.

Jeff gazed at her fondly, his smile a carbon copy of George's. "It smells delicious."

"Your cooking always is, Mum," George said. "Although Jules's might be even better. Last night, we had Chicken Cacciatore, didn't we, darling?"

Sarah's eyes hardened.

Jules blushed. While she made an effort for George, she wasn't a natural in the kitchen. Their meal had come from Marks & Spencer's, with a dash of brandy added — a trick she'd learned from Penny. "It wasn't up to Sarah's standard," she managed.

"So how are things, you two?" Sarah asked, considerably perkier.

"Well, we do have some news," George said.

"I knew it!" Sarah clapped her hands. "Congratulations."

"We've only booked a holiday," George said. "A long weekend in Paris, just after the election."

His mother deflated but rallied quickly. "The city of love. Remember when you took me there?" she said, nudging her husband.

Jeff ignored her. "I'll be glad when the general election is out of the way," he said. "The financial markets are unsettled. I hope John Major gets back in, and it's business as usual."

"Quite," George agreed. He wore his political heart on his sleeve; despite Jules's misgivings, he'd placed a bright blue Conservative poster in their front window.

"Major's too wet. I wish Mrs Thatcher had stayed," Sarah said. "Anyway, enough of that. What have you done to Damien, Jules? He's been so cheerful lately. Your German Club has made a good impression on him."

"Where is Damien?" Jeff asked. "I told him to come down from his room for twelve."

"I'll fetch him," Jules volunteered.

She dashed up the stairs, carpeted in a pink velvet pile. Given that a teenage boy lived there, it was remarkable that Sarah kept the place like a show home.

Damien's bedroom, too, was unnaturally tidy. Jules remembered posters on the wall as an adolescent — Duran Duran for her and the England football team for Greg — but Damien only had a school calendar. He sat at his desk with what appeared to be a miniature computer in front of him.

"Hi, Jules. Take a look at this." He pointed to the gadget: two slabs of cream plastic at ninety degrees to each other, a keyboard and screen with a hinge in between.

"What is it?"

"A laptop. Rufus gave it to me." Damien's face lit up. "Rufus is ace. He really gets me, you know? Thanks for telling me about the games testing."

"You're welcome. But did I understand right? That machine looks expensive. Are you sure he gave it to you?"

Damien tutted. "Yes, that's what I said. It's so I can help him design games. Can I show you one?"

"If it's quick. I've been sent to take you downstairs."

"Watch."

Damien typed a few letters. A figure appeared, picked out in dark grey on the lighter-coloured screen.

"A penguin?" Jules asked.

"Yes. He has to avoid rocks and sharks."

The penguin glided across the screen. Suddenly, a sawtooth line appeared below him and a straight line to the right.

"I'll get him jumping to that platform without falling on the rocks," Damien said.

He typed another command.

The penguin made it.

"What do you think? I haven't finished the sharks yet."

"It's very clever," Jules said. She'd rather relax with a book, but Damien deserved praise for his efforts.

"Rufus thought so too. He says I've got a future in the games industry, especially as I'm good at art. That's going to become really important."

"Have you shown your mum and dad?"

"No," Damien admitted. Switching off the laptop and popping it in a drawer, he whispered, "They think I'm going to German Club, remember? So don't tell them, Jules."

"Of course not." She placed a finger on her lips.

Chapter 11

September 2023

Brooklyn

Brooklyn's stomach ached with hunger by the time he'd finished shifting furniture. Nanna Lizzie usually sent him to work with a bag full of sandwiches. Today, he had nothing, and he'd only eaten half a packet of Jammie Dodgers last night. The biscuits had been lying on the side in Lizzie's kitchen, and he'd grabbed them as they left. Later, he'd shared them with Vix. At least she'd have a school dinner in her belly by now.

He decided to suggest stopping for lunch before hauling wood. But Ricky's phone rang at that moment, its ringtone a rap about bling, hoes and bitches. Brooklyn suspected Ricky had chosen it to annoy Simon.

After a quick discussion, Ricky ended the call and grinned. "You could use some extra cash, hey? The gaffer dun't pay more'n'ee needs to."

"He's okay," Brooklyn said, sure what would come next.

He wasn't wrong. Ricky said, "I've got a mate with a few bits that need storin'. Boxes and that. Can you puts 'em in your nan's garage? Fifty quid a week." He flashed a grin, revealing tobacco-stained teeth. "Cheaper 'n Safestore, so it's win-win, ennit?"

"Sorry, she wouldn't like that."

She wasn't his nan either. Brooklyn suspected Ricky was aware of that, but he couldn't begin to explain the complexities of his life. He was in enough trouble without letting Ricky near the bungalow, or storing whatever his workmate wanted hidden. Stolen goods probably. Or drugs.

Ricky face-palmed. "You're kissin' goodbye to easy money."

There was a loud, frenzied knocking on the front door.

"Oozat?" Ricky grumbled. "Another delivery, I 'spose. Come on, Brook."

But when they opened the door, an old woman stood at the threshold. Short and slight, with a choppy grey bob topping a white singlet and jeans, she looked as fragile as a wisp of mist. Brooklyn wondered if she was something to do with Ricky's side hustle. Her fierce expression unsettled him.

"Hello again, Miss," Ricky said, his tone ingratiating. "How can I help?"

"Mr Heath?"

She spoke with a plum in her mouth. It made Brooklyn even more uncomfortable, as if confronted by a schoolteacher in his weakest subject.

"We works for 'emm." Ricky's soft Bristolian lilt contrasted with her clipped delivery.

"Well, send him up to see me when he's here. Flat 2. This is not acceptable."

Ricky smiled at her. Brooklyn had seen that boyish appeal work on women before, although Simon was better at it. The boss followed through, too. For all his faults, Ricky didn't cheat on his wife.

"I'm not sure what we've done wrong." Ricky's baby face didn't waver. "I alerted you to a leak, mind."

"So?" the woman huffed, reminding Brooklyn not to underestimate little old ladies. "How did that canvasser get in? Did you leave the door open?"

"Um," Brooklyn said. He remembered seeing a wine crate wedged in the entranceway, but had no idea who had left it there.

Ricky interrupted. "We wuz bringing in furniture," he said.

"But—" Brooklyn said.

"So I see." Her eyes swept across the boxes stacked behind the men. "But you've finished now, haven't you? You should have closed the door. It's a security risk, especially for someone like me, on my own. Anybody can get in. There might be a burglar inside already."

Ricky still didn't put her right. What was he doing? He replied in the same drawl. "'Ee'd be doing you a favour, woonee? I've seen the mountains of stuff in your flat. 'Ee'd have to climb over 'em to get in."

Heat flared in her eyes. "They're not my possessions. Not exactly. I'm clearing my brother's flat, so whatever you're implying…"

Ricky stared at her denim-clad legs. "There's no need to be unfriendly. So you dun't live 'ere, then?" He sounded disappointed.

"I'll stay while I'm clearing the flat."

"And you're selling up after, I suppose."

She nodded. "As soon as I can."

"Then it's your lucky day. I've got a mate who does house clearance, 'aven't I, Brook?"

"Yes," Brooklyn said. He had no idea who Ricky meant.

"I'll get you a good rate. And I can fix up your flat for you, help you get the best price."

"Which bit of 'I'm clearing the flat' do you not understand? I don't have the money to pay anyone for anything. Close the door to the lobby behind you in future. I'll have to call the police if you don't."

Brooklyn gawped at her, alarm spiking at the mention of police. Suppose she summoned them, and they asked where he lived? One visit from a keen copper, and he'd be stuck behind bars. "There isn't a door to the lobby. Not from this flat," he said, fear sending his voice shrill.

She stormed off without acknowledging him. They heard her footsteps stomping upstairs and on the landing above. A door slammed.

"What planet is she on?" Ricky asked.

Brooklyn was still concerned about the police. "Do you think she'd complain to Simon? Or call the cops?"

"Nothing to complain about," Ricky said. "Go on, make us tea while I have a smoke."

He removed rolling papers and tobacco from his pocket.

Brooklyn refrained from saying Simon wouldn't approve. Ricky lit up outside if their boss or his clients were around; otherwise, he did what he liked.

"There's that canvasser. The one who caused the grief," Ricky said, glancing out of the window and knocking on it.

The young man turned, startled. He mouthed, "Yes?"

"Use the doorbell, mate, all right?" Ricky yelled.

"Sorry," the politician mouthed back. He donned a cycle helmet and unlocked a bike across the road.

"Tory," Ricky said with venom. "Made of money. Look at that, ten grand's worth of steel. Anywhere else in Bristol, they'd have 'ad the wheels off by now." He scowled. "Forget the tea, Brook. After that excitement, I needs a pint. I'm off to the pub. You stay in case Simon comes back. Unload the wood."

"But I'm starving," Brooklyn protested.

"I'll bring you a sausage roll." He paused at the threshold. "Tell Simon it's an estate sale, yeah? The old bag won't pay to fix the leak, but I bet Simon can nab her flat at a knockdown price. 'Ee'll like that." Ricky rubbed thumb and forefingers together. "Information is power, boy."

Brooklyn made another brew, adding six sugars this time. The hunger pangs waned. He brought in the oak, which had already been cut to size and was easy to manoeuvre. With his spirit level, he marked the walls of the alcoves, celebrating with more tea. He started fitting shelves.

His fingers were busy, but there was nothing to occupy his mind. His thoughts drifted to the evening, when he would collect Vix from school. What then? She might not like sleeping in the van, and nor did he, but they didn't have a choice. He felt lightheaded as the sugar rush wore off. Losing concentration, he tapped his thumb with the hammer.

It wasn't bruised or broken, but it stung. Brooklyn sucked the injured digit ruefully. He put the kettle on.

The back door rattled. Simon strode inside with an air of impatience. "Look lively, lad. Where's Ricky?"

Their colleague had been at the pub for over an hour. "He popped out for materials," Brooklyn lied.

Simon frowned. "How come he left the Transit behind? Hang on, I'll ring him."

"Want a cuppa while you wait, boss?"

"All right." Simon jabbed at his phone. "Ricky, mate, when are you coming back?"

Brooklyn couldn't hear the explanation. When Simon snapped the phone back in its case, he said Ricky was buying glue from the hardware shop in Clifton Village.

"Funny, I thought they closed at lunchtime," Simon added. "Anyway, how are you getting on?"

Brooklyn waved to the shelves.

Simon cursed. "I told Ricky to make them floating."

Brooklyn had heard him say no such thing. He gawped.

"Good workmanship, though," Simon continued. "The Rickster knows his stuff." His gaze flicked to the open door to the front room. "What's all that?"

"Furniture. It arrived earlier."

Simon swore again. "No way. I thought I'd cancelled the delivery. What was Ricky playing at? He should have phoned me when it arrived."

That was harsh, as they were supposed to be finishing off. Wasn't that why Leanne Heath had sent the flatpacks, sofas and rugs? But Simon's mouth was twitching. An explosion looked to be on the way. No point in making it worse.

Simon sucked his teeth. "We'll have to get it all moved. Although perhaps it can stay for a few days while I work out where to put it. I'm not laying out money for storage."

This didn't make sense. "Won't the client—" Brooklyn began to say.

He heard a door open. A blast of beery fumes heralded Ricky's arrival.

"Are you drunk?" Simon demanded.

"Just a cheeky pint," Ricky said.

"And the rest. You're not to drive the Transit in that state. Brooklyn will take it home for safekeeping. You can walk, mate."

"But—"

"No buts, Ricky. You want to drive, you don't drink. Simples."

"Boss, I came in my own van." Brooklyn pointed outside.

"Leave it there," Simon insisted. "Get the bus later and pick it up if you're that fussed."

Brooklyn didn't dare ask if Simon would pay the fare. His boss was in full flow and wouldn't like to be interrupted.

"That's enough from both of you," Simon said. "I've got news. Ricky, I want you in south Bristol tomorrow, on that summer house in Totterdown. You can walk there and all. Brooklyn — you'll be working on the manor in Somerset."

The manor was a stately home, Simon's largest current project. If it meant getting away from Ricky, that was fine with Brooklyn, but he didn't understand why Simon would send them both elsewhere.

"There's still a lot to do here, boss. How come you don't want me to finish?" he asked.

Simon scowled. "Our work on this flat is stopping now. The client was supposed to make a stage payment by lunchtime. He didn't, and I copped an earful when I phoned. He's cross about the ceiling, but does he think I work for love?"

He shook his head. "I'll see him in court. An hour earlier, and I'd have stopped the furniture coming here. And if I'd known you were buying all the wood upfront, I'd have put the brakes on that too. Still, we can use it at the manor. One door closes and another opens, eh? Let's load the van."

"Where's my sausage roll?" Brooklyn hissed at Ricky while they carried the remaining oak to the car park.

"I couldn't get one. The boss hauled me back too early." Ricky belched, an unappetising mix of beer and curry.

The last thing they needed was a repeat visit from the mad lady upstairs, but she'd obviously spotted Simon's Merc and twigged that the boss had turned up. She hammered on the door, demanding to speak to Simon.

Brooklyn and Ricky hunkered down in the back lounge, eavesdropping.

"Same old," Ricky whispered, yawning as she asked Simon why his employees were so careless. There she was, a woman on her own, exposed to the risk of burglary or worse.

"Ricky," Simon yelled.

Ricky winced. He sidled to the front room to face the music.

"How come you left a door open?"

"I didn't—"

"Make sure it doesn't happen again," Simon ordered. To the old woman, he said, "I apologise for the oversight. Now I assume my workman told you about the leak from your flat? Would you like to come in here and see the damage?"

She stalled him. "Well, I don't think I need to see it. I'll be checking on my insurance."

"You do that," Simon said. "Why don't I take a look at your bathroom now, and I can give you a quote for the insurance company? No obligation, obviously."

"That won't be necessary." She sounded stiff and awkward. "I'm sorry, but I must go. I have work to do."

"Here's my card." Simon proffered it, then closed the door. He pretended to knock his head on the wall. "Is she for real?" he asked.

"Piece of work," Ricky said. "Listen, that was her brother's flat, and she's clearin' it out for sale. The place is in a state and she says she can't afford to fix it. Could be an opportunity for you, Simon."

"Yes, it just might be." Simon fingered his chin. Mollified, he said, "Maybe I was too hasty. Ricky, you can't drive home, but Brooklyn can run you back. Give me your keys, mate."

Reluctantly, Ricky obeyed. Simon retrieved the Yale and clover mortice for the front door, and a key with a serrated edge for the back. He handed the remainder to Brooklyn. "That one's for the Transit, okay?"

Curiously, the jingling bundle included three keys very similar to the ones Simon had just taken. Shining silver as if newly cut, there was a Yale, a clover and a jagged edge. A fantastical idea began to take shape in Brooklyn's mind.

"Should I make a cuppa before we go?" he asked, walking through to the kitchen.

"No need. Why don't you stop early for a change?" Simon's mood had turned for the better since Ricky dangled the prospect of flipping the upstairs flat.

Brooklyn checked no-one was looking. He removed the shiny keys from the ring and shoved them in his pocket. Perhaps tonight wouldn't be a problem after all. Just wait until he told Vix.

Chapter 12

September 2023

Vix

Vix stood at the school gate, listening to Keisha and Aleisha without clocking a word they said. Their bus, which had always been hers too, was late. She hadn't intended to talk to anyone, wasn't in the mood for it, but the twins had waylaid her on the way out. Why the sad face, they'd asked, before inviting her to vent.

Vix had made up an excuse about the new GCSE classes over-stretching her. It was hard to raise a smile when she missed Nanna Lizzie so much. Pretending to be interested, she let the twins' conversation wash over her. Keisha stroked Aleisha's braids. They both favoured dreadlocks, unlike Brooklyn's girlfriend, who preferred a puffy Afro style.

He hadn't talked about Marley for a while, and she wondered if they were still together. A month ago, it had been Marley this and Marley that. Of course, the first flush of romance might have faded. She ought to ask him later. He surely wouldn't risk telling Marley what had happened now?

The bus arrived, putting to a halt at the stop down the road. "Coming?" Aleisha asked.

"No, Brooklyn will give me a lift."

"Brooklyn!" Aleisha giggled.

Vix glared. So what if her parents were Posh and Becks fans? At least, she guessed they must have been. They weren't around to ask.

She felt a pang of regret as Keisha and Aleisha boarded the bus. The twins had become her best friends since Ruby moved last year. Her departure had been abrupt; a care placement broke down, and the next day she was three hundred miles away. The girls messaged each other for a few weeks, hourly at first, then daily, and finally not at all. It wasn't the same as sitting in the next chair at school. Vix supposed Ruby had a new bestie in Blackpool.

The bus pulled away. Aleisha waved. Vix bit back tears. Yesterday, she'd been on that same bus, joshing with them, certain of her destination. Her stomach swirled. Where was her brother?

She shuddered. Tonight, she'd have to lie on the van's cold hard metal floor again. Brooklyn had piled on blankets, but the chill still seeped through into her bones.

"Hey, I hoped I'd see you."

Vix jumped and spun around. Beneath dark corkscrew curls, Cody beamed up at her.

"Where did you come from?" She couldn't stop herself from sounding cross, even though she liked Cody. He was in her class, sparky, not a creep like some of the boys. Perhaps he tried harder because he was so short. Even Vix stretched above him, and she barely passed the five-foot mark.

"Something getting to you?" Cody asked.

"No," she muttered, following up with, "Time of the month," to close the conversation down. Thankfully, it was a lie. She kicked aside the thought of van life with a period. There was another fortnight to work out how to handle it.

"Poor you," Cody sympathised. "Still up for Saturday?"

"Saturday?" What did he mean? Vix squinted at him.

"The demo. Climate change. Remember?"

"Oh, er, yeah." How could she have forgotten? She'd really wanted to go. That was how the trouble started with Nanna Lizzie, though.

Now the rally no longer seemed important.

"Still going?" Cody pressed.

"Sure." It beat sitting in Brooklyn's van all day.

"You sound out of it," Cody observed. "They're starting at eleven on College Green. Can you get there early? Meet outside the Chocolate House?"

"Sure, ten minutes before." That would stop him turning it into a date. He hadn't given any indication he fancied her, but you never knew.

Cody smiled. "Feel better soon."

He crossed the road, heading to the council flats where Brooklyn had turned his van around that morning. A family of five lived in a two bedroom apartment: his mum, dad, their twin babies and Cody. Vix had always felt sorry for him, cramped up with the squalling brats. Now, she was jealous. She wished she'd asked him if she could sleep over. They must have a couch or armchair to spare. Then again, he might misunderstand.

Vix wouldn't ask Cody to go out with her any time soon. She didn't need a boyfriend.

Maybe she should have approached the twins about a sleepover. It was too late now, and they'd have been suspicious.

For her own safety, she must push her friends away.

She'd have no-one left but Brooklyn. Tears wet Vix's cheeks as she waited for him.

Chapter 13

September 2023

Brooklyn

Brooklyn jolted in his seat when he saw the dashboard clock. Nearly 4pm. Vix must have already left school. Once they'd tidied up and loaded the Transit, he and Ricky hadn't gained any time at all.

Ricky noticed too. "So much for stoppin' early," he carped.

"Yeah." It was the least of Brooklyn's worries. As he started the engine, he hoped Simon would forget to dock his pay. The boss had had plenty of distractions. He'd gone to a meeting, argued with a client and encountered a crazy lady. There must be a chance.

Ricky continued to grumble. "Sheesh, you shouldn't have braked, Brook. How did you pass your driving test? And don't turn that way, it's quicker to the left. Then we wanna cut through Bedminster, okay?"

"I'm using the satnav." South Bristol was a closed book to Brooklyn.

"Well don't. What does a robot know? I lives 'ere, dun I?"

It wasn't a battle worth fighting. "You tell me the way," Brooklyn said.

"No, let me drive," Ricky suggested.

Brooklyn's shoulders tensed. "It's more than my job's worth. You heard Simon."

"But 'ee won't know," Ricky protested.

Brooklyn flailed for an excuse. They'd both be in trouble if the boss found out they'd flouted him.

"Simon might have hidden a camera in the cab," he said. There was no sign of one, but they were the size of a fingernail. He wouldn't put it past Simon at all.

Ricky gave up. "Okay, as I'm stuck with you behind the wheel, this is where you're to. You wanna head for the wood merchant, but instead of turning right, you go left, round the gyratory, and left again. Got it?"

Brooklyn hadn't, but he let Ricky yell directions like "Sharp left – now!" until they reached the point where Bedminster and Knowle West intertwined. Glastonbury Road was J-shaped, a long sweep of brick semis and bungalows similar to Nanna Lizzie's. Her front garden featured neat flowerbeds rather than junk and thistles, though. Even Brooklyn, irked by Nanna Lizzie's constant demands for tidiness, wasn't impressed.

Ricky didn't apologise for the rotting mattress outside his home, nor offer tea. He drummed his fingers on the dashboard. "You've got my keys, Brook."

Heart thumping against his ribcage, Brooklyn removed the Transit key from the ring. He passed the rest to Ricky. "There you go," he said, his tone nonchalant.

"Some's missing," Ricky stated flatly.

It was too much to ask, expecting him to overlook keys he must have only just had cut. Brooklyn widened his eyes, pretending innocence. "These are all the boss gave me," he said. "You saw him."

Ricky grimaced. "Okay, I'll ask Simon." He hopped out of the van, slamming its door.

Ricky must be bluffing. He'd surely imagine his cousin had caught him out. Brooklyn's hands trembled as he switched on the ignition. He decided to stop for food. A few minutes wouldn't make a difference when he was already late, and he'd spotted a convenience store.

After texting Vix to say sorry, he downed a bottle of Coke and a KitKat before setting off again. The sweet, creamy chocolate tasted better than anything he'd eaten for weeks. When a surge of energy hit him, he realised how hungry he'd been. Wedging a tube of Pringles to the left of the driver's seat, he helped himself as he drove. As he pulled into the car park opposite her school, only a third of the crisps remained.

Unlike the morning, there was no hustle and bustle. Vix alone stood outside the gate, lounging against a wall, hands balled into fists and eyes reddened. While she stared straight at him, she made no move to cross the road.

Brooklyn wound down the window. "Hey, Vix."

Her whole body jolted. "Brooklyn?"

She glanced left and right, and ran to him. "Why are you driving that?"

"Simon asked me to. It's fun. Really high up. Let me help you in."

Vix glared up at him as he opened the passenger door and held out his hand. "How can you be so excited about a van?" she spat. "We don't have anywhere to stay, I could be sent to the other end of England, and Nanna Lizzie…"

She climbed into the passenger seat, threw her backpack into the footwell, and turned her face away.

"Vix, there's a flat." His words tumbled out like a sudden gush of water. "It's in Cliftonwood, where I've been working. We can stay there as long as we're careful—"

She interrupted. "What do you mean, as long as we're careful?"

"Because Simon doesn't know. He has no idea I've got the keys. Vix, the place is nearly finished. There's everything we need. The bathroom's done, and the kitchen. It's nice."

He decided not to add, 'apart from the living room ceiling'.

"What if he finds out? You'd lose your job, Brooks."

"We've got bigger problems."

Watching her face crumple, Brooklyn regretted saying that.

"Listen," he said. "Why would anyone tell Simon? The owner's not in Bristol. They live in China, Hong Kong, or somewhere. And Simon's having an argument with them, so he told us to stop work. Nobody will go near that flat. If we keep our heads down, it's a place we can sleep."

He put the Transit into gear. "Anyway, do you like my wheels? It's fun sitting up this high. Like flying."

"Not electric, is it?" Vix mumbled. "Killing the planet like your other one."

She was silent for a while. He wondered if she'd fallen asleep, but when he snatched a glance, she was staring out of the window.

Traffic oozed slowly along the main road. Brooklyn appreciated why they called it a jam. At this time of day, the drive was like wading through treacle. He took a handful of crisps, cramming them into his mouth, relishing their salty tang. "Want some?" he asked.

"Not hungry."

"I'm starving. Can you cook us something when we get there?"

"Like what?"

He sensed a belligerent edge to her voice.

"I don't know," he said. "Meat and two veg, or a curry? You always do the cooking."

Vix sniffed. "Yes, but there was food in the house. Nanna Lizzie went to the shops and bought it. There won't be anything in this flat, if no-one's living there. Probably nothing to cook it with, either."

She blew her nose. When they stopped at traffic lights, he spotted her tears.

"Don't cry," he said softly, although the lump in his gullet suggested he felt the same. "There may be some kitchen things. Simon's wife ordered show home stuff. We can check what's there."

"Did she bring a fruit bowl, veggies and juicy steaks?" Vix held her head in her hands.

"We'll go out to the shops in Clifton Village." He didn't have much money, but there was enough to buy food, especially if he didn't pay rent to Nanna Lizzie anymore. The direct debit from his bank account must be stopped. He'd do it later with his phone.

A car braked in front of them, and Brooklyn returned his concentration to the road. It was pointless trying to talk to Vix. Nothing he said would cheer her up. Yet she seemed to brighten as they passed through the narrow streets of Cliftonwood.

"I'd like to live there." She pointed to a pink-washed cottage.

"The flat's not pretty like that," he admitted.

"Don't care. It's better than a van." She laughed, a golden sound: the first sign of lightness for twenty-four hours.

"Right."

Her eyes drank in their surroundings. He wasn't too keen on the area himself, Clifton Village being overrated and the beer overpriced. Friends occasionally dragged him to pubs there. He didn't enjoy it. Nobody spoke like him. They all had plummy voices.

Long before, he'd gone on a school trip to the suspension bridge, which he appreciated more. Like Brunel's other work, it had been ground-breaking. Imagine designing railways, boats and bridges, with everyone telling you they'd never work, then proving them wrong.

Brunel was a genius. Brooklyn loved the bridge's flawless engineering, its chains flying gracefully above the Avon Gorge. He'd ignored his teachers when they raved about the Georgian architecture nearby. Who cared about a load of old houses? Still, although Clifton didn't impress him, the flat was an amazing piece of luck.

"Here we are." He turned into Aldworth Terrace, pulled into the car park and helped her step down from Simon's van.

Brooklyn fiddled with the keys, recalling that the Yale and the clover opened the front door. He breathed more easily once they'd succeeded in entering the kitchen.

"Wow," Vix said.

Brooklyn grinned. "What do you reckon?"

"Flash, isn't it?" She ran a hand over the smooth granite worktops.

"We can make it cosy. Like I told you, Mrs Heath ordered furniture. We just have to unpack some and find what we need. Come and look, it's all in the front room."

That meant walking through the lounge. He realised his mistake right away, when she gawped at the hole in the ceiling.

"What's that?"

"It's what Simon and his client are arguing about. A leak from the bathroom in the flat upstairs. There's a crazy woman living there. She doesn't want to fix it."

"Won't it just get worse?"

Vix had a point. Brooklyn imagined their upstairs neighbour taking a bath and crashing down beside them. It gave him an idea.

"Maybe I could get her onside," he suggested. "If I did a temporary fix for her."

Vix wrinkled her face. "You're not a plumber. And you said we shouldn't tell anyone we're here."

"I'll say I'm working on the flat. She's seen me do that already, and she'll notice the vans, anyhow. Also," he pointed to the void above them, "there's rotten wood up there. She needs to make her floor safe. I can do that. And plumbing. It's not as hard as you think."

"If you're sure."

"I've watched Dave and Ricky do it."

"All right. Will you ask her?"

"After dinner."

Vix sighed. "Let's play hunt the saucepan."

"If we've got any, they're here." He led her to the front room.

Vix surveyed the packaged-up furniture. "I don't see any kitchen stuff."

Brooklyn ripped open one of the smaller boxes, producing three white china mugs swathed in bubble wrap. Vix popped the bubbles while he tried more packages. He found an artificial cheese plant, table lamps and a mirror.

"Um, what about an electric kettle?" he asked, remembering the tea kit.

"Yeah, I can boil eggs or pasta in it," Vix announced. "Possibly both."

"Better than nothing," Brooklyn said, suspecting they'd soon get sick of them. He would delve into the boxes again later.

"Give me twenty and I'll get some," Vix said.

"Wait." Brooklyn heard the thud of footsteps on stairs. The front door to the apartment lobby opened and closed. He gazed out of the window. "Come and see. It's the mad cow from upstairs."

Vix ogled her. "Looks harmless. Just an old lady."

"She's insane. Still, at least she's gone. Try to avoid her if you spot her again. I've got a reason to be here, but you haven't."

"Sure. Where's that money?"

He gave her the single twenty pound note sitting in his wallet. Ricky's tenner was already gone. "Buy bread and ham too, and make me sandwiches for tomorrow."

"Don't push it," Vix said.

She stayed until their neighbour was lost from view. Once she'd gone, Brooklyn made tea. He identified two flat-packed beds amongst the heap of boxes. Heaving one onto his shoulder, he removed it to a bedroom and laid out the pieces for assembly. He had black metal tubes of varying lengths, curly finials to cap the bed posts, screws and an Allen key. This was an easy job. He rigged the tubes together in twenty minutes.

A door slammed. He heard footsteps.

"Hello?" Vix said. "Oh, good. A bed." She sniffed. "You need a shower."

"Thanks. Tell me you bought soap."

"Yes, you lucked out."

His stomach rumbled. "What's for dinner?" he asked.

"Pot Noodles and boiled eggs."

"Tasty."

Vix ignored the note of irony. "You're right about the old lady," she said. "Out to lunch, for sure. I saw her in the supermarket, and she looked at me like this."

She peered at Brooklyn, bug-eyed.

He laughed. "Yeah, that's her."

"We walked back via the same route. You know, down Constitution Hill and along Aldworth Terrace? She was a few metres ahead of me, and she kept turning round and staring."

A frisson of alarm stiffened his shoulders. "Did she see you?"

"Probably. I tried to hide in shadows and doorways."

"Next time, go a different way."

"I wouldn't have thought of that," she said sarcastically.

He wasn't looking forward to it, but when Vix produced the hot food ten minutes later, he found it surprisingly tasty. She served the Pot Noodles in their plastic tubs and the hard-boiled eggs in mugs. They stood at the kitchen island, eating with Simon's teaspoons.

"I've got homework," Vix said. "Is there wi-fi?"

"Don't think so. Nobody lives here …officially. I'll try her upstairs – she might give me her code if I ask nicely."

Brooklyn finished his food, every scrap of it. Hunger still gnawed at his belly.

"Cornflakes?" He eyed the packet hopefully.

"That's breakfast," Vix snapped, then softened. "Okay, yeah, grab some for pudding."

Brooklyn ate a mugful. Emboldened by a sugar high, he left to visit their neighbour.

He bounded up the stairs two at a time, forcing himself to hurry. She gave him the creeps. The sooner this task was out of the way, the better. Music escaped from her flat: an insistent, drum-led beat which he recognised as an old song. Brooklyn jabbed the doorbell. Although the jangling sound was clearly audible, nothing happened. After half a minute or so, he pressed it for ten seconds.

He was about to give up when the door sprang open. The woman stood there, looking every bit as mad as he expected, eyes flashing feverishly. Then he noticed the carving knife in her hand. His heart stopped. He stepped backward.

At least she hadn't confronted his sister. Vix, tiny and unused to fighting, wouldn't have stood a chance. He was a head taller. Stronger too. A lucky punch might save him.

Getting away would be better still. Brooklyn inched back. If he was quick, he could turn and run, get downstairs before she even thought of throwing the knife.

The old lady snarled, "Why are you following me?"

Chapter 14

May 1992

Jules

"Why are you following me?" Jules demanded. "Couldn't you phone?"

"No. Suppose George took the call? You wouldn't want me talking to him, Jules, darling." Rufus lounged in the doorway, arms folded.

Behind her, a suitcase lay on the bed. It was the same four poster in the same plush rural hotel where she always rendezvoused with Malcolm. She'd hardly started unpacking the silky fripperies she'd brought to wear for him.

"We need to talk. Let me in." He uncurled his arms and planted a leg over the threshold.

"I'm expecting company. I thought you were—"

"You don't say. We can go to the bar if you'd prefer a conversation in public?"

She admitted defeat. "Okay. Ten minutes, then." Locking the door behind him, she asked, "What's up?"

"It's about Damien. He's stolen my laptop."

"A laptop? But he told me you gave it to him."

Rufus scowled. "He's lying."

"He invented some kind of game. Penguins. I thought he was working with you on it."

"Well, you thought wrong." Rufus paced the room. "I've got ten years' experience of game design. Do you think I need his help? Listen, I want the kit back. It's expensive. I bet the little devil's sold it to buy drugs."

"Drugs? But he's just a child. He wouldn't..." Her voice faltered as she watched his nostrils flare. She'd never seen Rufus in a rage before. It both frightened and unsettled her, as if a kitten had transformed into a rabid tiger.

Rufus glared at her. "Damien does drugs all right. Of course he'll lie if you ask him. Look, I don't care how you do it, but get my laptop back, okay?"

"I'll try."

She heard a key turn in the lock, then the rattle of the still-closed door being repeatedly pushed.

"I've locked myself in!" she yelled. "Silly me. Can you ask at reception—"

"Don't worry, I'll go right away." Malcolm's voice was muffled. "But why didn't you phone them from the room?"

"Oh dear." Jules forced out a giggle. She fiddled with her wedding ring. "I didn't think of that. I'm in such a tizzy."

Malcolm chuckled. "Just get yourself ready – well, perhaps not too ready. We may have to break down the door, after all. Back soon." His footsteps faded.

She exhaled, slumping onto the bed. "That was so close. You should go."

If Malcolm found Rufus with her, what would he think? He'd imagine she had another lover. Yet Malcolm was more than enough. Anyway, she and Rufus had never been attracted to each other.

For years, he'd been around in the background, part of a group of student friends. A drinking buddy, party animal and confidante, Rufus was good company. But now he seemed darker. Dangerous.

His eyes narrowed. "Before I leave, there's one more thing. Those kids you sent along last week – they're not taking it seriously. Find me a couple more, okay?"

He opened the door and lingered a moment longer. "Ciao, darling."

Chapter 15

May 1992

Jules

She'd dreaded that awkward conversation with Damien, avoiding eye contact when he arrived for his next German lesson. He forced Jules's hand by turning in such a poor piece of homework that she asked him to stay behind.

"Forty per cent, Damien? You can do better." She stared at him across her desk.

It was Damien's turn to avert his gaze. "Doesn't matter," he mumbled. "I'm dropping German next year, anyway."

Jules sighed. "That's up to you. But your parents will get your marks at the end of term, won't they? And I'm sure they'll be happier if this is a one-off and you meet your usual standard in future."

"S'pose I don't want to?"

"Out of my hands," Jules said. "You'll have to justify it to them. Look, is everything all right at home?"

"SNAFU. As usual." He flicked angrily at a loose strand of hair.

She caught a whiff of tobacco. Was he smoking too? Perhaps Rufus was right about the drugs.

"How's it going with Rufus's beta testing?" she asked.

His brows knitted together. "I don't care about his poxy games," Damien spat.

"He said you took his laptop without permission. Can he have it back?"

"He gave it to me. And no, he can't."

Damien met her eyes at last. He was either telling the truth or had become a good liar.

"Look, maybe you thought it was a gift, but Rufus doesn't. It's his word against yours. You don't want him going to the police."

Nor did she. George had friends in the force. If she ended up boxed in a corner by their questions, forced to admit to an affair, George would hear about it. Then what? The perfect life she planned, playing happy families, would vanish before it began.

Damien reddened. "Rufus can take a running jump," he said savagely. "I threw it in the river."

Jules's lips tightened. How would she explain to Rufus? She'd better offer to buy a replacement, and make sure to pay with cash. George's credit card was out of the question; he checked the statements too carefully.

"By the way," Damien said, his flushed skin paling again, "Steve Purslow told me he was going to test games for Rufus this week."

"Are you friends with Steve?" she asked.

"No. Purslow's a psycho." A wild glint shone in Damien's eyes. "Rufus won't know what hit him."

Chapter 16

September 2023

Juliet

Who was this – one of Rufus's victims? No, it was impossible. The gangling youth was much too old, and at the same time, too young. Damien and the others would be middle-aged by now. Still, she wanted answers.

As she waved the blade at him, he shrank back. His Adam's apple wobbled. Straggling, sandy hair stuck out in random directions. He'd never be Rufus's type.

"I'm not following you," he gasped. "I'm working downstairs – remember?"

He had the same Bristolian drawl as the builder who'd disturbed her shower that morning. Was this the younger colleague she'd seen? Now the youth mentioned it, his features did seem familiar. She spotted the toolbox in his left hand.

"Sorry," she said, dropping her hand to her side while still holding the knife. "It's just... well, you can't be too careful."

He nodded, still gawping at her. His mouth twitched on one side.

"I get it," he said. "A woman on your own. Listen... um, I heard you need some repairs doing, and you can't afford it? How about if I take a look? I'll see what I can do. No charge."

She gripped the weapon tightly. "Why would you do that?" she asked.

"Um... You'd, like, be helping us out. You see, we need to finish off Flat A."

He wanted to do her a favour? Her teeth unclenched, jaw softening in a reaction that was instinctive but unfamiliar. She gulped, realising she wanted to cry. "Well, you'd better come in," she said.

He gave a shaky laugh. "Um, can you put down that knife, please?"

Juliet wavered. It was her insurance policy, in case he was just pretending to be a workman. Yet she'd seen him carry materials and drive that huge Heath House van. Watching him closely, she placed the knife on a waist-high pile of old cardboard in the hallway. If she had to, she'd be able to reach for it.

She didn't warn him about the obstacle course that awaited him. There was a sharp intake of breath when he walked into the hall.

"Sorry," she said, as he nearly tripped over a stack of old paint tins. "The bathroom isn't as bad. I mean, my brother actually liked to take a bath."

"Um, that might be the problem." He sniffed. "Did you notice the leak? I can smell it."

"I blamed the drains." The pong had hit her the moment she arrived. She'd just got used to it.

"It's worse here than downstairs," he said.

She waved him through to the bathroom. "I should have said. I'm Juliet."

"Brooklyn."

"Oh, your parents—"

"Yeah. They liked David Beckham." Brooklyn's voice was flat.

She reddened. Of course, he'd heard it all before.

Brooklyn entered the bathroom and fumbled for the light switch. "You have a lot of shampoo."

"My brother was a hoarder."

"I guessed." He turned to face Juliet where she stood in the doorway, towering over her. That boyish grin lit up his sharp features.

To her surprise, she found herself smiling back.

"I will clear out all the junk," she said apologetically. "It's why I'm here, really."

"I reckon the bath is the problem," Brooklyn said. "I'll get the panel off. Okay?"

"Go ahead." She remembered George grumbling the construction industry ran on Typhoo and Radio 1. "Would you like a hot drink?" she asked.

"Yes, please. Tea, white, five sugars."

Five? Young people needed their calories, she supposed.

"Sorry, I don't have sugar." She hadn't found any in Greg's kitchen cupboards, although they contained teabags and instant coffee. The best before dates had expired, but they wouldn't poison anyone. At least she had milk. Earlier, eager to wean herself from the vegan diet imposed at the farm, she'd bought a pint.

Brooklyn clearly had a sweet tooth. "Maybe a biscuit with it?" he asked.

"I've got apples."

He settled for white tea and a Granny Smith. She delivered them to the bathroom, then left him to it.

He hadn't complained much about the detritus littering the flat, but embarrassment spurred her into action. She started filling the black plastic bin bags she'd picked up at the supermarket. Shoe boxes full of string, stacks of out-of-date discount coupons, a broken toaster: objects were piled seemingly at random.

"Brooklyn," she called, "Will the council take all this rubbish?"

He emerged from the bathroom, hair plastered to his forehead with what she hoped was sweat. "They'll take whatever you can stuff in their bins. If you want to be careful about recycling, it's complicated. Nanna — I mean, we, always check their website. By the way, I found your leak."

His eyes twinkled. He reminded her of a pupil seeking praise.

"Can you mend it?"

"I did. Temporary, like. Come and see."

There was barely space for both of them in the bathroom. The cubbyhole was crammed with as much sanitary ware as possible, the ugly green fittings scabbed with scratches and limescale. One corner boasted a cramped shower cubicle. The bath ran along a wall, with basin and toilet opposite. Against them, Brooklyn had propped the bath panel, a slab of plastic in a shade that didn't quite match.

Using his phone as a flashlight, he angled the beam under the bath's plughole. She saw the floorboards had been cut away.

Brooklyn seemingly guessed her thoughts. "The wood was rotten. Joists are sound, though. Lucky. Look over there. That's the outlet pipe. I've taped up the joint and stopped the cold tap dripping. That's sorted it." He nodded for emphasis.

"Thank you. It's kind of you."

His face lit up again. "Like I said, it's good for us too. Want the bath panel back on?"

"Yes, please." She regretted being so strident with the workmen earlier.

Brooklyn stood up, shimmying around her to pick it up. "You need to call someone in. Fix it permanent, okay? I wouldn't use the bath either."

She retreated to the hall to give him space. With a deft twist, he refitted the panel.

"Thanks," she repeated. More from politeness than a wish to spend time with him, she asked: "Would you like more tea?"

"I ought to get back," Brooklyn said, as she'd hoped. "Um, there is a way you can help. Can I use your wi-fi code?"

She stared at him, taken aback at the strange request.

Brooklyn must have sensed her disquiet. "Um, to listen to the radio on my phone? My pay-as-you-go ran out of credit."

Of course: tea and music. Nothing had changed in three decades. "It's gregprice1," she said. "All lower case."

"Um, would you mind writing it down, please? Spelling isn't my strong point."

"I'll get a biro." Juliet picked her way through the hall and to the lounge, where her laptop bag contained stationery. If Greg had buried pens among his layers of possessions, she hadn't uncovered them yet.

What did they teach kids at school these days? The less academic children had always been left behind, of course. She liked to think she'd been a diligent teacher, that she'd have made a difference to a pupil like Brooklyn. He didn't seem the type to have given his educators any trouble. Perhaps that was his problem. He would have skulked at the back of the classroom, keeping his head down, never admitting to difficulties.

Still, he was skilled with his hands, kind and polite. His mother must be proud of him. Juliet would have been. She'd have badgered him about that Bristol accent, though. Brought up in a Somerset council house, she'd learned to speak properly, so there was no reason why Brooklyn couldn't.

She handed him a scrap of paper with the code.

"Thank you," Brooklyn said.

"You're welcome." Juliet bolted the door behind him. The fleeting moment of empathy she'd felt for Brooklyn vanished as she focused on her own problems. Someone had followed her home from the supermarket. Juliet had felt their eyes boring into her back, had turned around and caught a glimpse of movement. She was sure by now that it hadn't been Brooklyn.

So who was it?

Chapter 17

September 2023

Vix

Vix sat at the kitchen island, perched on a folding dining chair. Opposite, messy hair haloed by the morning sun, Brooklyn crunched cornflakes. They'd opened more of the boxes without discovering plates or bowls. Brooklyn just spooned his cereal from a mug. Another held strong tea. With a final slurp of the hot drink, he stood up and stretched.

"Off to play football," he announced.

Vix glared at him, resentful that his Saturday morning routine was going ahead as usual. Brooklyn behaved as if everything was normal. Yet nothing would ever be the same again.

"You might wash up first," she grumbled.

Her brother had the grace to look sheepish.

"Sorry." He took crockery and spoons to the sink, rinsing them under the tap. They still didn't have washing-up liquid. She must buy some later.

"What are you up to today?" he asked.

"Homework. Might go to the library." She didn't need to, with access to wi-fi here. It was a convenient excuse to visit the city centre.

"Can you get another set of keys cut?" he asked. "I'm seeing Marley after the football. You'll be in when I come back, won't you?"

So Marley was still part of his life.

"Depends how late," Vix teased him. "Now Marley's sixteen and all."

Brooklyn coloured up. He was ridiculously easy to embarrass.

Vix relented. "Yeah, I'll be in. Listen, I don't know how much keys cost, but can I have an extra tenner for food?"

He removed two notes from his wallet, which, she saw, had been refilled.

"Thanks." She pocketed the cash.

Brooklyn slipped off to his bedroom, returning in his team's black and green striped kit. "Laters, Vix."

"See ya."

He left his own van in the car park, taking Simon's Transit. Yesterday, he'd explained to Vix that he'd use it as a runaround this weekend. That way, the boss paid for the petrol. If Simon complained about it, Brooklyn would claim it was free advertising. When he played amateur football on the Downs, he met rich people. Young accountants, lawyers and salesmen all joined in. They might want house renovations, or have friends who did.

As a child, Brooklyn had dreamed of scoring goals for Bristol Rovers. He'd told Vix this before she knew what a football was. For years, she'd regarded it as a fact. He was her wise, clever older brother, so of course she believed him. By the time she realised he wouldn't be a soccer superstar, Brooklyn had already shrugged off his disappointment. As long as he played the game at some level, he stayed happy. Nanna Lizzie had found him the apprenticeship with Simon, a job that suited him.

His future was mapped out.

Except it wasn't, if anyone found out what they'd done.

And what about her? Vix sniffed. Would she be allowed to go into nursing? It was all she'd ever wanted to do. She still planned to spend half her weekend on GCSE coursework, keen to get her grades. When she'd told Brooklyn she intended to do homework, she hadn't been lying. Not entirely. She just hadn't been specific on timing.

She rinsed out her own cornflakes mug. Afterwards, she put on trainers and checked her phone for the way to College Green, where the climate rally would take place. It was a twenty-minute walk. Vix smiled with relief. Although she paid half fare, and a bus trip was only a pound, she must count every penny. Brooklyn's wages were all they had, and Simon Heath wasn't generous.

She plotted her route: along Aldworth Terrace and Aldworth Road, then down steep Constitution Hill and Jacobs Wells Road to the harbour. Through the kitchen window, she glimpsed a fine day, the sky blue and cloudless. Gentle breezes ruffled a pear tree in the small garden next to the car park. Vix had noticed fruit weighing down the branches. Tomorrow, she'd test it for ripeness.

She shrugged on a grey parka over her T-shirt and jeans, and made for the front room. Another resident was leaving the lobby. Just her luck. Vix heard the click of a door and the clatter of heels. She peered through the window.

The old lady from Flat 2 emerged, formally dressed in a black trouser suit and court shoes, steel-grey bob brushed back. A blue paper face mask hid her features, but it was definitely her. Like Vix, she was skinny and only around five feet tall. Evidently, her paranoia extended to germs as well as people.

69

The woman had pulled a knife on Brooklyn. If Vix hadn't already had good reason to avoid Juliet – what a ridiculously romantic name for an old witch! – that alone would have convinced her.

Vix let Juliet make her exit before she slipped out too. Unfortunately, their neighbour appeared to be heading in the same direction. Her heels tapped out a rhythm towards Aldworth Road. With a glance over her shoulder, she turned left towards Constitution Hill.

Vix hung back, darting behind the trees planted at intervals along the pavement. These mature specimens stretched as high as the rooftops. Perhaps they'd been there for centuries. Vix recognised them as beeches from the oval, slightly pointed leaves, some of which had turned autumnal brown. She'd learned about trees from Nanna Lizzie, the knowledge imparted conversationally when little Vix was taken to the park. How she had shrieked in delight as Lizzie pushed her swing.

Vix bit her lip, blinking away a tear and wishing she could compartmentalise her feelings. Brooklyn seemed to do it easily.

When she reached the junction with Aldworth Road, Vix turned right, away from Constitution Hill. It was vital to avoid Juliet. If the crazy woman twigged that people were living in the flat conversion, who knew what she'd do? She might call Simon Heath, whose number was plastered all over his van. Even Brooklyn needed to be careful. His cover story lacked plausibility; no builder worked 24/7.

Vix checked her phone, seeing that a nearby footpath led to the harbourside. Her route took her past cute cottages and grand houses to a steep flight of stone steps. Vix hastened down them and through a tunnel at the bottom. Here, a modern block of flats had been built around the old walkway. Traffic zipped along the road in front of her, while opposite, small boats bobbed on sparkling water.

Vix drank in the sight of houseboats and motor cruisers moored nearby, kayaks racing through the harbour and the SS Great Britain in the distance. Then she turned away and half-walked, half-ran past the blue and cream buildings of the City of Bristol College. She was late.

Competing smells of curry, fried onions and vanilla wafted towards her. Vix sniffed appreciatively. A wall of noise increased in volume, almost deafening her as she approached the grand brown brick sweep of City Hall. Her senses were pleasantly overwhelmed, crowding out dark memories. Vix embraced the sensation. She edged around the side of College Green, ignoring the stalls, placard-holders and musicians filling the grassy triangle. Apart from the line of children queueing for face painting, everyone seemed much older than her.

"Grab a whistle, my lover." A bald man with a grey beard down to his waist sprang in front of Vix, thrusting a green lanyard at her. She noted the small silvery object attached to it.

"I'm sorry, but I can't afford—"

"No charge, my dear."

"Thanks. Can I take one for my friend too?" She hoped Cody was still waiting. Looping both lanyards around her neck, she waved to the whistle man and dashed off. She skirted the crowd and arrived at the foot of Park Street, a steep hill lined with shops and bars. They charged the sort of prices that meant Vix only window-shopped. The Chocolate House, popular with students, was just a landmark to her: across the road and a little way up the rise.

Vix exhaled in relief at the sight of Cody's black frizz. He lounged with his back to the Chocolate House window, gaze fixed on his phone.

"Hey, Cody."

"Vix. I was messaging you. Want a brownie?" He handed her a cake wrapped in greasy paper.

A gorgeous chocolatey smell rose from the package even before she unwrapped it. Vix took a bite, relishing its fudginess.

"Lush," she said, taking care not to spread crumbs. "Did you get it here?"

He pointed back to the green and said, "No. From the vegan stall. It's pay what you can." He added, "I had two for breakfast. Anyhow, come and get a banner. Spike says we can take one."

"Who's Spike?"

"He's a fixer. You'll see." Cody stuck his phone in his jeans pocket. To combat the breeze, he wore a black hoodie. It dwarfed him; Nanna Lizzie would have claimed it had growing room.

Vix followed him back across the road. A trio of musicians, men in their twenties tuning guitars, nodded to him.

"Seen Spike?" he asked.

"Outside the hotel." One of them jabbed a finger towards the Marriott. The grand sandstone pile dominated a corner of the green, rising above a bird poo-splattered statue of Queen Victoria.

Cody weaved through the throng, spotting gaps easily. Vix dived after him, spirits buoyed by the brownie and the smiling faces around her.

"There he is."

71

In the circular cobbled lane around Victoria's statue, protestors surrounded a stationary SUV. The driver had wound down his window. He was haranguing a tall man with a shock of turquoise hair. Given the music and hundreds of loud conversations, Vix merely caught fragments of the argument.

"I'll run you all down!"

"Please be patient, sir, I'll ask them—"

A toddler ran across her path. Vix tripped, face flying towards the cobbles as the infant skipped off unscathed.

With an uncanny sixth sense, Cody twisted around, grabbing her arm. "You 'kay, Vix?"

"Yeah," she responded automatically, distracted by the SUV's sudden movement. With a curse from the driver and a roar from its engine, the vehicle shot forward.

By some miracle, all the pedestrians jumped out of its way. Fists pounded the doors as it disappeared into an underground car park.

"Spike?" Cody appealed for attention from the turquoise-haired man, who, lips curled in a snarl, turned his back on the hotel.

"Yo, Cody." Spike's face, tanned and lined, was older than Vix had expected. It settled into an amiable expression. "What's up, my friend?"

"You said there were banners?"

"Yeah, James will sort you out. Say I sent you." Spike waved towards a younger fellow, blond and clean-cut, dishing out flags. His eyes fixed on Vix's. "Are you okay? You seem somewhat enraged."

She hadn't even realised that her shoulders were hunched, her hands bunched into fists. "That car," she gasped.

"He isn't worth space in your brain," Spike said. He shook his head. Sunlight glinted off a silver, balloon-shaped stud in one ear.

Why didn't he understand? "It's his sense of entitlement," Vix said. "He thinks he's more important than anyone else. That's why—"

"—he drives a Chelsea tractor," Spike finished for her. "You're right. As I always say, don't get mad, get even. Interested?"

"Yes." Cody spoke before Vix even drew breath.

Spike reached down to clap him on the shoulder. "See you later at the Green Man," he said.

Chapter 18

June 1992

Jules

"Best steak I've had this year," George commented, cutting another bloodied slice. He preferred it rare, the way it was served to him when they holidayed in France. Not that those short breaks were the main event. He'd also whisked Jules to St Lucia, Acapulco and Bali. Thailand would be next.

Jules blushed, and topped up their glasses. She'd cooked a special meal tonight, with Bull's Blood wine, which tasted delicious with beef. Later, they would attempt once more to make a baby. George enjoyed ribald jokes with his friends about it. He had fun trying, he told them.

No-one need know about Malcolm's extra help. Surely a baby would be on the way soon? Then she'd be faithful to George again, the wife he deserved.

She glugged her wine, letting a soft haze of alcohol overcome her unease. It wasn't just guilt that set her on edge, but the strain of appeasing Rufus. The dynamic of their friendship had changed, and not for the better. He'd become cold and demanding, impatient for more games testers.

George took a final mouthful and set down his knife and fork.

"Hey," he said, "I forgot to ask. What about the boy in the Floating Harbour?"

It sounded like a riddle. She smiled at him. "Do tell."

"Well…" George leaned forward, clearly eager to impart juicy gossip. "I'm surprised you haven't heard. Merv said he did a press conference this afternoon. It's not every day he finds a dead body."

It wasn't a joke, then. "Your policeman friend, Merv? How awful for him."

"Don't be silly. He didn't fish it out himself. Merv has minions for that. Listen, it's a pupil from your school."

Jules froze. "Who?"

Suddenly, she felt stone-cold sober. Casting her mind back to the day's classes, she tried to remember who hadn't turned up.

She fought a sudden urge to vomit. "It couldn't be Damien, could it? He wasn't at school today."

"What?" George scowled, his tone sharp. "Of course not. I popped into Mum's earlier, and Damien was up in his room, doing homework. What's this about him skipping school?"

She backtracked. "Well, maybe I got that wrong. He just didn't come to my class, that's all."

"I'd have skived off German too, if I thought I'd get away with it," George said. "Don't fret, he's alive and well. Not like the poor little lad lying stark naked in the water. Strangled, not drowned. Has to be a kiddy fiddler, doesn't it?"

Bile rose again. She hoped her dreadful suspicions were unfounded. "Did Merv give you a name?"

"Stephen something."

"Purslow?" She retched.

"That's right. Jules, you've gone green. Did you know him?"

She nodded, mouth closed. Stumbling to her feet, heartbeat roaring in her ears, she ran to the cloakroom under the stairs. She was only just in time. Afterwards, sobbing and howling, she wondered how she'd been so blind.

When had she seen Rufus with a girlfriend? He'd fooled her with smoke and mirrors — rueful jokes about chasing women, blind dates that never worked out.

George banged on the door. "Jules, are you all right?"

She couldn't face him. "Leave me alone," she mumbled, making a puking noise. The real thing followed swiftly.

Through tears, her mind raced. How many teenagers had she sent to Rufus? She went through their names: nine of them, all males. The girls weren't interested. Rufus hadn't complained about that, or even remarked on it.

The lads might have tested video games. After all, Rufus did run a successful business; George had invested in it. But that wasn't why Rufus wanted those boys.

Poor Damien. What had Rufus done to him? Jules shuddered, her stomach lurching again. She'd have to tell the police and somehow avoid mentioning her affair. After all, she'd been innocently helping a friend, hadn't she?

The drifting odour of a cigar suggested George had returned to the dinner table. Unable to look him in the eye, she crept upstairs to use the master bedroom's trimphone. Her hand shook so much, she could barely punch in 999.

Chapter 19

June 1992

Jules

Stiff, steely, white-hot with rage like a poker pulled out of the fire, Jeff Sharples ranted.

"You won't believe what I've been through. Two hours, sitting in that room at Bridewell—"

Jules could picture it too well: the tiny, barred windows, damp stains on the ceiling, mingled smells of sweat and mould. Then there were the police, pushing her for details of Rufus's misdeeds, impatient with her answers. She'd told them about everything, except the affair. Relieved when she was finally allowed to stumble into the dark night, she'd repeated it all to George.

But the investigation had begun quickly, and less than twenty-four hours later, her father-in-law had stormed around to her home.

"—with my son telling them he's a homosexual." Jeff infused the word with scorn. He stabbed the air with a finger.

"Damien isn't gay, Dad," George interrupted. "He's a mixed-up kid, for sure, but only thanks to that monster. Look, we can arrange therapy for him."

Grateful for his support, Jules flashed him a half-smile. He refused to meet her gaze.

"Therapy? But then people will find out," Jeff said. "Your mother won't cope. She's in pieces already."

"She'll have to get used to it. We'll be dragged through the mud, no matter what." George frowned at Jules, leaving no doubt who he blamed. "Jules will be asked to give evidence. And I invested in Cameron's latest video game, an investment that's just gone south."

Jeff's eyes snapped around to meet his son's. "You didn't borrow to fund it, did you?"

George blanched. "What? No, I never over-commit myself. But the tasty return he promised will be a big fat zero once they lock Rufus Cameron up. Honestly, I hope they throw away the key."

"How could you do this to us, Juliet? To Damien?" Jeff demanded.

George, his face stony, said nothing. Both men waited for her to speak, but what was there to say?

Over and over again, she'd asked herself how she'd failed her pupils so badly. Since her trip to the Bridewell police station, she'd had a sleepless night; an awkward, silent breakfast with George; and a day when the school buzzed with horror at Steve's death. Jeff was right, it was her fault, but Damien wasn't the only victim. She imagined little Steve, bravely fighting back and dying for it.

How many other boys had Rufus hurt? She'd bet money it wasn't just the ones she'd sent his way.

She hated herself. Worse, fear's frosty tentacles tickled her spine. If her lie was discovered, she'd lose her husband. And thanks to her, a child had lost his life.

Chapter 20

June 1992

Jules

When they came for Jules at six in the morning, she'd been awake. That was a piece of luck. The police didn't need to batter down the front door, attracting attention in this quiet, upmarket suburb. George would have been mortified.

She'd listened with horror as they arrested her for aiding and abetting the indecent assault of a minor. Not murder, though. She was thankful for that.

George's parting words, hissed as she was bundled out of the door, were, "I'll get you a top lawyer," followed by, "Don't let the neighbours see you." There was little she could do to stop them, except enter the police car as quickly as possible.

It didn't seem real. Barely functioning after a sleepless night, her eyelids drooped. The journey to Bridewell, the Victorian police station in the city centre, took fifteen minutes in the best of traffic. To Jules, it seemed instant, like stepping in and out of a lift. She must have slept at last.

A man sat waiting for her in the interview room: no lawyer, but George's friend from the Freemasons, Merv. Immaculate in a well-cut suit, smoking his usual Marlboro Lights, he rose to greet her. His tall frame dominated the space.

"Hello, Jules." Bleary eyes beneath his trendy glasses gave the only indication that Merv wasn't a morning person. He nodded to his colleagues. "May we have a word in private?"

Once they'd left, Merv sat down again in one of the moulded plastic chairs. He gestured for Jules to do the same.

"Here." He pushed a plastic cup of pale brown liquid towards her. Another, half-drunk, sat on the table before him. "Tea, with two sugars. Don't argue, just drink it. You'll need it."

She took a sip, sweet and lukewarm. It tasted terrible; they wouldn't even drink this in the school staffroom. "Thanks," she muttered.

"You're welcome." Balancing his cigarette on a well-used tin ashtray, he steepled his fingers under his chin. "You're in big trouble, Jules. Aiding and abetting indecent assault – you're looking at prison. And you'll never be able to work with children again."

She gawped at him. "But I didn't do it." Her brain didn't seem to work, and she floundered for words. "I mean, Rufus asked me to find games testers for him, that's all. You can't believe I—"

"What I believe, or don't believe, doesn't matter." Merv's tone was sombre. "George will ask me to make them go away. But I can't make them go away. These are serious allegations and we have witnesses. So—"

"Who are the witnesses?" she interrupted.

"You'll find out soon enough. But here's a question for you. Do the names Rufus Cameron and Malcolm Jenks mean anything to you?"

The room began to spin.

"Careful." Merv moved the tea as she slumped forward.

"Malcolm?" She could barely speak.

"You had an affair with him, didn't you?"

They knew.

Her mouth opened and closed without a sound.

"Malcolm has been very helpful," Merv said.

"He told you I did this?" Tears welled at his betrayal. They didn't love each other, but she'd imagined some affection between them. Yet he'd lied to the police about her.

"Do you need a tissue?" Merv removed a small, cellophane-wrapped pack from his pocket and passed them over to her. "Help yourself. No, he didn't say that. But what Malcolm did tell us backs up Rufus's account, or part of it. Malcolm Jenks would also like to make this go away. He has a wife and, what, eight children? But he's a public-spirited citizen keen to assist in a murder inquiry. He recognises it's his duty to testify. And with his lover on trial for serious offences, he's going to have to."

"I didn't—"

"Well, Rufus would disagree there. And he wouldn't have met Stephen Purslow but for you. But whatever the truth of that, the facts of your relationship with Malcolm Jenks will come out in court. George will learn about Malcolm sooner or later. It's up to you whether you warn him before the media get hold of it."

"Is that likely?" Still dizzy, she longed for a sip of tea, however disgusting. Her hands shook so much that she'd spill it, however. She left it alone.

Merv frowned. His eyes were sympathetic. "I'm afraid the vultures circle around the court."

He took a drag on his cigarette. "That brings me to the question of solicitors. George has told me he'll pay for the best. But if he falls out with you – which is possible – you may find yourself without legal representation. I strongly recommend you ask to see the duty solicitor."

Jules reeled again. The day had hardly started, and it was already getting worse.

"Okay," she managed, "but how do I know they're any good?"

Merv blew a smoke ring. "Oh, take it from me, Alison Lambert is very good. She does this all the time." He grinned. "George wouldn't agree, of course he wouldn't, but our lady lawyers are the best in Bristol. They have to be."

Jules nodded. You had to be twice as good as a man to progress in your career. The feminists called it a glass ceiling, and it existed in her field too. She still hoped to be head one day. Whatever George thought, she'd juggle it with kids and housework. It was called having it all.

But it was beginning to seem she'd have nothing.

Chapter 21

September 2023

Juliet

Juliet winced at her throbbing feet, blistering from unfamiliar shoes. She regretted making the effort to dress smartly, now she'd had to walk two miles into the centre of Bristol. After scaling the heights of Constitution Hill to catch a bus from Clifton Village, she'd found the stop wasn't in use. A kind soul told her traffic was diverted because of a march in the city centre. How lucky that she'd left early.

She wouldn't be late for Hugh Wimbush, but she'd be limping by the time she arrived. Had she known, she'd have asked Hugh to rearrange. Then again, that might have meant waiting for weeks. He'd kindly offered to help her free of charge, so she couldn't pick and choose the slot in his diary. This Saturday was the only date he'd suggested. He felt obliged to visit his office at the weekend to catch up, he said.

She was almost there now, teetering down Park Street, exercise bringing a flush of heat. Her face itched. She ripped off the mask, which had been a mistake. She'd hoped to avoid attention. The mask had the opposite effect; as no-one else wore one, it made her conspicuous.

The Clifton bus would have travelled via Park Street. Today, a barrier at the top of the hill kept it free of vehicles. Unnervingly young cops stood by. Juliet imagined their eyes on her back. Her spine tingled. Once, she'd believed the police existed to protect decent citizens. People like her. Then she'd been arrested.

Thirty-odd years had passed, yet she couldn't forget. Would Hugh recollect the case? His colleague, Alison, had been convinced she'd keep Juliet out of jail. If only she'd been right.

Juliet tried to focus on the sights and sounds around her. The elegant Georgian terraces along Park Street were as she remembered, although a rash of coffee bars and Chinese restaurants had sprung up on their ground floors. She recalled headshops and secondhand clothing stores catering to students. The new outlets seemed more upmarket, the kind of places she would visit if she had either money or friends.

A cacophony of whistles, chants and thumping music disturbed her thoughts. It rose almost to ear-bleeding levels as she neared the bottom of the hill. Obviously, a protest was taking place on College Green. Some things never changed: Bristolians loved a demo.

Telling herself she wasn't used to city noise after the peace of the farm, Juliet crossed the road. Pain surged through her feet, but the extra steps were necessary to avoid the crowd.

Curiosity overcame her, though. She glanced at the green, where hordes of earnest, scruffy demonstrators chanted 'No to fossil fuels'. A group to the side held banners declaring 'Stop The War.' Juliet nodded approvingly. If only wishing for the common good would somehow bring it about.

She shook her head bitterly, and began to move on before her gaze was drawn to the rally's focal point. A giant of a man worked the crowd, broadcasting slogans with a microphone. As his audience cheered, she realised he wasn't ludicrously tall after all, but standing on a soapbox. His spiky aqua hair also added height. Beside him, a figure she recognised was hanging on his every word. Clean-shaven and preppy, James Sharples seemed out of place, like a perfectly clipped rosebush among weeds.

Unexpectedly, James made eye contact. He nipped across the traffic-free street.

Juliet glanced around, seeing no escape route. At least his parents were nowhere in sight.

"Miss Price, isn't it? Are you joining us?" he asked, with the enthusiastic air of a new puppy.

Juliet squinted at him. "I thought you represented the Conservative Party, not the Greens?"

"Quite so," James said. His smile didn't waver. "There are no silos among us today. Climate change brings every stripe and colour together. It's common sense to combat global warming. Many of my Conservative colleagues agree, and where they don't," he shrugged his shoulders, "well, I'm working within the party to change their minds."

The spiky-haired fellow glared in their direction. He began a speech, rousing the crowd. Charismatic, his golden voice rose and fell for effect, its tone persuasive. Despite his honeyed words, his expression remained fierce. He seemed familiar, although the reason escaped her. She'd never spent time with crusties or hippies. The few New Age travellers who made their way to the farm, attracted by a vegan commune, were swiftly deterred by religion and hard work. Juliet was sure she hadn't spotted him among their number. Had she seen him on TV?

"Who—"

"I'd better go back," James said, before she had a chance to quiz him. "Good to meet you again."

He had sensed his leader's gaze, just as Juliet had felt uncomfortable earlier under the unseen eyes of the stalker. Fortunately, he or she seemed to have absented themselves. She'd experienced a twinge of fear upon leaving the flat in Cliftonwood, but nothing since.

"Nice to see you, too," Juliet said. He did seem a decent young man. That wouldn't be George's influence. Penny might be an opportunist, but she deserved credit for James.

Juliet's breathing slowed as she put more distance between herself and the rally, its noise dissipating. At the edge of the Floating Harbour, she took a moment to get her bearings. The Hippodrome still dominated St Augustine's Parade to the left, a straggle of families queuing outside it. Late night chippies, shuttered against daylight, clustered on the corner. Apart from them, the centre of Bristol had smartened up. The pedestrian square by St Augustine's Parade boasted a line of fountains rather than the scrubby shrubs she remembered. To her right, derelict old wharves had been swept away. Smart bars lined the harbour; balconied flats loomed, shiny and new, in the distance.

It was seductive. Yet this city wasn't safe. The man with aqua hair had stared at Juliet as if he knew her. Was he one of Steve Purslow's relatives?

Rufus had living victims, too. They wouldn't let go of their pain. Nor would their families. Dozens, if not hundreds, of people must hate her still. Emotions might have calmed while Rufus rotted in prison, but only an idiot would bet on it.

No way should she stay in Bristol.

She hurried to Hugh's office. Wimbush Berryman had moved. Alison had worked in a labyrinth of corridors and cubbyholes near the law courts. The modern, mirrored block on Marsh Street couldn't be more different. Juliet peered at her reflection, smoothing her bob. Satisfied, she pushed at the glass revolving door. It didn't budge. Luckily, she had a mobile phone, a luxury on the farm, but one she'd insisted on because of her translation clients. A call to Hugh produced an apology and his assurance that he would be right down.

Moments later, he appeared: a little gnome of a man, skin shrivelled like an old apple. He scarcely outstripped Juliet in height. His clothes fitted her perception of his age: old-fashioned dark suit, white shirt, silk tie and black and grey brocade waistcoat.

Hugh introduced himself, although she didn't doubt his identity once she heard his voice. In person, his tone came across exactly as it had on the telephone: deep, friendly and reassuring. The contrast with his colourless appearance was striking.

He held out a hand.

She hesitated, wishing she'd ignored him when his grip turned out to be clammy and limp.

"So sorry," Hugh repeated. "My support staff don't come in at the weekends, although if I needed help with IT, your brother was most flexible."

He tutted. "A sad loss."

"So he worked for you?" Juliet had no idea what Greg had done since 1992.

"Yes, and others. Your brother was an IT consultant for a number of small businesses in Bristol. Our helpdesk, you might say. Got me out of a tight spot several times."

Juliet found it hard to reconcile Greg the respected computer expert with Greg the hoarder. She didn't dare ask Hugh if he'd visited the flat.

"It was the least I could do to assist him in his divorce. And on this sad occasion now." Hugh gestured to a lift, its doors decorated with a huge photo of the Clifton Suspension Bridge. "Please. We'll go to my office."

The small cabin's steel walls closed in around them. Juliet's heart rate quickened. This metal box was barely large enough to hold them both, but she couldn't insist on using the stairs. It would be unreasonable. Hugh, with his thinning white hair, wrinkles and long red nose, must be nearly a hundred years old. Anyway, thanks to her labour in the fields, she had issues with her lower back. Twinges spiked through it in sympathy with the agonised throbbing of her feet. She'd been walking for too long. Better travel to his office swiftly, and sit down.

The lift clanked to a halt on the top floor, its doors opening.

"This way." Hugh guided her past a reception desk and into an airy, open plan room. Neat rows of blank monitors stood on empty tables. Only the hum of air conditioning broke the silence.

He held a glass door open for her. It didn't bear his name, but inside, Hugh had marked the territory as his. Law books and folders were laid out on a solid dark wood desk, a piece which had clearly moved to the new office with him. Framed portraits of a wife, children and grandchildren decorated walls in a tasteful off-white shade. There was a pleasing absence of clutter.

"Like the view?"

Juliet nodded. "Lovely."

Hugh's window overlooked rooftops, the spire of a church and clouds scudding across the blue sky. Ironically, the Wimbush Berryman offices probably spoiled the scenery for workers in the surrounding buildings.

Hugh gestured to tub chairs placed around a highly polished oak table. "Do take a seat. Would you like coffee? The girls aren't here to make it, but there's a machine."

"Yes, please."

He left for a few minutes, returning with two mugs of frothy beige liquid. "I didn't ask what you'd like, so I hope a latte will suit you. It's my favourite."

The aroma reminded her of holidays in France. At the first sip of punchy, creamy coffee, she was sitting at a pavement café in St Malo, George brushing windswept blond curls from his eyes. Seagulls squawked overhead. A plump toddler singled her out for a smile, evoking bittersweet feelings. She was trying for a baby with George, months turning into years, with no child turning up.

Hugh's soapy aftershave banished thoughts of salty air. He'd pulled up a seat beside her, setting down his drink next to a blue cardboard file.

Juliet caught a blast of bad breath. She edged her chair away.

He moved the file towards her, opening it and leaning in closer.

Juliet took a mouthful of coffee to counter the smell. She suspected he was a smoker, the type who would claim law was a high-pressure job. He should try teaching.

"Here we are." Hugh ran his finger down a piece of A4 paper. "The statement of assets. First and foremost, we have your brother's flat. You'll see that, after the mortgage, its equity value is estimated at thirty thousand pounds. What are your intentions for the property, if I may ask?"

She winced. "I'm going to sell it. Is that really all it's worth? I thought Cliftonwood had come up."

"It has. You were last in Bristol, when…?"

"1992."

"Ah, yes. Cliftonwood has indeed 'come up' since then. But your brother bought the property four years ago."

"After his divorce?"

"Exactly so. We offer a full conveyancing service, by the way. I have excellent contacts with estate agents. If you wish, I can ring one of them and arrange it all for you. You needn't set foot in Bristol again, mmm?"

Was that his game? Juliet bristled. She imagined the flat selling for a knockdown price, with Hugh and his estate agent cronies pocketing a fat commission.

"I'll stay for now. There's a lot of junk to sift through." She had nowhere else to live until she received the proceeds, anyway. Thirty thousand pounds wouldn't buy much, perhaps only a caravan, but she could rent. She didn't care where, as long as it wasn't Bristol.

"A house clearance firm —" Hugh stopped, evidently sensing Juliet's reluctance. "Shall we go through the other assets, such as we've identified?"

'Sundry furniture and effects' were valued at a thousand pounds. Juliet considered this an overestimate until Hugh pointed out it included Greg's state-of-the-art TV and a highly specced laptop. A bank account contained two thousand pounds, some of it earmarked for utilities and insurance. Three clients owed sixteen hundred pounds between them. Hugh promised to send them letters and help Juliet with an insurance claim for the leak.

That left one item, a car with a distinctive number plate. She hadn't noticed it parked at Clover House.

"Where is it?" Juliet asked.

"Try the garage," Hugh advised. "It's the one on the left in the row behind your flats. We took the AutoTrader figure of nine thousand pounds for the Skoda, but the personalised plate is potentially valuable in its own right. GREG 107 may appeal to a man blessed with the same name."

"Do you have a key for the car?"

"I'm afraid not." Hugh's rich voice suggested sympathy and regret. "Hopefully, you will find it as you clear the flat. I can assure you it wasn't cremated with your brother, in case you had concerns around that. Funeral directors are most particular in checking the pockets of the deceased. Batteries can cause explosions."

He closed the folder. "So there you have it. A modest estate. No life insurance, as your brother had no dependents. We have been prudent in our valuations, and a few assets may realise a little more. You should inform me if they do, but don't worry about tax. The total is well below HMRC's threshold."

"Thank you for going through it. And all your hard work." Just as she spent hours translating a short commercial document, Hugh would have done extensive research to produce that single A4 sheet.

"You're most welcome." Hugh fixed beady brown eyes on her. "You know, you're not what I expected."

What did he mean? Nosiness got the better of her. "And that was?"

He ogled her. "You may remember my colleague, Alison Lambert? She worried about you. Said juries never trust a beautiful woman, or a clever one. I think the words she used were 'double whammy'."

Alison hadn't mentioned that to her. Would she have done so in Alison's place? Probably not.

She'd been so naïve. Alison, the duty solicitor at the police station, would persuade the cops they'd made a mistake. Then, as her day in court approached, she was sure justice would prevail. How stupid she had been. She wasn't so trusting now, and hardly flattered that Hugh had anticipated a bimbo.

Nausea swirled in the pit of her stomach. She gazed out of the glass door at the silent, creepy open-plan office. They were alone. No-one but Hugh knew or cared that she was there. Signposts had been in front of her all along, topped with red flags, and she'd ignored them.

"How is Alison?" she asked, hoping to deflect him.

Thankfully, it worked. "She retired last year, alas. A sad loss to the firm, but she was determined to take her pension and move on from the law."

Hugh blinked, mouth pursed as if disbelieving that anyone would wish to leave the legal profession. He added, "But she was a criminal lawyer, as you are aware. Alison dealt with sad situations and mixed with quite unsavoury types, present company excepted. She always felt you got a raw deal."

"The jury's verdict was a shock to me." It shouldn't have been. Her trial had been brutal. Yet, whatever they thought, she hadn't known the truth about Rufus. She hadn't even suspected until it was too late.

"Alison is a good judge of character," Hugh said. "She hoped, I think, that you would put the case behind you and find peace. I'm sure the delightful Sister Anya helped you do that."

Juliet had many words for Anya, but delightful wasn't one of them.

"It's a farm where you live, isn't it?" Hugh probed. "Outdoor work, fresh air, tranquillity?"

If you didn't mind the side order of religion. And she didn't live there anymore. "I did some labouring," she said. Enough to give her a bad back. "But mostly, I worked as a translator. Initially for the community, and then commercially. It was a useful source of income for them."

"Was?"

Goodness, Hugh was sharp.

"That's right," she admitted. "I've left."

"A big adjustment for you. Not so much as when you joined, I suppose. I've heard them described as a cult."

"They are. But it was a safe space. And they wanted me."

Of course they did. She brought a divorce settlement with her, marketable skills and nimble fingers. None of that had crossed her mind. She'd seen a hiding place, and jumped at it.

It was the best choice she had. The only choice. Bile caught in her throat. She remembered the first night in prison: banging and catcalls from the other cells, angry cries of 'Juliet, Juliet'. The newspaper headlines. Family and friends turning their backs.

No-one else wanted her.

In the circumstances, she'd make the same decision again. But perhaps she'd gone wrong in staying so long.

"Things changed," Juliet said. "Anya felt I wasn't paying my way since demand for my services declined. Many of my old clients turned to Google. You can't compete with free."

"Indeed not." Hugh chuckled. "I say, if you can't beat them, join them."

"As I said, I'm grateful for your kindness."

She'd misjudged him. Her stomach settled, the quiet surroundings no longer sinister.

"If you need an urgent German to English translation any time, just get in touch," she offered. "I'm right up to date with the language. I took a few clients with me, and intend to make a living from it."

It helped that she needn't pay for accommodation for the time being. Luckily, Anya hadn't appreciated Greg's estate had any value. Juliet imagined Anya changing her mind: encouraging Juliet to stay with the cult just a few months longer until she'd been thoroughly fleeced.

"There's no question of taking up teaching again?" Hugh asked. "I suppose at this stage in life… No, forgive me. The criminal record precludes it."

"I've come to terms with that."

And the lack of relationships, children, and the rest of the future she'd projected for herself. Juliet bit her lip. Hugh's sympathy was almost too much to bear.

"Good, glad to hear it." Hugh finished his coffee and leaned closer. "But if you need someone to talk to, I'm always here."

His breath remained rank. Juliet coughed.

"Between you and me," Hugh said, "I believe selling up and leaving Bristol would be the right thing to do. People have long memories and powerful friends, George Sharples in particular. And Rufus Cameron must be eligible for parole by now. He may be out, for all I know."

She gaped at him. "But he's on a life sentence," she gasped.

"With a minimum term of thirty years, which has expired. Look, are you all right? Let me fetch you a glass of water." Hugh's thin-lipped mouth settled into a rictus. Presumably, he intended a reassuring grin.

He patted her arm before standing up and leaving the room.

Lightheaded and leaden-footed, as if all her blood had drained downwards, Juliet gripped the edge of the table. Having steadied herself, she stared out of the window at the city's rooftops. Rufus was walking the streets below. She'd been convinced someone was spying on her. Now she knew who.

Hugh returned with her water. "Drink this and take deep breaths," he said. "I didn't mean to alarm you unduly."

It was too late for that. Rufus was already stalking her.

Juliet gulped from the glass, hoping to quell her panic. It didn't work.

"You shouldn't fret too much. There are safeguards around parole. Mr Cameron wouldn't be released unless he displayed remorse and wasn't considered dangerous."

"Of course he's dangerous." Her voice trembled.

Hugh regarded her kindly. "People change. And the Parole Board can impose conditions. He might be forbidden from setting foot in Bristol. You may like to check."

"I will." She found herself unable to string a longer sentence together. Anyway, she couldn't prove Rufus was still a liar and a psychopath, even though she was sure of it. Whatever he told the Parole Board, whatever conditions were imposed on him, Rufus would do exactly as he pleased. What did he have in mind for her?

Chapter 22

September 2023

Vix

"Got anything left?" Cody squinted up at the stallholder. The sun, still high in the sky, intensified the lurid orange of her hair.

She stopped boxing up her remaining goods. "Only mushroom pasties." A silvery pin glinted on the tip of her tongue as she spoke. It matched the jewels in her nose and eyebrows.

"Can you afford—" Vix began.

"Pay what you can, all right?" the stallholder said. Suddenly, she chuckled. "Go on, these are the last two. Call it a pound and you can have both, one for you and another for your girlfriend."

Vix glanced at Cody. He'd ignored the comment, which was probably for the best. She decided not to explain. "Thanks," she said, grabbing one of the pastry parcels.

It was still hot. She took a bite, enjoying the flaky texture and garlicky filling. "Lush."

"Home-made this morning. I thought you looked hungry, hun. And it's packing up time, isn't it?"

The rally was over. Ten minutes ago a police officer had tapped Spike on the shoulder. Spike had nodded, thanked the crowd and told them to leave.

Only a few stallholders remained, and teenagers seeking freebies.

"You coming to the Green Man?" Cody asked.

Vix blinked at Cody. "What is it – a pub? We'd never get served." Nor could she spare cash for drinks, and doubted he had any either.

"It's Spike's boat," Cody said with reverence.

Vix gawked at him. "You're crushing on Spike?" If Cody was gay, it was the school's best-kept secret.

"No." Cody's tone was dismissive. "He's my friend, that's all. You'll like him when you get to know him. He's interesting."

"Where's the Green Man, then?"

Cody flicked his thumb towards the lane between the Marriott and Bristol Cathedral. "The harbour," he said.

Nanna Lizzie had explained to Vix that Bristol's Floating Harbour was so-called because boats could float on it. That seemed a statement of the obvious. What else would a boat do? It was a short walk away, through the lane, down steps and past a museum.

When they arrived at the stretch of water, Cody pointed across it to the other side.

"You're kidding me," Vix complained. "That's the SS Great Britain."

She'd heard too much about it from Brooklyn. He idolised the engineer Brunel, who had designed the massive steel ship in ancient times. After a school trip, he wouldn't stop talking about it for weeks. Only the Clifton Suspension Bridge eclipsed its popularity.

"Spike lives in the marina next door," Cody said.

That did sound interesting, but there were no bridges close to the SS Great Britain, and they'd have to walk for miles.

"Won't it take ages?"

"Catch the ferry?" Cody suggested. "I'll pay."

About to point out it wasn't a date, Vix realised from his shining eyes that it was a treat for him.

"Sure," she said.

The Bristol Ferry Company's long yellow boat bobbed towards them, heading for the nearest landing stage. As it slowed, they easily matched its speed, dashing along a narrow walkway beside old brick warehouses. They'd been converted into bars and cinemas; Brooklyn occasionally took Marley here. Vix pressed her lips together. She'd forgotten all about her brother and Nanna Lizzie in the excitement of the rally. Maybe that was a good thing. She couldn't change the past, and worrying wouldn't alter the future. A distraction might help.

The ferry journey delivered that. She and Cody stood on deck, holding onto a rail as a breeze whipped her face and hair. Seagulls glided close by, shrieking warnings. The boat wobbled up and down on the rippling water. Its engine thrummed. The noise altered to a sputter on the approach to Wapping Wharf, and the craft came to a halt. A deckhand threw a rope to moor, fixing steps to the bank. Vix joined the line of passengers queueing to depart.

"It's the next stop," Cody hissed.

She giggled. "This is fun."

"I know." His eyes sparkled.

New passengers boarded, jostling the teenagers for space beside the railings. Obstinately, Vix stood her ground. Only a minute or two later, they docked in the shadow of the SS Great Britain, their yellow ferry like a goldfish beside a killer whale.

Cody scrambled up the steps, offering Vix his hand.

She braced herself against the harbour wall instead. "Where are the houseboats?" she asked.

"This way."

She followed Cody past the sightseers milling around the ticket office. The crowds thinned quickly once they left the tourist attraction behind. Shuttered warehouses, offices and other old buildings huddled around deserted lanes.

Vix's excitement fizzled out. "Why are you leading me away from the water?"

"I'm not."

A moment later, they rounded a corner, and the Floating Harbour came into view again. By a boatyard, vessels lay moored in neat lines: motorboats, barges and sailing craft as well as dwellings. Vix approved of their orderliness.

Cody pointed to the central pontoon. "The Green Man's along here."

Vix couldn't tell which boat he meant, but she registered a problem. "How do we get in? I saw someone use that gate, but I bet it's locked."

"Let's try it."

She was right, though. The metal barrier, taller than either of them, hardly rattled when they touched it.

"I'll call Spike," Cody said.

Vix spotted a familiar flash of aqua. Standing by a long, thin vessel, Spike waved to them.

"Yo! Come on down. We have samosas."

"Let us in, Spike," Cody bellowed.

Spike saluted them. He strode to the gate and punched a combination into a pad to the side. The gate swung open.

"Welcome to the Green Man," he said, ushering them into the marina. "How do you like her?"

He was staring at Vix. Bewildered that the Man appeared to be female, she replied, "It looks nice."

She'd never set foot on a boat, or even been this close to one, but it was obvious Spike itched for a compliment. He clearly looked after the Green Man well. As Vix neared it, she noticed how the dark green paint gleamed in the sunlight. Shades of jade, black and gold picked out its name and the image of a man's head. Hair and beard surrounding it like a halo of flames, his face appeared godlike and stern.

91

Spike jumped down onto a small triangular deck, its point butted up against the pontoon. "Hey, Cody and Cody's friend. Make yourselves comfortable."

"I'm Vix." She followed Spike onto the deck. Apart from the apex, the sides had rails, with rough wooden benches lining the deck's edges. Blond James sat on one, a tray heaped with pastries beside him. Opposite, a pink-haired young woman petted a small brown dog. Snuggling on her lap, the animal gazed up at her in adoration.

"My name's Teena," she said, adding, "Spike, James and Gaz. The fur baby."

A gust of wind ruffled Teena's mane. Her floaty skirt swirled around Doc Marten-clad ankles. She shifted along the bench, pointing alongside. "Sit here. There's plenty of room."

Vix joined her, leaving enough space for Cody. Spike took a seat next to James. He passed the tray to Vix, wafting curry spices across the deck. Gaz whimpered softly.

"Try a samosa," Teena said. "They're vegan."

"Are they home-made?" Vix asked, remembering the pasty stall.

"Not by me," Spike chortled. "I microwaved them, though."

Vix took one and nibbled the edge. "Thanks. It's tasty."

Gaz wriggled from Teena's grasp and stared pointedly at Vix. He began to slobber.

"Ignore him," Teena said. "He's had three."

Too weak to resist the animal's soulful brown eyes, Vix fed him crumbs. "What kind of dog is Gaz?" she asked. "A border terrier?"

"Might be," Spike said. "He's a rescue. Another boater died, and I took him on. My partner wasn't best pleased."

"Thought you lived alone," Teena said.

"Too right. A simple life for me. It used to be way more complicated."

That settled any possibility of Teena being Spike's partner. James could be, if Spike was gay. They might live apart. In vain, Vix kept an ear on the conversation for clues while the three adults took stock of the morning.

"Did you get all the banners back?" Spike asked.

"Apart from the ones that fell apart," James said. "Over-enthusiastic waving."

"Not ours," Cody said, to laughter.

"You protest too much," Spike said. He turned to James. "Who was the woman you spoke to when we were getting started? Business suit, grey hair, bright blue eyes?"

"They are distinctive, aren't they?" James agreed. "The first thing I noticed about her. I met her canvassing."

"A posh Cliftonian, is she?"

"Cliftonwood."

That sounded like Juliet, but why would Spike be interested in her? Anyway, she'd last sighted her mad neighbour heading for Clifton Village. Vix dismissed the thought. She picked up another samosa, and continued to eavesdrop.

"Cliftonwood isn't posh?" Teena asked.

"Not as. I live there," James admitted. "She's not far from me. You know the seventies flats in Aldworth Terrace?"

"Can't say I do, lover. Or anywhere else that rich, self-satisfied nobs live," Teena sneered.

"Can we avoid a class war?" Spike asked. "Cody, how do you think the rally went?"

Cody's face lit up. He was obviously pleased to be consulted, even in a shameless attempt by Spike to change the subject. "Over two thousand people there, I bet," he said. "That's a success, isn't it?"

"Nothing on Bristol Live yet, though. Or on 24/7." Teena scrolled on her phone. "Social media's better. There's a pic of that scumbag driving straight at me." She angled the screen for Spike to see.

A seagull swooped close by, not quite reaching the boat but near enough to cause a rush of air. Gaz snarled at it.

"Good boy." Spike petted him. "Send him packing."

"Vermin, like Chelsea Tractor drivers." Teena pursed her lips. "You saw the guy on College Green, yeah? He used that vehicle like a weapon. I could tell from his eyes. He was excited, planning to run me over like it was a video game."

"They should ban those big cars," Cody said.

"Child killers," Vix agreed.

"I met a child killer once," Spike said. "Want to hear the scariest thing about him?"

Vix nodded.

"He looked like you and me," Spike told her.

"Not anyone I know. You could see that guy was a psycho," Teena insisted. "His piercing dark eyes..." She quivered.

"Whatever," Spike said. "Anyhow, we'll teach him a lesson. Him, and the others like him."

"Got to go," James said. "Canvassing, you know?"

"All right, Tory boy." Spike's tone was good-natured. "I'll tempt you from the dark side one day."

"No chance. See you around." James hopped onto the pontoon.

Teena stared after him. He spoke to a boater near the gate, slipped through, and selected a bicycle from several locked onto railings. "Nice bike," she said. "Is he really a Tory?"

"Yeah. Everyone makes mistakes. He's turned out well considering his dad is such a moron." Spike opened the door to the cabin. "We've got new volunteers, Teena, so let's step inside for a chat. Mind your heads and feet, gang. There's a couple of steps down, and the ceiling's low."

Unsure what to expect of a houseboat's interior, Vix goggled at the kitchen in front of her. Like a rich kid's doll's house, it was tiny but luxurious. She couldn't imagine Spike choosing marble worktops and gold taps. He didn't look wealthy, or behave that way.

"Wow," she said.

Spike laughed. "You should have seen it before I whitewashed the paintwork. No holds barred. Cherubs dancing on the ceiling, gilded woodwork, nymphs and shepherds on the cupboards. My partner loved bling."

Teena picked up on the remark. "He did, did he? Not anymore?"

"He's dead. We travelled the world together, but all good things must end. The Green Man is my only keepsake."

"Quite a legacy," Teena said. "You miss him?"

"I miss a lot."

Vix leaned against the counter, its coolness chilling her through the parka's flimsy material. She missed a lot too: Nanna Lizzie's smile, the scent of her clothes fresh from the washing line. Blood pounded through her temples.

"What's wrong, Vix?" Cody asked, his voice sounding so distant it hardly intruded into her thoughts.

A sudden warm, moist pressure on her hand jolted her from the waking nightmare. Gaz nosed her, licking her fingers. Vix stroked behind his ears. "Just thinking."

"Hey, I'm sorry. I can get too intense," Spike said. "Sit down. We'll all fit round the table in the dinette, if we're friendly."

"Can you give us a tour of the boat first?" Cody asked.

94

Spike laughed. "I think we can spare a minute. It won't take any longer."

Spike's dining area was visible from the kitchen, as was a lounge beyond with a TV screen on the far wall. Narrow and compact, the micro-rooms flowed into each other. In the dinette, an L-shaped bench, padded in red velvet, surrounded two sides of an oblong table. The flat surface, fashioned from dark wood, boasted an inlaid design of flowers in mother-of-pearl. Despite a few scratches and nicks, Vix appreciated why Spike hadn't painted over it. The table was a work of art as well as making effective use of the space.

Spike pointed to a sliding door beside the TV. "The bathroom's through there."

Teena opened it, gesturing to the others to follow. They crowded inside. Like the rest of the boat, this miniature room spanned the full width and made maximum use of space. A full-size shower cubicle and sink, with the obligatory gold taps, had been shoehorned in. The walls were tiled in a mural of Neptune driving a chariot pulled by seahorses. The god, picked out in cobalt on a white background, bore a remarkable resemblance to Spike.

Teena gaped at the toilet. A scalloped gold lid topped a pan decorated with blue seashells. "Spike, that is some throne," she said.

"You like it? Me too. It's an eco-friendly composting model. No disgusting chemicals."

"Doesn't smell too bad," Vix said.

"Try it if you like. I'll move the audience on," Spike offered.

"No thanks."

"What about the bedroom?" Teena asked.

"That's private. Come on, we've got planning to do."

A tang of curry spices hung in the air as Teena wriggled into the corner of the L. Cody and Vix followed.

Spike sat beside the pink-haired girl. "Let's talk SUVs. We hit them where it hurts, right, Teena?"

Teena made a fist. "Deflated tyres, deflated egos."

"You can't drive a car with a flat, but it's not criminal damage," Spike said. "The tyre doesn't need repairing, just pumping up. But these selfish morons are always in a hurry, right? They'll get up in the morning, start up the car, and learn they're not getting their own way for once."

"We go out at night," Teena said.

"I'll show you how it's done." Spike tapped his phone. In the living room beyond, the TV sprang to life. "This is a YouTube video explaining how to let air out of a tyre. It's simple. You see that valve, the little tube accessed between two spokes of the wheel?"

He paused as the video played without sound. Freezing it for a moment, he said, "You unscrew it, then apply pressure to the pin in the centre. That lets the tyre down. You see he's nudging it with a screwdriver?"

The short film began again. "We use a lentil. A stone would do it too. You place it on the pin, then screw the cap back on the tube. If you can't hear air come out, do it again. Then move on to the next one."

"It takes a few hours, so when the egotists wake up, the tyre's flat as a pancake," Teena said.

"Wow." Vix laughed, beaming at Spike and Teena. "So it's that easy?"

"It's that easy," Spike repeated. "We're doing Clifton tonight. Want in?"

"Sure." All the tension she'd been holding in her shoulders had vanished. Vix felt alive. Of course she'd join them. She lived in a flashy flat near Clifton now, didn't she? And she could sneak out with her own keys. That reminded her that she needed to get them cut. She must buy food too. Brooklyn constantly complained there wasn't enough.

She eyed up the half-full tray Spike had brought inside. "Sorry. Got to go. Can you spare any more samosas?"

"Help yourself," Spike said. "I'll see you tonight at 2am, right? Wear dark clothes and a mask. Gloves, to avoid fingerprints. Can you remember that?"

"I'll bring lentils," Teena said.

"Right. You can't have enough lentils. We're meeting in the old St Andrew's churchyard, Vix. Know it? At the end of Birdcage Walk."

"Sure," Vix said. She had no idea where it was, but Google would tell her.

Cody left too, blinking when he emerged from the cabin onto the Green Man's sunny deck. "Cool boat," he said, as they strolled away. "I'd like one when I've got a job. Or I might try van life."

She flashed him a sharp glance. "Living in a tin box? No thanks."

Cody seemed taken aback. They walked in silence to the ferry stop. He inspected the timetable. "We just missed one."

"Never mind."

From the look of relief on his face, Vix suspected he didn't have money for another journey. Yet the path hugging the harbour would only take them twenty minutes to walk. Her energy levels had zoomed into overdrive, boosted by samosas and the prospect of punishing SUV drivers.

"Are you coming tonight?" she asked.

Cody pulled a face. "I can't, with buses and that. How will you even get there from Henleaze? It's miles from Clifton."

"You're right." She'd nearly given herself away. "Maybe I'll ask my brother for a lift. Or tell Spike I'll help him when he does the cars in Henleaze. Do you have his number?"

"Yeah. I'll message it to you."

"Thanks."

How close was Cody to Spike, and should she even care? Perhaps she'd ask Spike that evening. Whatever Cody thought, Vix would be in Clifton tonight. Those child-killing SUV drivers were in for a shock.

Chapter 23

September 2023

Brooklyn

He'd scored three goals, which made him the man of the match. That meant buying drinks for his teammates afterwards. Short of cash, Brooklyn pleaded a hot date. It was partly true – he intended to see Marley. The guys accepted his excuse with laughter. Everyone knew Marley was over sixteen now.

He didn't go straight to Marley's, though. Instead, he drove back to the bungalow. Until last week, he'd have called it home without a second thought. Now the dormer windows stared at him like reproachful eyes. He didn't fancy entering the house. Parking Simon's Transit on the drive, he opened the garage.

It was a single storey separate from the main building, a solid brick structure with double wooden doors. They were old-fashioned, of course, unlike those elsewhere in the street. Nanna Lizzie didn't see the need to replace them, especially when Brooklyn kept them in good condition. His dexterity had been obvious from an early age, possibly a skill inherited from his father, whoever that was. Brooklyn had no memory of him, and little enough of his mother.

Tools were stacked tidily in the garage, the lawnmower in its place, clean and oiled. Nanna Lizzie insisted on it. For once, Brooklyn was grateful for her fixation on order. He opened the door to the back garden, plugged in the mower, and began cutting the lawn.

Like football, this was part of his Saturday routine. All three of them had their own chores to do. Nanna Lizzie managed the finances, shopping and most of the housework. Vix cooked. He was expected to mend, fix, garden and put out the recycling. Brooklyn realised he'd missed the collection this week.

After leaving clippings on the compost heap, he scanned the flowerbeds for weeds. Nanna Lizzie always inspected them and told him what to do, but he recognised bindweed, dandelions and rosebay willowherb. He pulled them up and stuck them in her green bin. You couldn't leave them with the compost, where they'd spring into life where you didn't want them.

He brought the mower through the garage to start on the square of lawn at the front. Stan, who lived across the road, was tinkering with a motorbike on his drive. He waved at Brooklyn.

Pasting on a grin, Brooklyn waved back. He didn't know Stan well. The man was in his thirties, an engineer from — where? Poland, probably — with a young family. Both Nanna Lizzie and Vix babysat his kids occasionally.

Stan ambled over. "New van?" he asked.

"It's my boss's. Mine's in for repairs." Brooklyn flicked a switch and began cutting the grass.

Stan wasn't so easily deterred. "I haven't seen you for a while," he yelled over the mower's thrum.

What was wrong with Stan? They'd been neighbours for years, during which they'd barely exchanged two words. Why was he so chatty now?

"I've been at my girlfriend's," Brooklyn said through gritted teeth. He made a show of concentrating on the lawn.

"I haven't seen Liz lately, either," Stan observed. "Is she okay? She told Agata she wasn't well."

"News to me. She's fine," Brooklyn said, gripping the mower.

Something in his expression must have told Stan to back off. The Pole said, "Good," and returned to his mechanics. Occasionally, he looked in Brooklyn's direction, a watchful expression on his face.

Brooklyn refused to make eye contact. He finished trimming the lawn. Without glancing back at Stan, although sure the neighbour's gaze was fixed on him, he returned the lawnmower to the garage. Again, he tidied away the clippings. He cleaned and oiled the mower. Finally, he surveyed the back garden, inhaling the fresh grassy smell.

With a deep breath, he prepared to enter the house. His reluctance ran deep, but Vix would appreciate the kitchen things. Cooking with a kettle limited her options. They were both sick of Pot Noodles by now. He was hungry, too, and there was food in the kitchen. It had only been a few days; the fridge's contents wouldn't have spoiled yet.

He forced himself to unlock the kitchen door. Flies buzzed angrily at the window. Brooklyn's appetite vanished, bile rising to his throat as he imagined what had attracted them. Then he noticed a stack of dirty dishes festering in the sink. That was Vix's responsibility, but he didn't blame her. They'd both been in a hurry to leave.

Nanna Lizzie's words resounded in his head — 'Break the habit of a lifetime' — as he squeezed Fairy Liquid onto a sponge and cleaned up.

Already sweating when he entered the kitchen, he nearly choked on the humid air rising from the sink.

Brooklyn ran the cold tap and splashed water on his face and neck. Its welcome chill almost made him smile. For good measure, he smoothed his flyaway hair. Hopefully, Marley would see he'd tried.

He looked for a newspaper to swat the flies and realised Lizzie's Daily Mails had piled up by the front door. The newsagent's bill was attached to one of them. They would have to pay it, and he'd ask Vix to cancel deliveries. She was good at paperwork. He still struggled with letters and numbers, seeing them jump around the page. Nanna Lizzie had arranged for his reading to be tested. Following this, he received a transparent plastic sheet in a sickly green shade. He was supposed to clip it over books and screens. It didn't help much.

Brooklyn scooped up the newspapers and letters, junk mail and all, and shoved them into a plastic carrier bag. He would give them to Vix to deal with.

Next, he turned his attention to the cupboard with pots and pans. He filled three more carrier bags with saucepans, knives, utensils, plates, bowls, cutlery, and by emptying the fridge. As he opened the latter, a cold blast of air cut through the warm kitchen. Taking a moment to relish it, his gaze lit on the chest freezer in the corner. Only a week ago, he would have reached inside for an ice cream. He shuddered. It held contents he didn't wish to think about, couldn't afford to dwell upon if he wanted to remain sane.

Nausea gripped him again. Swallowing, he grasped kitchen roll, towels and a chopping board, threw them in the bags and gathered them up. He hurried out, dumping them in the back of the Transit. Tyres squealing, he swung the vehicle out of the drive and hit the road. It didn't even occur to him to keep to the speed limit, a sedate twenty miles an hour.

Sweat trickled down his back, plastering his T-shirt to it. Slowing down on Henleaze Road, a strip lined with crowded pavements and busy shops, he was convinced pedestrians were looking at him. He pulled into a side street, parked and lay back against the headrest, breathing in short jerky bursts. Marley expected to see him in ten minutes, but he couldn't turn up in this state. He looked awful. Worse, suppose she worked out what he'd done?

She would never know. No-one would. Somehow, he'd find a way through this.

Brooklyn took control of his breathing. In and out, in and out. He must focus on the good in his life. Eyes tightly shut, he concentrated on bringing an image of Marley before him, letting her citrussy perfume tickle his nostrils. He could almost reach out and stroke that cloud of soft hair, touch her warm, toffee-coloured skin. Desire gripped him, his breath quickening again, but at least his panic had eased enough to drive. He made his way to St Michael's Hill.

Marley lived in one of the oldest parts of the city. Like Cliftonwood, not every building had been standing for centuries. Handsome Georgian terraces jostled up against the university's Brutalist concrete. Her family's brown brick cottage sat in an enclave of social housing, accessed via a pedestrian lane. He had to park on the main road. Brooklyn glanced around for traffic wardens before choosing a spot on double yellow lines, by the coffee bar where they'd arranged to meet.

Marley was nowhere in sight. His mouth twitched at the corners. He called her without getting through.

Seconds later, a message buzzed his phone. 'Running late. Come round to house.'

He'd only been there once, purely by chance. His then-girlfriend had dragged him round to meet online buddies from Canada. They turned out to be Marley's cousins, four of them, and he still had no idea how they had all found beds in the tiny cottage. He'd spent hours playing video games with his girlfriend, Marley, her little sisters and the cousins. Marley's smiley blonde mother had made pancakes with maple syrup. They had been a large group, joking around, all squashed into a poky living room. He'd sat on the floor.

Everyone said Cotham School was for the rich kids, but Marley's family weren't like that. Her dad was a civil servant and her mum worked as a VA, whatever that was. Marley said it meant giving support to small businesses. Her parents wanted Marley to train as a lawyer. Brooklyn doubted Marley's mum would either remember him or approve of her daughter going out with a carpenter. He hoped Marley answered the door herself. She was expecting him, wasn't she?

Down an alleyway and past a children's playground, small kids shrieking, he found the path where Marley's house stood in a terrace of four. It was distinguished from the others by its striking pink door, the colour of bubblegum. Baskets of fragrant white blooms hung on either side. In the front garden, bees buzzed around a neat oblong bed of lavender. Its order and symmetry had passed him by last time. Not now;

after all his weeding and mowing, Brooklyn appreciated the care involved.

He rang the doorbell, stepping back as the door opened and his fears were realised. It wasn't even Marley's mother who stood in front of him. Tall, dark and grey-bearded, the man could only be her father. He occupied the entire doorway, towering over Brooklyn, who was hardly short himself.

"Yes?" Keen brown eyes swept over Brooklyn. At least he wasn't scowling yet.

"Is Marley ready?"

"Ready for what?" Her father's forehead creased.

"We're going out to a film. Elemental."

"She's seen it already with her sisters."

"Sorry, I didn't know. Um, she said she wanted to go."

Despite his jitters, Brooklyn tried smiling. Being polite and friendly went a long way in appeasing Simon Heath. Perhaps it would work on Marley's dad.

"Well, she's drying her hair or some such. Come inside and wait."

Reluctantly, Brooklyn trooped in after him. He braced himself for the third degree.

The door opened straight into their lounge, as tiny as Brooklyn remembered. A sofa and three chairs clustered around the TV, which was set to Sky Sports. Pundits were analysing the latest scores.

A can of lager sat on a folding table beside one of the chairs. Marley's father took this seat, stretching out his impressively long legs. He gestured to the sofa. "Robins are losing," he observed.

"Good," Brooklyn said, wishing right away that he hadn't. Suppose the man was a Bristol City supporter?

Luckily, they were both of one mind. Marley's father grinned. "Are you a Gashead like me?"

"Born and bred," Brooklyn said.

"You can't be all bad, then. What's your name? I'm Errol."

"Brooklyn."

"No way." Marley's father laughed, a sound that ended abruptly when he asked, "And how old are you?"

"Nineteen." Brooklyn resisted the temptation to add, "Sir."

"Thought you would be. Don't you think Marley's a bit young for you?"

"She has," Brooklyn struggled for the right words, "a mature outlook."

"That she does," Errol agreed. "It's going to stand her in good stead when she goes to university to do law. You see where I'm coming from?"

Brooklyn saw only too well. "My sister's going to uni too. Nursing."

Errol nodded. "Glad to hear it. Victoria, is it?"

Brooklyn's neck prickled. "How do you know?"

"I put two and two together. You're Liz Novak's foster kids, aren't you?"

"Yes."

"A wonderful woman." Errol's eyes twinkled. "How is she?"

Brooklyn's heart skipped a beat. "Um, okay," he stuttered.

"Give her my regards." Errol smiled. "I used to see her on my beat all the time, but I was moved to St Paul's. Then I got a transfer to Traffic. You know how it is."

Brooklyn didn't, but he couldn't ignore the strident alarm bells. Fearing Errol's answer, he said, "What's your job, then?"

Errol twisted his face, clearly surprised. "I'm a police officer. Didn't Marley tell you?"

"No."

"She hasn't said much about you either, Brooklyn. Your name, for starters. Or your line of work."

"Carpenter." He omitted the apprentice part.

"Nimble with your fingers, no doubt?"

"Yes." Unsure where the conversation would lead, Brooklyn decided to say as little as possible. Anyway, it was the best strategy for dealing with the police; everyone knew that.

"That figures. I've spoken to your mum often enough about shoplifting. Don't look so shocked. Yes, I know her and all."

"I don't."

"Guess she's not in touch. She was in a bad way when social services called us about you two. So were you. Heartbreaking, the state of you when Liz Novak took you on." He shook his head.

Brooklyn remembered the man he supposed was Vix's dad. Dead eyes. A tattoo on his neck, like an intricate spider's web. Shouting. Pain. Bruises.

His mother hadn't protected him. She wasn't violent herself, but she'd largely ignored Brooklyn. Fragments of memory came to him: long hair, tuneless singing, then snores while baby Vix screamed in her cot. Suddenly, the police were there. Had they broken down the door?

After that, he never saw his mother again.

No-one told Brooklyn or Vix why they'd been removed from her less than tender care. By now, he could guess. Then, he'd picked up snippets by eavesdropping. He listened intently when Nanna Lizzie spoke to doctors or teachers or kind ladies who visited and made a fuss of him. Some were Lizzie's friends, while others were social workers. As an adult, he was no longer of interest to them. Because Vix was in a long-term placement, they rarely bothered with her either. That would change in a heartbeat if Errol got a sniff of problems in the household.

He realised Errol expected a reply.

"No," Brooklyn said. "Um, we're not in touch."

"Keep it that way," Errol said. "You're better off where you are. Liz is the closest thing to a saint in today's world. Although if you're nineteen, she isn't fostering you anymore, is she?"

Brooklyn squirmed. "I pay rent."

Errol nodded. "Good lad. Don't forget to mention me to Liz, will you? Now, where's that daughter of mine? I keep telling her she'll be late for her own funeral."

He left his chair, standing at the foot of the staircase, which was uncarpeted and made of polished pine. "Marley!" he yelled. "Brooklyn's waiting."

She dashed down. The steps were the open type with a single rail at the side. Brooklyn enjoyed a fine view of Marley's golden legs, white trainers thudding on the wood, before the rest of her appeared.

Errol looked askance at his daughter's frilly pink minidress. "What are you wearing, my girl? You forgot your jeans."

"I can't get changed, I'm late." She pouted.

Brooklyn caught her eye and gave the merest hint of a headshake. He would explain later that it wasn't worth picking a fight over clothes. Errol seemed uneasy enough about their relationship, Gashead or not.

"I guess it only takes two minutes," Marley said, huffing. She stomped back upstairs.

Errol slumped in his chair again. He toyed with his phone. "I'm setting a timer."

Brooklyn sensed he'd outstayed his welcome. "She won't be long, will she?" he said, hardly bothering to hide his dismay.

"With women, who knows?" Errol said. "By the way, Marley can't stay out past nine. Did she tell you? No, I thought not. She's working tomorrow. Part-time job at the supermarket. That's how she pays for all those dresses."

He chuckled. "Women are all the same, my daughters included. Trouble."

In Brooklyn's opinion, Marley was worth it. She returned in skintight white denims, showing off her legs to perfection. The dress was still in evidence, loose and flouncy, swinging around her curves.

"Satisfied?" she asked her father.

"It'll do. Don't be late."

She crouched next to his armchair, snuggling into his shoulder. "I'll be back on time. Promise."

"I'm relying on you," Errol said, with a pointed glance at Brooklyn.

"Um, nice to meet you." Brooklyn parroted a phrase Simon Heath used with people he needed to impress. He stood up and headed to the front door.

"Nine o'clock," Errol said, his words carrying the unspoken threat 'I know where you live'. And while Errol was wrong about that, Brooklyn foresaw a heap of trouble descending on him if Marley's father started looking.

Chapter 24

September 2023

Juliet

The eerie sense of being watched didn't leave Juliet as she scurried away from Hugh's office. Protestors had dispersed and the roads reopened. Buses were running again. She waited at the stop on College Green for the number eight to Clifton Village, hanging back to let other passengers on first. As the last to board, she'd be certain she wasn't followed.

She alighted opposite a supermarket and popped in to buy fresh food. It made no sense to waste money on tins or dry groceries. The flat was well supplied with a varied selection, Greg having stockpiled them along with everything else. She chose cheap bread, oil, and vegetables. The packs of bacon in the fridge reminded her of the builders and their sandwiches. Recalling that heavenly aroma, she added streaky rashers to her basket. It would be the first meat she'd eaten since leaving prison.

Back at the flat, salivating in anticipation, she found a frying pan. The built-in hob was stacked high with cookery books, trays and towels, thankfully all clean. She removed the items, balancing them on top of other piles of junk. As she fried three rashers, her mouth watered. The delicious smell alone made her efforts worthwhile.

At last, Juliet sat on the sofa to eat. Her first crisp, salty crunch of bacon represented freedom. It was intoxicating. Hardly stopping for breath, she devoured the rest.

Sated, she looked around the room with dissatisfaction. So much needed to be thrown away. Her top priority must be tracking down Greg's Skoda, though. It was valuable. She could sell it, or even live in it. Yet she hadn't seen a key for either the car or garage. Where would Greg have left them?

Juliet started searching his computer desk, the easiest option. Remarkably, it was free of clutter. The two drawers contained leads, USB drives, pens and other stationery, all tidily arranged. Sadly, she failed to find keys. She checked the pockets of an anorak, which had been left on a hook by the front door as if Greg would retrieve it at any minute. That produced nothing either. She supposed Hugh's team had been through it to look for Greg's credit cards, as the loans had been identified and settled.

Finally, she struck gold by emptying the contents of his wardrobe onto the bed. The Skoda fob, a garage key attached, lurked within a suit jacket's inside pocket. On a mission, Juliet slipped into her coat and out of the flat.

The apartment block hadn't been especially well designed. There was no back door from the lobby to the car park. The old shop and its storerooms, the only accommodation on the ground floor, wrapped around the stairwell. Simon, or whoever was paying him, would make a pretty penny from the conversion. Leaving the building by the front, Juliet walked around the driveway at the side. This gave out into the car park, with the garages arrayed in front of her, five in a row with white up and over doors.

Which was Greg's? She recalled Hugh mentioning the one on the left. It seemed a likely candidate, shabbier than the others, edges darkened by moss and lichen.

The key turned in the lock. Juliet spent a split-second enjoying her triumph. She pushed tentatively at the door, managing to open it without hitting herself. There it was: GREG 107, a black Skoda Superb. A wide, executive style, it barely fitted in a space built for the smaller vehicles of yesteryear.

She caught a hint of Turtle Wax in the stuffy air. Greg had always looked after his cars, she recalled. He'd continually washed, buffed and tinkered with his first, a secondhand Mini acquired in his teens. The Skoda had a showroom gleam. Why was an upmarket model worth only nine thousand pounds? It wasn't like Hugh to make a mistake. Juliet wondered if the car was older than its appearance suggested, a beloved motor which Greg had fought to keep in his divorce.

Muffled sounds drifted towards her: a woman's voice, singing against a drum-heavy background. The music appeared to come from the old sweetshop. Simon Heath's men must be listening to Radio 1; it was why they'd asked for the wi-fi code. But why were they working over the weekend? Juliet glanced at the vehicles in the car park. Simon's white van wasn't there. Perhaps she'd imagined it. The noise had stopped. She cupped a hand to her ear, hearing only the excited chatter of children playing hide and seek in the distance.

A lump came to her throat. Away from the farm, no longer worn out by labouring, German lessons and translations, she had too much time to think. Too much time to dwell on the life she might have had.

She'd better return to the flat. However tempting to take Greg's car out for a spin, she wasn't insured to drive it. Its MOT had probably expired. Did she even have a driving licence anymore? Her old paper document had vanished years ago. There was a new sort, with a photo; she probably needed one of those.

A flicker of movement in the ground floor window caught her eye, but when Juliet peered through, she saw no-one. Debris had been removed from the floor, although the hole in the ceiling remained. She hoped Hugh would persuade the insurers to pay. He'd offered to try. She replayed their conversation in her mind, stopping at the point when he mentioned Rufus. She'd been negligent. The hunt for Greg's car had diverted her from an essential task: finding out whether Rufus was in Bristol.

Despite her aching feet and creaking knees, she ran back into the building and thundered up the stairs. Inside, without even sitting down first, she switched on her laptop. It took less than a minute to flick through the opening screens, but it felt like hours.

She Googled.

On a government website, she discovered the Find A Prisoner service. If he remained in jail, they'd tell her which one, as long as Rufus gave permission. That wasn't likely to happen. Only the police had an automatic right to information. Or his lawyer.

Juliet hugged herself, blinking through tears of frustration. Her only chance lay in pretending to be Rufus's lawyer. Which law firm had he used in 1992, and what was the man's name? She remembered a solicitor, young and keen, passing notes to the barrister with the thankless task of defending Rufus in court. Defending the indefensible. It was over for Rufus as soon as young Damien took the stand.

Although an old case, its high profile ensured the details were easy to find online. Too easy. A picture of her younger self popped up, straplined 'The Face of Evil'. Headlines screamed of the sleazy teacher from hell, of Bristol's Hindley and Brady.

Her tears flowed in earnest. She wasn't evil. She hadn't been evil. But nobody believed her.

Alison had, she realised. Hugh did. And she already knew you couldn't trust everything in the papers.

She dried her eyes, made a cup of tea, and gritted her teeth to start looking again. Nothing recent caught her eye. That suggested Rufus remained inside. His release would surely have created a media storm. A couple of true crime bloggers had written long accounts of the case, and she found the lawyer's name buried in the detail.

Thirty minutes later, having set up a plausible gmail address, she emailed Find A Prisoner under the guise of Andrew Robert Mayne. Luckily, he still worked for Quicksilver solicitors.

Now she had to wait, and hope.

Chapter 25

September 2023

Vix

At the wail of her phone's alarm, Vix snapped awake. She stretched and threw off the duvet. Dim rays from the phone's screen highlighted the cover's leopard print pattern. Reminded of Nanna Lizzie's fluffy slippers, Vix sniffed and looked away.

No half-remembered dreams intruded. She must have been deeply asleep, yet Vix felt fully alert, pumped with energy. For a moment, she listened for signs of Brooklyn stirring, afraid her alarm had disturbed him. His snores told her otherwise. With her phone's flashlight, she found her clothes and pulled them on. Next, she artfully draped the duvet over a pillow. The huddled form would fool Brooklyn if he peeped into the gloom.

Although there was a wall switch for a pendant lamp, the fitting on the ceiling was empty. A mirrored chandelier lay in a box, waiting to be attached. Brooklyn had refused to do it. He wouldn't even switch on the bare bulb in his own room, scared of making the neighbours suspicious. Vix agreed, but she wasn't looking forward to the shorter evenings ahead. Homework would be even more of a challenge than usual.

Stealthy as a cat, she tiptoed into the corridor outside her room. Brooklyn's door stood ajar, a faint lemony scent lingering in the air. Vix recognised it as Avon. Keisha and Aleisha's mother wore it. She supposed Marley did too.

Leaving the flat was tricky. She used the kitchen door, because it had only one key. Turning it softly, she opened the door with barely a sound and shut it with the faintest of clicks.

The car park lay in silence, moonlight reflecting off Simon Heath's white van. Vix crept past, following the driveway around the side of the building. She wore dark clothing as Spike had commanded, blending into the inky blackness. Not that anyone was about to see her. Aldworth Terrace was deserted, its houses slumbering blind below the starlit sky. Trees and shrubs cast fantastical shadows. It was easy to see why small children believed in monsters.

Autumn's chilly air prickled her cheeks, serving only to raise her excitement. It felt like Christmas morning. She slipped quietly through Cliftonwood, skulking close to walls when taxis passed her.

A party was in full swing at one house, with windows lit and raucous chatter. Vix sped up, pulling her parka hood tight around her chin. She stuck hands in pockets. With only a pale face on show, she would fade into the background. But her effort proved to be pointless, as nobody broke away from their revels to look.

She neared the top of the Avon Gorge, where the roads flattened out on the approach to Clifton Village. Her phone told her she was virtually upon Birdcage Walk, the rendezvous. Where was it, and the church Spike had mentioned? She almost missed the set of steps leading upwards across a grassy bank. At the top, she noticed an ornate gateway, imposing enough for a churchyard. Vix tiptoed through.

She found herself in a small park, an avenue of trees beyond, their topmost branches curving to form an arch. It could be Birdcage Walk. There was no church, though. Then she spotted five dark figures standing in the shadows.

"Spike?" she whispered. As balaclavaed heads turned, Vix realised her mistake.

She hadn't worn a mask.

Making her way to the group, she hesitated, feeling tiny and insignificant. They were all much taller than her. Surely they knew what they were doing, and she hadn't even practised. Nor could she tell which was Spike, if he was here at all.

"Vix." He stepped forward, holding out a long black scarf. "Use this."

"Thanks." She smiled before wrapping it around her face.

"No problemo. And you'll need these. Cup your hands."

From a water bottle, he poured out a measure of lentils. "Stick them in a pocket. Are you ready?"

"Waiting for anyone else?" Another male voice, this one deeper and irritable.

"No, Bob. Can you pair up with Vix? She's new."

"Can do." Bob sounded unimpressed.

"You two can do Worcester Terrace, all right?"

"Sure," Vix said, eager to please.

Bob grunted.

"Right, off you go."

Vix heard Spike give instructions to the others as she followed Bob through the avenue. Lanky and fit, he set a cracking pace. She struggled to keep up.

"Hey, can you slow down?" she whispered.

111

He strode forward without replying. Half-running, she kept up with him. They passed a wide road with bus stops, another park, a school.

"How far is it?" she asked.

"It's over there," Bob hissed, a sharp edge to his voice as he pointed ahead. He sounded middle-aged, like a less pleasant version of her maths teacher.

Vix took out her phone to check the map. "I can't find it."

"You don't need that. Switch it off." He stopped and folded his arms. "And be quiet, will you? Make too much noise and you'll attract attention."

What was it about old men, that they felt entitled to treat you like a kid? Spike had included her in his circle, inspired her to slip out at night to save the planet. Thanks to Bob, that camaraderie was over. Vix pulled a face, then realised he wouldn't see it. Mute, she marched alongside him.

They rounded a corner. A long, thin, tree-lined garden backed onto a road. There, a string of expensive cars stood in the shadow of a wall. Stone steps led to a row of balconied villas above. Vix approved of the set-up. They'd be safely out of view; the vehicles sat below the line of sight from the residents' windows.

"Can you see anyone?" Bob asked, his tone softer now.

"No."

"Grand. We tackle one car at a time. You take the left, I'll do the tyres on the right. Got it?"

"Sure."

"Then let's go." He nodded to a vehicle, its squarish black hulk gleaming in the moonlight.

"Toyota Land Cruiser 250," Vix read aloud.

Bob glared down at her. "What did I tell you?" he snapped.

"Fine." She held his gaze until he looked away. Her stomach might be churning, but she wouldn't let him push her around. If he complained to Spike and she wasn't invited again, so be it. Only a weakening sense of loyalty to Spike stopped her from stomping away, screaming so loud that the whole neighbourhood descended on Bob.

Without another word, Bob knelt next to one of the back wheels. He motioned her towards the other.

Vix crouched down beside it. This was it. Beneath the scarf, she beamed, arguments forgotten. She could do this.

The moon's rays provided enough light. She located the valve. Her fingers, stiff from the cold, fumbled to unscrew the cap. The tiny, thimble-shaped object slipped from her grasp.

Bob noticed her sharp intake of breath. "What now?" he muttered.

"It rolled away. Under the car."

"Well, find it. No theft or criminal damage. Understand?"

Vix flicked on her phone's flashlight, dazzling herself. Luckily, the cap wasn't far, just an inch or two away. She retrieved it, then fished in her pocket for a lentil. She pressed it against the valve pin. A satisfying slow hiss told her she'd got it right. Shoulders hunched with concentration, she replaced the cap over the lentil. Then she bunny-hopped to the front of the car.

"Hurry up," Bob complained. He was on his feet, stretching and rubbing his lower back. Perhaps he was simply grumpy with pain. Except for his name, she knew nothing about him.

She finished and made for the next vehicle at the roadside.

"Leave it," Bob said. "Electric. There," he pointed, "we'll do the VW."

Vix almost matched his pace on that one. They fell into a companionable rhythm, working on another half dozen cars. She smiled to herself, imagining a black cloud of anger descending on Worcester Terrace when the residents awoke to flat tyres. Shame tomorrow was Sunday. They wouldn't be in a hurry to drive to their high-powered, self-important jobs. Maybe she'd suggest coming out the following evening too. Spike would listen to her, wouldn't he? He treated her like a human being rather than an irritating brat.

Bob snapped his fingers. "One more. My joints are playing up."

"Shh." Vix couldn't resist it, despite the glare she received. She scowled back, momentarily losing concentration and tripping on a pothole. Her scream was instinctive as she felt herself pitched forward. Hands reaching out in vain, her right shoulder connected with a red Mini. They hadn't even planned to attack this car. It jolted as Vix slammed against it.

The alarm blared. Headlights flashed. "Run," Bob yelled.

Stunned, her shoulder sore, Vix stumbled to her feet. She stared at the space he'd occupied. Bob had put his words into practice. He was already out of sight.

For a split-second, she wondered what to do. Then she saw squares of yellow light appear in the villas looming above. A window opened. Vix ran, panting, back towards Clifton Village. She hardly cared where she went. All that mattered was escaping Worcester Terrace. Only the taste of blood in her throat and a painful stitch in her side caused her to slow down.

Chapter 26

September 2023

Rufus

A day didn't get much better than this. Fair enough, Rufus's back was killing him after a morning of lettuce-picking, but it beat being stuck in a cell. He'd enjoyed the wind whipping through what was left of his hair, the smell of soil and leaves, the vista of rolling Kent countryside. Of course, he had Brexit to thank for that, as he'd just learned. The Poles had all gone home, John complained. Rufus had been in prison when they'd arrived in England after the EU expanded in 2004. He was still there when they left. While he'd ignored the referendum, given that he couldn't vote, he was happy to reap the benefits.

There were four of them out on the farm today. The other lads weren't nonces like him, but none of them had a go. You had to leave your baggage behind to get a transfer to an open prison. Besides, he worked out, keeping his muscles ripped despite his advanced age. When it first sunk in that he'd spend half his twenties and all his thirties and forties rotting in jail, he'd nearly gone crazy. But the alternative was worse, as his dear old mum said, and he realised he had to get on with it. He'd taken every opportunity to work out, to keep his body and mind active. There had been degree courses, self-help training and books. So many books. It was all that reading that would, finally, lift him out of the garbage heap where the courts had thrown him.

John, the farmer, was pleased with their work. He'd taken them out for a pint and a ploughman's, strictly against the rules, but it was an open secret that John was a decent fellow. Good-looking too, with that little kiss curl on his forehead. He must have been cute as a teenager.

"What're you in for?" John asked, swigging his Bishop's Finger.

You didn't ask a man that, but he wouldn't know.

"Drugs," Rufus said, wishing he hadn't downed his ale so quickly. It was strong, especially when you weren't used to it.

Dessie, one of the other lads, nudged him. "Nah, you ain't," he said. "But—"

He didn't finish. Right at that moment, their food arrived. Somehow, as plates and cutlery were set down, Rufus spilled the dregs of his pint on Dessie. The skimpily clad waitress distracted Dessie so much that he forgot to kick off. Everyone else was too hungry to care.

Rufus polished off the best meal he'd enjoyed in thirty years, and wandered off to the gents. At first, he stepped into the beer garden to look for it. A customer told him the loos were inside the pub, which took him by surprise. He hadn't figured the place was so upmarket.

Another man was finishing up at the urinals, a weather-beaten chap wearing a beanie hat and a high-vis jacket. He nodded to Rufus, zipped himself up and stood aside for him. Then he spoke. "Rufus Cameron?"

Instantly on a war footing, Rufus jerked a finger in the general direction of the garden. "He's out there."

Beanie Man's voice and body language weren't aggressive, but Rufus didn't plan to take a chance. He sized up the stranger. The guy was younger and taller, although Rufus was no midget himself.

"Shame," Beanie Man said. "I've got news of interest to him."

"Is that so?" Rufus asked, his tone casual while he weighed up his chances of winning a fight. He reckoned fifty-fifty, unless there was a knife. Then all bets were off.

Beanie Man peered into his eyes, as if expecting Rufus to say more. Then he shrugged. "I hear Rufus wants to rid the world of a snitch. Well, we're on the same side. I can find her for him."

"Who are you talking about?" Only one female fitted the description. Curiosity piqued, Rufus waited to see if this new friend was the real deal or a random liar.

"Jules," Beanie Man said. "The sometime Mrs Sharples."

Bingo. He'd love to meet Jules again, preferably with a deadly weapon in his hand. It was an ambition, an obsession even, which he'd admitted to no-one. How amazing that this stranger not only shared his dream, but had guessed it was his dearest wish and had sought him out. On the day before his parole hearing too.

What a coincidence.

"So where might she be?" Rufus asked, edging away.

"Bristol. Cliftonwood. But she plans to move on soon, so you'll need to act fast. Let me help. and I'll tell you the precise location when you're out. Where will you be living?"

It was tempting, and if the guy wanted to kill him, he could have slit his throat already. Even so, Rufus's instincts screamed at him to say nothing.

Beanie Man squinted at him.

"Send a letter to Rufus's solicitor," Rufus said, deciding to maintain his pretence whether Beanie Man believed him or not. "Andrew Mayne at

Quicksilver. Care of, to be opened only by Rufus. Marked private and confidential."

He wasn't handing over his widowed mother's address to anybody. Hopefully, he'd be staying with her rather than in a bleak hostel. Andy Mayne thought he could swing it.

She'd welcome Rufus with open arms. Bless her, she still didn't think he'd done it. The jury had got it wrong.

He knew they'd got it right. Rufus was guilty of every single offence with which he'd been charged, and many more that the police hadn't discovered.

Still, it was all behind him now. He was a reformed character, full of remorse and determined to stick to the straight and narrow. He hoped the Parole Board believed that little fairytale.

Chapter 27

October 1992

Jules

Jules's hopes for a glimpse of normality were dashed. She wasn't transported from jail in a police car, but a windowless Black Maria. It decanted her into a service yard at Bristol Crown Court. She was manacled to a prison officer and marched through corridors to the dock.

"Sit there," Rita, the prison officer, hissed.

Rita was not chatty. Both officers and inmates at the jail seemed to decided Jules was guilty. She looked forward to proving them wrong.

In common with the other seating in court, her bench reminded Jules of a church pew. It was padded, presumably more for Rita's benefit than hers. The two women sat next to each other in silence. Then Jules heard a scuffle behind her, a command to "Get on with it", and Rufus parked himself on her other side.

He wore a tweed jacket, a square choice for him. Alison Lambert had counselled Jules to dress conservatively too. 'No trousers, hem below the knee.' She'd chosen a plain black shift.

"Jules," Rufus whispered, "don't think you're strolling out of here."

"Shut up." The male guard by Rufus's side scowled at him.

Jules shuddered, turning her face away. So close to Rufus that she could smell his sweat, it was impossible to ignore his baleful presence. Yet she must try.

She scanned the chamber, her gaze alighting first on the public gallery to the left, behind the witness box.

George sat in the front row.

Perhaps he cared after all. Her heart leaped.

Would he take her back?

If the baby growing inside her was his, then maybe. They weren't divorced yet.

Since her arrest, they'd had no contact, except through lawyers. He didn't know she was pregnant. She'd told no-one, not even Penny.

Unease tightened her stomach as she wondered for the hundredth time if Malcolm was the father. In that case, she'd stand no chance with George. But suppose George himself had stuck a bun in the oven, as he liked to put it? When this nightmare was over and she was free again, he might forgive her.

Jules tried in vain to catch his eye. He was looking down at something, probably his Psion Organiser. She'd given him the gadget for his birthday, and he'd become addicted to it, his Filofax consigned to the bin. Was that how he felt about their marriage? It couldn't be, or he wouldn't be here.

Penny arrived, slipping in beside George and waving to Jules. "Good luck," she mouthed.

At least Jules had one true friend. Apart from Alison, only Penny had visited the prison. She'd brought chocolate, books and conversation. Most important of all, she'd been good company. For those precious hours, Jules pretended she had a life. They discussed novels, politics and fashion. Penny had asked whether she should dye her hair blonde. Jules had encouraged her to. It was the right decision: the fresh style suited her.

How kind of Penny to devote her half-term holiday to supporting Jules. No other family or friends had bothered to turn up. The remaining seats in the public gallery were occupied by journalists and an assortment of gloomy individuals who were probably relatives of the victims. Jules recognised Steve Purslow's older sister sitting with a pair of angry-looking adults. Pity, sorrow and guilt gripped her. If only she'd had an inkling of Rufus's true nature.

The judge sat across the room with the clerk at a desk in front of him; the empty jury benches were to the right; and the dark-robed lawyers in the middle. As Jules watched, the clerk stood up and demanded silence.

Chatter in the gallery came to an abrupt halt.

The clerk, an elderly gent with the red face of a drinker, wore black clothes like the other functionaries. Whatever his other skills, he boasted an impressively loud voice.

"Rufus St John Torrance Cameron," he announced, "you are charged with the murder of Stephen Wayne Purslow. How do you plead?"

"Not guilty," Rufus replied firmly.

"You are further charged with indecent assault on Stephen Wayne Purslow. How do you plead?"

"Not guilty."

"You are further charged with gross indecency…"

There followed a litany of crimes involving boys identified as A, B, C, D and E. Rufus denied them.

119

Already wobbly after a bout of morning sickness, Jules tasted bile. She imagined the terror that Steve and the others must have felt. And it was her fault.

"Juliet Dawn Sharples," the clerk said. "You are charged with aiding and abetting the indecent assault of Stephen Wayne Purslow. How do you plead?"

Her heart pounded. "Not guilty."

She gave the same answer to the charges involving the other boys.

The clerk nodded and sat down again.

"Please bring in the jury," the judge requested.

An usher went to fetch them. He returned so quickly that Jules was convinced the twelve jurors had been waiting outside. She scrutinised them as they filed in. All would have a hand in her fate.

A mix of ages, races and genders, the jury offered a welcome splash of colour in the sombre courtroom. Jules noticed a red dress, striped ties, even a retro Mohican haircut. A few whispered to each other. There was a delay while each was sworn in, and the clerk read out the charges to them. The judge then introduced Alec Underwood, the prosecuting barrister.

Underwood was a similar age to the clerk, but unlike him, didn't have the appearance of a man who enjoyed life. Tall, gaunt and pale, his face was nearly as colourless as the grey wig above it. His ears stuck out. Nevertheless, as soon as he spoke, he commanded everyone's attention.

"Members of the jury," he began, "this is a very sad case. A teenager with a bright future had it cruelly snuffed out. You will hear that he fought for his life, but to no avail. And five of his classmates suffered almost unmentionable harm at the hands of his murderer."

He coughed. "Unfortunately, you will be asked to listen to details of what they went through. It will be difficult for you. I assure you that I find it agonising too. But I urge you to remember how much harder it is for the innocent victims, who will bear the effects for the rest of their lives.

"Our case is this. Mr Rufus Cameron, the man before you in the dock, is a paedophile. And Mrs Juliet Sharples, the woman sitting next to him, is a teacher who procured boys for him to abuse. One of those boys, thirteen-year-old Stephen Purslow, was killed by Mr Cameron, and his body dumped in Bristol's Floating Harbour. He was trussed up in a bin bag. Like a piece of trash."

Having infused his last sentence with anger, Underwood paused to let the jury digest it. Their expressions were bleak. As one of the women began to sob, an usher passed over a box of tissues.

"Please continue, Mr Underwood," the judge said.

"Yes, Your Honour. Ladies and gentlemen, I appreciate these are upsetting crimes. I am sure you will agree that it's important that those responsible are justly punished. It's the least we can do for the victims and their loved ones. Sadly, we can't turn back the clock.

"The defendants, Mr Cameron and Mrs Sharples, deny all the charges. Indeed, Mr Cameron claims he lent his flat to Mrs Sharples to pursue affairs both with her teenage pupils and with a Mr Malcolm Jenks."

The courtroom appeared to shake and spin. Juliet clutched Rita's arm. "Going to be… sick," she stuttered.

For a split-second, Rita gaped, then collected herself and asked the judge if they might be excused. She pulled Jules to her feet. With the help of a female usher, she rushed Jules to a toilet.

Dizzy and shocked, Jules threw up.

"Want to splash water on your face? Clean up a bit," the usher suggested.

Jules nodded, still weak at the knees. She tidied herself up while Rita looked on, silent and disapproving.

"Ready to go back?" the usher asked, glancing at Jules's belly under the loose dress.

She wasn't showing yet. Had the woman guessed? Jules simply nodded. She allowed herself to be shepherded back to the dock.

"Ah, Mrs Sharples returns after that courtroom drama," Alec Underwood said. "May I carry on, Your Honour?"

"Please do."

"As I was saying, Mr Cameron alleges Mrs Sharples had sexual liaisons with male pupils, and with Mr Jenks. It is she, he says, who must have murdered Stephen Purslow.

"But we say otherwise. You will note that Mrs Sharples has not been charged with murder. The Crown is not accusing her of indecent assault herself, only in aiding and abetting Mr Cameron to do it. Thanks to painstaking detective work, you will be hearing from some of Mrs Sharples' pupils. They tell a different story from Mr Cameron. We say, and we will prove to you, that Mr Cameron cravenly murdered young Stephen and foully abused other children. We will show you that Mr Cameron has told lies.

"But that's not to say that Mr Cameron has lied about everything. And while there is no proof whatsoever that Mrs Sharples seduced teenage boys, she is not pure as driven snow. She is a married woman who did indeed conduct an affair with Mr Malcolm Jenks."

Underwood halted for enough time to give his words emphasis, but without attracting a comment from the judge.

"You will hear from Mr Jenks too," Underwood said. "He will tell you he has never met Mr Cameron or been to his flat. He does not know Mr Cameron. Lucky him. But Mr Cameron knew about this affair. And he persuaded Mrs Sharples to deliver up her pupils to abuse for his gratification.

"What pressure he may have brought to bear, we cannot be certain, but I ask you this," Underwood scanned the jury, slowly making eye contact with each one, "if you wanted to keep a secret, would you destroy innocent children's lives to do so?"

Chapter 28

October 1992

Jules

Alec Underwood had questioned the night shift worker who found Steve's body in the harbour, and police who were called to the scene. He was telling a story, deploying his witnesses for dramatic effect.

With the air of a magician pulling a rabbit from a hat, he announced that his next witness was Mr Malcolm Jenks. For good measure, he reminded the jury that Jules and Malcolm had been intimate whilst married to other people.

Jules twisted her hands together. He might be the father of her child. How would he react when he found out?

A door opened next to the public gallery. Malcolm swaggered into the court. He didn't even glance at Jules.

Her gaze flicked to George. There was a tightness around his eyes.

An usher brought Malcolm to the witness box, and Underwood began with the formalities.

"Good morning, Mr Jenks. I am Alec Underwood, counsel for the prosecution. As a matter of form, may I ask you to confirm your name?"

"Of course." Malcolm, in his trademark red braces, seemed entirely unfazed. "I am Malcolm Edward Jenks."

"Thank you. I must now ask you to take an oath on the bible, or you may alternatively choose to affirm that you will tell the truth."

"I'll take the oath."

The usher handed him a battered bible and a square of card. Malcolm read from the latter, "I swear by almighty God that the evidence I shall give shall be the truth, the whole truth, and nothing but the truth."

"Thank you," Underwood said. "May I ask if you know either of the defendants, Mr Rufus Cameron and Mrs Juliet Sharples?"

Malcolm made a show of staring at each of them, leering as he looked Jules up and down. "I don't know Mr Cameron at all. Mrs Sharples, I know very well."

"How do you know Mrs Sharples?"

"As I say, very well indeed." Malcolm licked his lips. "She's a good lay."

There were giggles in the public gallery. A male juror uttered a loud, braying laugh. George's face turned puce, and no wonder, given such a coarse remark.

What had happened to her caring lover? Jules flushed, gawping at Malcolm. He didn't return her gaze.

"Can we have order, please," the judge snapped.

Once quiet was restored, Underwood started again.

"I think we need to put your comments into context, Mr Jenks. I'll ask a few more questions, if I may. First of all, how did you meet Mrs Sharples?"

"Oh, I made an effort to," Malcolm said. "Having done business with her husband, I was extremely keen to meet her."

That was news to Jules, and presumably to Underwood as well. A flicker of surprise crossed his face.

"How so?" Underwood asked.

"He's an angel," Malcolm said.

Laughter erupted again.

"Would you care to explain?" Underwood said.

"George Sharples provides investment funding for small businesses, such as my own. He took a stake in my company. I believed we were sharing profits fifty-fifty. Hands up," Malcolm's body language mirrored his words, "I should have employed a lawyer. I did eventually, when I realised I'd got virtually nothing and George was taking a fat cheque every month. It cost me a fortune to buy him out."

"I am sorry to hear that," Underwood said. "So how does this relate to Mrs Sharples?"

Malcolm sniggered. "George boasted too much about his trophy wife. I'd seen his photos. He'd had my money, so it was only fair that I got to have her."

Jules froze.

"That was your motivation for starting an affair?"

"For starting it, yes." Malcolm smirked. "She was easy. A bottle of wine, and she's anyone's."

His attentiveness had been a smokescreen. An act. Sobbing, Jules saw George storm out of the room. An anxious Penny trailed after him.

"And you continued to meet Mrs Sharples?"

"For sex. Yes, she couldn't get enough. My wife had just given birth, so it took the pressure off her. Even though she'd insisted I had a vasectomy after she fell pregnant again…"

Blood pounded in Jules' temples. She wasn't expecting Malcolm's baby. There had never been any chance of it. If only she'd known.

Chapter 29

October 1992

Jules

The next witness was a child, so the judge asked the public to clear the court. From the dock, Jules watched George leave the public gallery. He appeared to be grumbling to Penny, stabbing at the air to make a point. Jeff Sharples did that too when overcome by anger. Like father, like son.

The judge glared at the reporters, who hadn't moved. "This witness is Boy A and is to be referred as such outside this court. While we may use his name during proceedings, you must not do so, nor identify him in any other way. Do I make myself clear?"

They nodded. They appeared on high alert, eager to hear the Crown's star witness. The jury sat upright too, interested expressions on their faces.

Jules turned to see Damien enter the courtroom.

She felt a wave of hatred from Rufus, sullen in the dock beside her. Clenching her fists, she hoped Damien's evidence would convict him.

Damien would prove her innocence too. As soon as Jules had met George's cherubic little brother, there had been a rapport between them. Damien would know she'd never expose him to harm.

He'd speak up for her.

She was sure he'd be excited later, when he found out he'd be an uncle.

An usher, a middle-aged woman, made sure the boy was comfortable in the witness box. Then Alec Underwood started his examination. He asked Damien to confirm his name.

"Damien Peter Sharples." Damien's voice wavered between treble and bass. Everything about him screamed of awkwardness: his pale face, sloping shoulders and twitching lips.

Jules hoped he sensed the sympathy she felt for him as, gripping a bible, he swore the oath. But Damien kept his eyes fixed on Underwood, as if viewing the occupants of the dock was too much to bear.

"Let's begin at the beginning," Underwood said. "Damien, how did you come to meet the defendant, Rufus Cameron?"

Damien hesitated. "Through Jules," he said eventually.

"That would be the second defendant, Juliet Sharples?"

"Yes."

"How do you know Jules?"

"She's kind of like my sister-in-law," Damien muttered. "And she's a teacher at my school. I'm in her German class."

"And being your sister-in-law, as well as your teacher, would you say you liked her? Got on with her?"

"Suppose so." Damien shrugged.

"And do you … did you trust her?" Underwood glanced at the jury to make sure they'd hung onto the past tense.

"Yes."

"Can you remember how or when Jules introduced you to Rufus?" Underwood asked.

Damien looked down at the floor. "She said he needed a beta tester for his computer games."

"Did you understand what she meant by that?"

"Yes."

"I don't play computer games, Damien. I don't even have a computer. Can you explain what a beta tester does?"

Damien gaped at him. "Well, we play a new game to see if it's good. And say what we think. This is, like, before anyone else gets to see it."

"That sounds fun." Underwood's eyes twinkled. "It's an important job, I can see that. How did you feel being asked to be a games tester?"

"Good. I like games."

"When would you do this games testing?"

"After school."

"Would you tell your parents what you were doing?"

"No."

"Oh. Why not?"

"Jules said to tell them I was doing extra German."

"Just to be clear, Damien. Jules told you to lie? To your parents?"

"Yes," Damien said.

The atmosphere in the courtroom was unnaturally still, as if everyone was holding their breath.

Underwood continued remorselessly, steering Damien to tell the story he wished the jury to hear. "And where would this games testing happen?" he asked.

"At Rufus's flat."

"At Rufus's flat? Not at school?"

"No, not at school," Damien said vehemently. "At his flat. That's what I just told you. And I told the police."

127

"Forgive me for repeating myself, but this is important, Damien. Your parents thought you were at school, taking extra German lessons, when you were actually at Rufus's flat playing computer games?"

"Yes."

"Damien, besides testing games, did you ever expect to do anything else at Rufus's flat?"

"No."

"But did other things besides testing games happen?"

Damien paused. His pale face reddened. "Yes," he said.

"Did you tell anyone else what was happening?"

"No."

"Earlier, you said you trusted Jules. Was there any reason you didn't tell her?"

Damien's tone was accusatory. "They were old friends, her and Rufus. She knew what he did. She knew all along he..." He exhaled loudly, screwing up his eyes.

Damien so obviously wanted to cry. Despite her horror at his words, Jules wished she could envelop him in a huge hug. Nobody offered him any comfort, or even a tissue.

"I see," Underwood said, his tone gentler than usual. "I'm sorry, this may be difficult for you, but we must now discuss what actually happened when you were in Rufus's flat."

Chapter 30

September 2023

Rufus

He was selling himself. Just like the old days, when he made a pitch to investors, except now he was the product. Shiny and new, the reformed Rufus.

As he entered the hearing room, he noticed differences from the rest of the prison. The paintwork wasn't scratched or absent. Pale peach walls, with a big screen mounted on one of them, gave an airy feel. The usual smells — boiled cabbage, disinfectant and worse — fell away. Instead, Rufus caught notes of polish, aftershave and Nina Ricci's L'Air du Temps.

Maybe that perfume would be his lucky charm, the scent of freedom. His dear old mum always dabbed it on her wrists before an evening out. When his parents left their children at home, he could do as he pleased. Drink their whisky. Terrorise his sisters or annoy the au pair. Although a certain au pair got his own back. Rufus shut off that train of thought.

Luckily, his mother wasn't here to listen to him admit his crimes. She'd paid for Andy Mayne to accompany him, though. And Rufus's solicitor was worth his considerable weight in gold.

"Good morning, Rufus." No longer young and thin, Andy manoeuvred his bulk out of a chair that was too small for him. He held out his right hand.

Rufus shook it, while focusing on the trio seated across the oval, pale wood table. A woman in a navy trouser suit and glasses, blonde hair scraped back in a bun, had a businesslike air. Two men flanked her, both more casually dressed. One of them, young enough to be Rufus's son, wore a canvas jacket, T-shirt and jeans. A stud glinted in his nose. The other, a bald fellow the size of a heavyweight boxer, had dressed in a red jumper and chinos. Interestingly, he'd positioned himself some distance along the table from the woman. It suggested they weren't best of friends, although it might meant nothing at all.

Rufus would wait and see. He smiled at them.

They stayed where they were.

The woman smiled back. "Welcome to your Parole Board hearing, Rufus. Do sit down." She pointed to the vacant seat beside Andy's.

Rufus did so. Another wave of perfume hit him, along with a sense that she really cared. That he wanted to spend time in her company. He didn't want her to leave.

What was all that about? He couldn't afford to freak out now.

"I'll make the introductions, and then explain what will happen in the hearing," the woman said. "I'm Jeanette, and this," she gestured to Canvas Jacket, "is my colleague, Dave. Then, to my right and your left, we have Marcus."

They each said, "Hello," Marcus in a pronounced Scottish accent.

"As you know," Jeanette said, her tone upbeat, "we are meeting to decide on your suitability for parole. We've already read various reports, of which there were quite a number."

Rufus had expected to see a thick paper file at her fingertips. Instead, while Andy had a dossier in front of him, the panel members used laptops. Enviously, Rufus observed the thin, silvery machines. Computer kit had come a long way.

"Victims of your crimes, or their relatives, are permitted to speak at the hearing. Only one person has indicated they wish to do so. That's Shirley Wilks, who will join us via video link."

"I thought she was coming in person," Andy said. "Didn't she insist on a face-to-face hearing?"

"She's still ill," Jeanette replied.

Rufus recognised the name. The hearing had been delayed because of her. Once he'd dealt with Jules, he'd add Shirley to his hit list.

"After that, we'll ask you a few questions, and you'll have an opportunity to tell us anything you think we should know," Jeanette said. "So, without further ado, let's get started. Marcus, can you patch in Shirley, please?"

"Okey doke." Marcus clicked the mouse a few times. His brow furrowed. "Not seeing her yet. By the way, just so you're aware, we'll use our laptops because the big screen isn't working."

That was typical of prison life. Rufus doubted it was the first time Marcus had encountered the problem.

"Any luck?" Andy said, as Marcus's frown deepened.

"No."

"Try sending her an email," Andy suggested.

"Not a bad shout," Marcus admitted. Another couple of clicks later, he sighed. "She's emailed us. Her wi-fi is down. She's requested an adjournment or deferral."

"How come her email works, but not her wi-fi?" Dave asked.

"Search me," Marcus said. He turned to Jeanette. "Can we discuss this privately?"

Rufus sensed tension from Andy. Good. The lawyer was paid to stop Shirley derailing him again.

"May I say something first, please?" Andy asked.

Jeanette nodded.

"My client has already suffered a deferral because of Shirley Wilks' illness," Andy said. "He didn't complain. In fact, due to his utmost sympathy for Mrs Wilks, he did not oppose the deferral. But now we hear that she is unwell again. And suddenly has issues with her wi-fi. She wants another delay. I fear this is a deliberate obstruction, and it's unfair to my client. He's keen to leave prison and atone for his misdeeds."

Rufus made eye contact with Jeanette, eliciting an empathetic nod. He bet she'd been trained to interpret body language. Just as well he'd devoured countless books on it.

She'd be easy to get onside. He wasn't so sure of the other two, especially Marcus.

"Can I take it you've already read Shirley Wilks' victim impact statement," Andy continued. "Surely that is sufficient to take a view?"

"We've been through all the reports, as I said." Jeanette's bespectacled gaze swept around the men on either side of her. "What do you think, Dave, Marcus? Andy raises a fair point."

"I believe Shirley has a right to be heard." Marcus leaned back, meaty arms folded. "It's clear she was deeply affected by her little brother's murder. It is not an exaggeration to say it ruined her life."

"Yes, I got the gist," Dave said. A stray sunbeam glinted off his nose stud.

"She would only be reading out the statement she's already given us," Andy said. "Isn't that right?"

"Yes," Marcus said, "but the point is to empower Shirley to make a personal connection with the panel, and I embrace that."

At least he was no longer insisting on discussing it in private. Rufus had a chance to win him over.

"I can only stress how sorry I am," Rufus interjected, palms open in front of him. "Poor Shirley…"

He paused, allowing Andy to interrupt. They'd planned what the lawyer would say about her.

"You may recall from the trial summary that Mrs Wilks and her brother were already known to the police before his sad death," Andy said. "She'd received a caution for cannabis use, and he for being drunk and disorderly, despite his tender age. That doesn't excuse what my client did, and he wouldn't claim it does, but it casts doubt on his culpability for all Mrs Wilks' problems. Then we have other victim impact statements that show my client in a different light, don't we? Damien Sharples, for example."

"Ah, yes," Jeanette said. "Mr Sharples, who has waived his anonymity. Boy A. He bears Mr Cameron no ill will and feels he has suffered punishment enough."

That was decent of Damien. Rufus wondered what he was doing now. He'd been a creative lad, with a good eye for graphics. Hadn't he developed that penguin platform game? Not bad for a first-timer on a DOS-based PC.

"I think we can carry on," Jeanette said. "Okay, guys?"

"Fine with me," Dave said.

"Yes," Marcus grunted.

Rufus almost fainted with relief.

"So, let's focus on you, Rufus," Jeanette said. "Having denied all charges against you in 1992, your written statement tells us you accept you're guilty of murder and child abuse. What made you change your mind?"

Rufus hung his head. "Well, it wasn't the jury's verdict," he said, taking care to look her in the eye. "I was in denial for a long time, trying to dissociate myself from those terrible crimes. Indeed, I didn't want to believe my compulsion had made me carry out such dreadful deeds."

The catch in his voice was clearly audible. Good. He'd spent months practising it.

"It's been hard coming to terms with my wrongdoing. I did a lot of work on myself in prison. Courses. Group work with other sex offenders. I take full responsibility for what I did. My punishment was justified. Thirty-one years."

"Interesting. You mention a compulsion," Marcus said. "Tell us about that."

"I was abused myself as a child," Rufus said, aware no-one could disprove it.

"There are details in the psychologist's report," Andy pointed out. "I imagine it's painful to talk about it, Rufus. Marcus, is this really —"

132

Sure that Marcus would insist it was necessary, Rufus gilded the lily. "Don't worry, Andy. I owe Marcus an explanation."

He cleared his throat, all the better to appear upset. "I conflated sex with love," he said. "The boys... I thought I loved them. It makes me feel sick now. I could never, ever harm another human being again."

"You killed one," Marcus said.

He would like to kill Marcus. After thirty-one years, it was like being back in that courtroom.

"I didn't know my own strength as a young man," Rufus said. "It was a moment of madness. I am deeply sorry."

Wide-eyed, he flashed an imploring glance at Jeanette.

She picked up the cue. "What do you plan to do if you're released?" she asked.

Dave added, "You were a games designer, I believe. A rapidly changing world."

"I've kept up to date," Rufus said, an outright lie, as the constraints of prison made it impossible. If they queried it, he'd bamboozle them with information about computer languages. Their eyes would soon glaze over.

They didn't follow up, so threw in another falsehood. "I'm keen to make a living again. Pay my taxes. Contribute to society."

"Obviously, the taxpayer stumps up a substantial amount to keep a man in prison," Andy said. "More than the fees at Eton, if we can believe the newspapers."

"I've heard that one before." Dave laughed.

"We need to be sure he's not a danger to the public," Marcus said. "You can't put a price on that."

"I understand your concerns," Andy said. "And with appropriate conditions, I'm sure you can eliminate any risks you perceive."

"You've seen the offender supervisor's recommendations, no doubt?" Jeanette asked.

Rufus held his breath. As a minimum, he'd have to keep away from children. However, options such as tagging were listed merely as possibilities.

"Dave, Marcus and I will have a discussion afterwards," Jeanette said. "Any further questions, guys?"

"Not from me," Dave said.

"No," Marcus muttered.

"Very good," Jeanette said, her expression open and voice warm. "Thanks for meeting us, Rufus. And Andy. We will make our decision within fourteen days. You'll be advised."

"Thank you." Rufus inhaled her perfume one more time, smiling at her to cover his jitters.

He'd done his best.

Was it enough?

Chapter 31

September 2023

Juliet

A gust of wind blew through the lounge, bringing a spritz of moist air. Papers flew off Greg's desk. Doors slammed. Shivering, Juliet unlatched and closed the window. Despite the cost, she'd have to put the heating on. A freezing flat wouldn't cut it with the estate agents.

She scanned the room. Heaps of junk still lay scattered around; fewer of them, since she'd stuffed the worst of it into the bins outside, taking bags of low-value items to Clifton's charity shops. Anything she thought would sell easily, she'd listed on eBay. That aspect of twenty-first century life had passed her by on the farm, but she'd learned quickly.

She'd also discovered Amazon and ordered flat-packed cardboard boxes. Deftly, she constructed half a dozen, piling the remnants of the hoard into them. Once she cleared the sofa and hid boxes behind it, the room looked more presentable.

Greg's kitchen was tidier too; just as well, as it was hardly bigger than a cupboard. Juliet reached into a wall unit for filter coffee. The packet was way out of date. She ripped it open, spooning grounds into a mug and topping it up with hot water. You were supposed to make coffee for house viewings, weren't you? She wouldn't drink this – she'd have to strain it through her teeth – but the aroma did the job. When she left the mug perched on the bathroom sink, she no longer smelled mould.

She turned to the bedroom next, more of a problem because she hadn't sifted through it yet. Perhaps she'd contacted the estate agents too early, but she needed to sell. It took months, didn't it? When she and George married and moved into their dream home in Stoke Bishop, he'd sold his little starter flat. She recalled it taking a long while.

That dream home must be where he lived with Penny, where they'd brought up James. She could Google it, but why torture herself? Of course George had moved on. He'd done so with indecent haste, but he'd had good reasons.

She should forget him, and Bristol too. The city, this unsafe haven of ghosts and stalkers, had reopened old wounds. The sooner she got rid of Greg's tatty apartment, the better.

What would Hayley, the estate agent, be like? The name sounded young. On the phone, the girl had been professional and charming. They were always looking for stock in Cliftonwood, Hayley assured Juliet, and it would be a pleasure to view the flat. Mid-afternoon would be perfect.

With an hour to go, Juliet chucked some of the junk onto the bed, smoothing the duvet over it. Then she assembled more boxes and began to fill them.

A buzzer sounded. She made her way to the intercom. While she never had visitors, she occasionally brought deliveries into the lobby. The other residents of the block, presumably out at work all day, received parcels from a host of big-name clothing brands. She must live near the best-dressed people in Bristol.

"Hello?" She posed it as a question, not a welcome.

"It's Hayley."

Juliet jerked back from the intercom. "I thought you were coming at three?"

"I'm sorry, didn't you get my text? My previous client cancelled, and you did say you were in a hurry, so I tried to get to you sooner."

She was in a hurry to sell. That's what she'd said. An extra thirty minutes would have made a difference to the bedroom's appearance. But Hayley was here now, and it would be rude to turn her away.

"Come on up," Juliet said, buzzing Hayley in.

The estate agent's arrival was preceded by the clicking of stilettos on the stairs. Juliet guessed they were the same height, but Hayley's strappy black sandals gave the illusion of tallness. She wore pearls, presumably fake, and a clingy, knee-length dress. It perfectly matched her wavy brown hair, displaying her figure and tanned legs too. For a customer-facing role, pretty twenty-something Hayley certainly looked the part.

She had an engaging manner as well. "Lovely to meet you," she bubbled, shaking Juliet's hand with just the right level of firmness. "This is a delightful location. I can't wait to see your flat."

"Would you like a cup of tea or coffee?" Juliet asked. Too late, she remembered the mug in the bathroom. Still, Hayley wouldn't realise why it was there.

"I've just had one, thanks." The estate agent flashed a toothy grin and fluttered her lashes. They were long, as fake as the rhinestones on her perfect pink nails. Close at hand, Juliet detected perfume: a sweet, musky scent that smelled expensive.

George, who had taken Juliet to task over her grooming — the word had a simple, innocent meaning in the last century — would have approved. Men would be drawn to Hayley, a clear advantage when she was selling your flat.

"Let's go through to the lounge," Juliet suggested. They would begin with the best room.

"Lots of light," Hayley said, staring at the mustard-coloured walls and adding, "That's a bonus, and the sunny colour makes the most of it. Beautiful views too. You can see the hills at Dundry."

You could also see the roofs and TV aerials of houses lower down the slope of the Avon Gorge. Juliet warmed to Hayley for accentuating the positive.

"How about the kitchen next?" Juliet asked. "That won't take long. It's small, I'm afraid."

"What you'd expect in a one bedder," Hayley said. "I wouldn't worry about it."

Considering the size of the room, Hayley spent ages in it. She opened the oven, fridge and washing machine, running a finger over the work surfaces which Juliet had freshly cleaned.

"Hmm." The estate agent pursed her lips. "When was this last updated?"

"I don't know. It was my late brother's. I think I said?"

"Yes, of course. A bachelor pad. Well, do show me the rest."

It was downhill from there.

Observing the faded floral wallpaper and clutter in the bedroom, the best Hayley could manage was, "It's a good size."

In the bathroom, the coffee had failed to mask the mouldy odour after all, although Hayley blamed it on mildew in the shower. "I had hoped to take photos," she said, "assuming you want to instruct us, of course," – an increasingly rare smile played on her lips – "but it would help to have a good clean first. A spot of bleach, say."

Just as well she hadn't seen the flat before Juliet set to work on it.

"I thought you sent a photographer round?" Juliet asked.

Hayley laughed. "They might have in the old days. I do it all with my phone. Room measurements too. I can make a start if you'd like to go ahead?"

That was pushy. They hadn't even discussed money yet.

"How much is the flat worth?" Juliet asked. "My solicitor got a probate valuation, but I'm hoping for more."

"Difficult to tell," Hayley said. "Most buyers in this area expect an older property, something quirky."

Those quirks presumably didn't include a bathroom in urgent need of repair.

Hayley continued. "We see a lot of interest in flats from students, doctors and other young professionals. Unlike families, who will spend time and money putting their stamp on a home, our bachelor pad buyers want somewhere they can move into right away. If you spent thirty thousand pounds on upgrading, you'd get it back."

"And if I don't?"

"Then it'll be reflected in the price, and the property will take longer to sell." Hayley wasn't smiling anymore.

"So how much would I get in this condition?"

Hayley named a figure. After fees and mortgage, it would leave Juliet with forty thousand pounds. "I won't lie to you. It might take a while. You'll find it will go quicker with a deep clean and a paint job."

"Perhaps I should talk to the competition."

Hayley shrugged. "They'll tell you the same. Unless they're lying to get your business. Walk around locally and you'll see all the Sold signs are ours. Not meaning to boast, but we know what we're doing."

Juliet believed her. She had chosen the agents for that reason. Their orange SALE AGREED placards were ubiquitous in the neighbourhood.

"Fine. Give me a week," she said.

"Perfect," Hayley said, beaming again and moving in for another handshake. "I'll email the paperwork and we'll arrange a date for photos."

Juliet ushered her out. Once she'd closed the door, she slumped against it, listening as the tapping of Hayley's heels grew fainter. She could tidy, clean and slap on paint, but what would a buyer's survey reveal? Heaviness infused her limbs. She staggered back to the lounge and collapsed, exhausted, on the sofa. Her eyes were swimming, the chipped woodwork and ugly walls mocking her.

In her handbag nearby, her smartphone made the grunting noise that signified an incoming message. She didn't get many. Perhaps someone was offering work. Juliet retrieved the phone and checked.

She had a text from Hugh. 'Look at the news. Rufus Cameron has had a parole hearing.'

Juliet trembled, the phone slipping from her fingers. With a crash, it hit the floor.

She heard what appeared to be an answering thud from the flat below. How was that possible? The builders must have finished; she hadn't seen Simon Heath's van for at least a week.

Could it be an animal, like a rat finding its way into the rotten floor space? Juliet gulped back vomit at the notion. Yet unappealing though it was, the alternatives were worse.

Chapter 32

September 2023

Brooklyn

The manor in Somerset, all creamy stone and mullioned windows, looked the part when viewed from the road. However, its grand exterior hardly hinted at the tasks required inside. For decades, the place had been used as offices. Simon's client wanted it converted into luxury flats. Tired sixties fittings had been stripped out, walls knocked through or built up, and now the shell was being transformed.

Today, Ricky Tamm was there too with Simon's Transit, his sins forgiven. Brooklyn had been required to hand the keys over to him earlier that week. It paid to be related to the boss.

The two of them were replacing floorboards. In practice, it meant Ricky lounged around with a cup of tea, watching the apprentice do the work. Brooklyn didn't mind. He enjoyed the resinous smell of new wood, the way focusing on the task occupied his headspace.

It was different when Ricky insisted on talking.

"What ya doin' tonight?"

"Seeing my girlfriend."

"What's she like, then, this Marley?"

"Nice." He didn't remember mentioning her name to Ricky before, but perhaps he had. Anyway, people gossiped.

"You got in 'er knickers yet?"

"None of your business."

"That's a no, then." Ricky smirked. "I can get you pills that'll help. Or do it like the gaffer with the champagne and roses. Pricey, mind."

"Thanks, but no thanks."

Brooklyn narrowly avoided hitting his thumb. He wished Ricky would leave him alone to concentrate. "Her dad's a police officer," he said desperately.

Ricky spat out a gobbet of phlegm. It missed Brooklyn's ear by a whisker, landing with a plop behind him.

"Who needs that? Give 'er the boot, mate," Ricky suggested.

Brooklyn imagined Errol's relief. He didn't reply.

"Cat got your tongue?" Ricky asked. He finished his tea with a loud slurp. "Time for a cigarette break."

Brooklyn didn't ask him what he was taking a break from.

As the crow flies, he wasn't far from Vix's school. The river got in the way, though. Outside the centre of Bristol, there were few places where you could cross the Avon. When Brooklyn left for the evening, he drove through wiggly country lanes to the M5. Once he'd soared over the river, he would come off the motorway.

In the afternoon sun, he had a grandstand view of the container port of Avonmouth with its chimneys and wind turbines. There was plenty of time to gaze at it, because the traffic was almost at a standstill. His van had barely made it into second gear. Brooklyn switched on the radio for a traffic report.

"Due to an accident on the A38, the M5 is running slow in both directions," he heard.

Tell him about it. The A38 was miles away, but it was a major route and its problems cast ripples across Somerset and beyond. At least the radio began playing his favourite Sam Fender song. Brooklyn sang along with enthusiasm, if tunelessly. When he did this at work, they told him to stick to carpentry.

He crawled off the M5 at Cribbs Causeway, past newbuilds sprouting like a thicket of trees, swanky car showrooms and hotels. Abruptly, the landscape changed to council houses and skyscrapers. The traffic thinned. Brooklyn hummed in time with the radio, looking forward to his date. They wouldn't be going anywhere fancy – he couldn't even afford a cinema ticket this close to the end of the month, especially at the prices you paid in the evenings. The weather was fine, so perhaps he would drive Marley to the Downs. There was free parking, and plenty of green space. He'd find a quiet spot for a cuddle. Before leaving the flat, he must brush his teeth.

He slowed on the approach to Vix's school, spotting his sister chatting to that kid again. Brooklyn brought the van to a halt beside her, pressing a button to wind down the window. "Hey, Vix. In here."

She spun around and huffed. "No need to shout." Turning to her friend, she said, "See ya."

The boy stared after her as she climbed in beside Brooklyn.

"Who's that? Black guy," he asked, hitting the accelerator hard. The van rocketed away.

"Trying out for Formula One?" Vix shot back. "Brooklyn Barber, the next Lando Norris."

"You didn't answer my question."

"That's Cody from my class. We were talking about climate change."

"Not your boyfriend."

"I don't have one. Boyfriends are for losers, whatever Marley thinks."

"Don't be a jerk about Marley, or you're walking home."

"About that." Vix sounded less snippy, more serious. "I want to start getting the bus again. Then I can hang out with my friends. Cody, for example—"

Despite the warm air inside the van, a chill ran through him. "Vix, no. Too risky, okay?"

"I need my life back."

A cold sweat gripped him. "One day. When I finish my apprenticeship. I'll earn more money—"

"No, Brooks." Vix's voice quivered. "You don't see it, do you? We'll be found out way before then. I just want to have a normal life while I can, or close to normal. Before they send me away like Ruby, or put us in prison, or whatever they're going to do."

"Not prison. We didn't kill anyone," he said, in an attempt to convince himself.

"Speak for yourself," Vix said. "I'll still be chucked into a home hundreds of miles away, like a piece of rubbish. So don't tell me there's sunshine and rainbows down the road."

"I wouldn't sugarcoat it, but," he reached for the words, "let's go on like this for as long as we can, okay?"

"Suppose."

She was silent for the rest of the journey. He cranked the radio up. As he turned into Aldworth Terrace, he saw the crazy woman, Juliet, marching towards Clover House. He nudged Vix. "Wait till she's inside, yeah?"

"Sure."

He let the engine idle. As soon as Juliet entered the lobby, he drove into the car park around the back. A couple of spaces were overlooked only by the windows of Flat A. Brooklyn chose one of these.

"Quick," he said. "Back door?"

They crept inside. Vix was gentle with the kitchen door, opening and closing it with barely a sound. Almost as if she'd practised.

"Can you cook something fast?" he asked. "I'm seeing Marley."

She pouted, throwing her backpack onto the worktop. "What did your last one die of?"

It was one of Nanna Lizzie's stock phrases. They both realised as soon as Vix said it.

"Sorry." Vix's eyes glistened. "Brooks, you could have said before. I was going to make veg curry."

He blanched. "No meat? Anyway, Juliet will smell it."

"She won't know it's us," Vix said reasonably. "Besides, we should eat less meat to save the earth. And money. And… I need help with my homework. If I can't see my mates, I'll have to ask you."

Brooklyn gaped at her. What planet was she on? He had a handful of terrible GCSEs. "You'd do better to ask Google," he said. "What subject?"

"History."

"I was ungraded in it."

Vix sighed "Nanna Lizzie always helped."

Brooklyn's cheeks grew hot. He stretched out his arms and hugged her. Neither of them were touchy-feely with each other, but he sensed she needed it. "I'll take you to the library. Late opening, isn't it? I'll drop you round, go see Marley, then get you after."

"No, don't bother." Vix brushed away a tear, sniffing. "They close at seven. It won't give you enough time with Marley. I'll go online like you said. And we've got baked beans, so I'll heat up a can. Quick enough for you?"

He nodded. "I brought a tin of frankfurters from home. Could we have those too?"

She pretended to puke. "You can. I'm not eating pig's bits. I'll cook them up for you, but that's it."

He showered, hoping the extractor fan wasn't audible elsewhere in the building. Sound travelled through the apartment block in unexpected ways. Sometimes, especially in the living room, he heard Juliet speaking in a foreign language.

Vix made tea and toast as well as warming up the cans' contents. He bolted the food down, splashing extra milk in the tea to cool it. His stomach gurgled. If he was hungry later, he'd grab a bag of chips on the way back.

Vix seemed calmer when he left. "Have fun," she called, without looking up from the laptop she'd perched on the work surface.

Outside, the rush hour continued. He'd never understood why people called it that. The busy times lasted longer than an hour, and nobody rushed: traffic trickled slowly through the city's narrow streets.

Marley stood outside the coffee bar near her house, scrolling on her phone.

"You're late," she said.

"Traffic."

"Oh yeah, Dad was saying. They closed that main road." She planted a light kiss on his lips, briefly, as if a butterfly's wings had brushed them. "He's been talking about your foster mum a lot. Lizzie?"

"That's right."

"She sounds lovely. I'd like to meet her. Can we go round to yours?"

"Not tonight. She's," he racked his brain, "out at bingo."

"Shame. You did give her his regards? He wanted to know if she remembered him."

"She thinks he's a nice man," Brooklyn lied.

How long could he maintain his deceit? He stared at Marley, overwhelmed by her sheer presence, wishing to hold on to the moment forever. Yet Errol was right. So was Ricky. He had no future with Marley, especially once she found out what he'd done. And he couldn't keep such a monstrous secret forever.

Chapter 33

November 1992

Jules

Now it was Jules's turn in the witness box. Her chance to set the record straight.

Except she could hardly speak. Because this morning, she'd lost so much blood that it felt like the biggest period ever. And she knew what that meant.

Her baby was dead.

Her life had no meaning.

Who cared what happened next?

She sensed George's hostile gaze behind her. There would be no reconciliation. She had nothing to offer him.

A twinge of pain spiked in her belly like the aftershock of an earthquake. When the usher handed her a bible and a printed card, she stared at them as though they were rare and exotic, items she'd never seen before.

"You're required to swear this oath," the usher whispered.

"Thanks," Jules muttered. She glanced at the jury, the most important people in the room. Today, they appeared as monochrome as the barristers, stuffy in black robes and white wigs. All joy and colour had been sucked from her world.

Alec Underwood strode forward to face her. "What is your name?" he asked, somehow injecting a sneer into the question.

"Juliet Dawn Sharples."

"Please swear the oath, Mrs Sharples."

Jules clutched the bible, her gaze flicking again towards the drab, unfriendly jurors. She read out the card. "I swear by Almighty God that the evidence I shall give shall be the truth, the whole truth, and nothing but the truth."

"Mrs Sharples. You are the wife of Mr George Sharples, I believe. Is that correct?"

"That's right." Trying to focus through her agony, she wondered why he'd bring George into it.

"And we've heard from," he consulted a notebook, "Mr Malcolm Jenks, that he had an affair with you. Can you confirm you had an affair with Mr Jenks?"

"Yes."

A collective intake of breath resounded through the room. Did they think she'd deny it?

"Did you also have an affair with Rufus Cameron?" Underwood asked.

Jules reeled as another spasm surged through her. "No," she gasped.

"Because he wasn't sexually attracted to you?"

"No. I didn't—"

"No is sufficient for now, Mrs Sharples. Now, we have heard, not just from Boy A, but from Boy B and Boy C that you arranged for them to visit Mr Cameron's flat after school and to lie to their parents about it. Is that correct?"

"Yes, but—"

"Answer the question, please, Mrs Sharples. Yes or no?"

"Yes." Her legs quivered beneath her, and her eyes swam. She stared at Underwood. How could he twist every little thing she said?

"Boy A is, in fact, your own—"

The judge interjected. "Mr Underwood, may I remind you that Boy A must not be identified. Can you phrase your questions accordingly, please?"

"Of course. Sorry, Your Honour." But Underwood had made his point, and the jury had noticed. They glared at her.

"So, Mrs Sharples," Underwood continued, "why were you so keen to introduce Mr Cameron to your teenage pupils?"

"He needed beta testers for his computer games."

"That is the cover story you gave the boys, yes," Underwood said, lip curling. "Surely you were aware, even if they weren't, that Mr Cameron accessed formal channels for games testing?"

She gawped at him. Rufus's profession was so far removed from everything she knew.

"No," she gasped. "Rufus didn't tell me that. He asked for help."

"Why would you put yourself out for Mr Cameron at all?"

"We were friends."

"Oh, come now, Mrs Sharples." Underwood shook his head. "You told the police that Mr Cameron was aware of your affair with Mr Jenks, did you not? Yes or no?"

"Yes."

"But you didn't tell them when you made your first statement, did you?"

"It wasn't relevant," she retorted.

"Surely the police should decide that, and this court? Still. You admitted it when challenged by the police, did you not?"

"Yes."

"Yes. Exactly." His voice echoed with triumph. "We will hear more from Mr Cameron later, no doubt, but I ask you to consider this. If Mr Cameron had remained in ignorance of your affair, would you have been so eager to help him?"

"No," she answered truthfully.

"Whatever pressure he put you under — you may call it blackmail, even — it is no excuse for breaking the law. Mrs Sharples, you knew full well what Mr Cameron was about. Yet you delivered up those innocent young children into his hands?"

"I didn't know about his... preferences..." she said.

Underwood scoffed. "You can't pull wool over the jury's eyes, Mrs Sharples. Why would a woman who deceived her husband bother telling the truth now? You're lying to save your own skin, aren't you?"

"No," Jules whimpered, sobbing.

"Crocodile tears," Underwood observed. "You're crying for yourself, aren't you, because you've been found out?"

"No..."

"No further questions Your Honour," Underwood said, as the jury scowled at Jules.

A dull ache in her abdomen intensified until it felt like a red-hot knife. It was hard to concentrate. Viewed through a mist of tears, Underwood, the jury, the judge and the rest of the court seemed far away. She noted Underwood sitting down, while her defence barrister rose to her feet.

Alison had gone to university with Lucy Lillingstone, and rated her highly. They'd planned the points they wanted Jules to cover in her evidence. But Jules hadn't had a chance to speak to either of them this morning.

She wasn't sure she could take much more.

Lucy smiled sympathetically, youthful features at odds with her archaic wig. She addressed the judge. "Your Honour, may I suggest a short break, please? For the comfort of the court, and to allow my client to collect herself."

147

He nodded. "Yes. Back at eleven o'clock."

The court reconvened. Eyes hot from weeping, her body sore, Jules trembled in the witness box.

"Mrs Sharples." Lucy's gentle voice contrasted with Underwood's aggression. "Tell me about your job. You're a teacher, aren't you?"

"Yes, I teach German at secondary school." Was she allowed to say which one? Surely not if it helped the public identify the boys.

"And when did you decide to become a teacher?"

"I can't remember… I've always wanted to do it."

"We might call it your vocation, then," Lucy said. "What do you think of your job?"

"I love it. I'd do anything for my pupils." A cramp almost bent Jules double, crushing the enthusiasm she'd hoped to convey. Her words emerged flat and leaden.

"You'd never deliberately expose them to harm, would you?" Lucy asked.

"No. Of course not." Jules took a deep breath, and the physical pain eased. Her mental torture, the knowledge of what she'd lost, did not.

"We've heard, of course, that some of them sadly did come to harm," Lucy said, her tone compassionate. "And for the benefit of the jury, it's worth pointing out that you suspected Rufus Cameron of foul play, and immediately went to the police. We'll talk about that in a moment. First, can you explain how you knew the defendant, Rufus Cameron?"

"I met him as a student in Bristol. We had mutual friends. He was always around." Jules's voice, echoing through her skull, sounded like another person.

"And what did you think of him?"

"Rufus was friendly. Charming. Normal." Jules shook her head. "He chased girls. It was almost a joke, that he was so unlucky in love."

"You didn't know his interests lay elsewhere?"

"No. I never imagined it. I mean, I even set him up on blind dates with women." How could she not have spotted Rufus's true nature? Yet, however much she'd sifted through her memories, she hadn't found a clue.

"Why did you keep in touch with Rufus after university?"

Jules had asked herself the same question, over and over. "We both stayed in Bristol. Looking back, I think he kept in touch with me, rather than the other way round. He'd ask me out for a drink every so often. Because he designed computer games and my husband invests in new technologies, I introduced them. My husband put money in his business."

"You arranged for Mr Cameron to meet your husband as a favour to a friend?" Lucy asked.

"I guess so. Rufus always wanted favours. And I didn't think it would do any harm."

"You were being kind to a friend, as any reasonable person would," Lucy said. "And was that how you came to introduce some pupils to Mr Cameron?"

"Yes." Jules gulped. "Rufus asked me to help him find beta testers for games he was developing. He said his target market was thirteen-year-olds. So, I asked… Boy A, if he would like to try out the games. I thought it would be a treat for him."

Her reply took every scrap of energy from Jules. She wished only to retreat to a dark corner and lick her wounds. Even though she, Lucy and Alison had planned this line of questioning, it was tough.

"You meant well, then," Lucy said. "Boy A said that you advised him to tell his parents he was taking extra German classes. Is that right?"

"Yes, I'm afraid so." Jules began to shake. "They're strict with him. They wouldn't have let him do something frivolous. Something joyful. It was such a small lie. Or so I thought…"

"How do you feel about it now?" Lucy asked.

"I regret it. More than I can say." She was still trembling.

"Of course," Lucy said. "We already know you wouldn't purposefully put your pupils in harm's way. You are devastated, I assume?"

"Yes."

"So when did you realise you'd made a terrible, terrible mistake?"

"When George… when my husband told me Steve Purslow's body had been found in the harbour." Jules felt a lump in her throat. "Then I remembered strange things about… Boy A and Rufus, and it made sense."

"What sort of things?" Lucy's eyes were kind.

"He fell out with Rufus. Started smoking. Sulked. It was so unlike him. Then, when George said Steve had been murdered, I just knew. It was unthinkable, but I had to confront it."

"So you called the police?"

"Right away." Jules broke down in tears again. "I wish I'd realised sooner."

Lucy turned to the judge. "No further questions, Your Honour."

But as Underwood stood up once more, a wolf intent on ripping out Jules's throat, the jury's stony faces said it all.

They didn't believe her.

Chapter 34

October 2023

Brooklyn

For the first time, Brooklyn's monthly wage went into his account and stayed there. In the past, three hundred pounds would have gone straight to Nanna Lizzie in rent. Vix checked the post he collected from the bungalow, and said Lizzie's bank account wouldn't miss it. With her pension and the income for fostering Vix, there was enough to cover the bills that went out by direct debit. That meant no-one would be chasing her for payment. No-one would be looking for her, Vix or Brooklyn. Asking questions.

As soon as he'd collected Vix from school, they drove to the nearest discount supermarket and filled their baskets. That included cheap cuts of meat, which Vix promised to cook even though she wouldn't eat it.

"It's time you learned your way around the kitchen," Vix said, once their purchases were stored in the smart, glossy cupboards.

"Why? I thought you liked cooking."

"That's not the point. I've got homework to do while it's light." As the nights darkened, the flat grew gloomy inside.

Brooklyn squirmed. "Can't you go to the library? Anyway, I can't cook. Tried it at school. I was rubbish."

"You left three years ago. And you'd better learn, hadn't you? Marley's planning to be a hotshot lawyer, not your personal slave."

His shoulders slumped. Everyone but him and Marley seemed to expect they'd have split up by the time she achieved her goal. He didn't want to talk about it.

"Well?" Vix said.

Brooklyn sighed. "What do you want me to do?"

"There's the chopping board. You peel and halve those potatoes. They need to be boiled. Then slice an onion, and I'll fry it with the sausages."

To his amazement, Brooklyn found he enjoyed it. Manipulating a knife and peeler was no different from taking a saw to a piece of wood. At school, he'd been distracted by his friends when the teacher gave instructions, then he'd looked at the recipes and struggled to read them. When Vix explained step by step, it was easy to prepare food. They sat down to sausages, mash and onions: a meaty meal for him and a vegan one for her.

"That was lush," Vix said. "Well done."

Brooklyn laughed. "You're so obvious."

He washed up, had a shower and left her to her homework. Later, they both sat cross-legged on her bed, watching TV on her laptop: a quiz show, a holiday programme and a sitcom that Vix followed. Brooklyn's mind started to wander. He frowned. Lost in the sights and sounds of the screen, he didn't need to think. But if he used his brain, if he worried about their secret being discovered, fear gripped him.

He glanced at Vix, noting the tension in her jaw, the hands scrunched into fists. Beneath her silence, she was brooding on their problems. And he was powerless to help.

At ten, Vix yawned.

Brooklyn did the same. "Bed?" he asked.

"Yeah. Night night." She switched off the laptop and lay down.

Her breathing slowed, face and shoulders relaxing. "This is way better than living in a van," she murmured.

The tightness in his own muscles began to ease. In finding the flat, he'd done something right for a change.

"Night night," he echoed, slipping off to his bedroom.

He had no recollection of falling asleep or dreaming until he was suddenly aware of a lot of noise. A man spoke, his voice loud and high with excitement. There was a woman too, giggling and shrieking. Both sounded drunk and happy.

Brooklyn rolled over onto his side, clutching the pillow around his ears. He willed the unwanted dream to go away. It didn't. The rowdiness increased in volume. Doors opened and closed, snatches of conversation drifted past his ears. The woman was the most beautiful girl her partner had ever seen.

Despite his lethargy, Brooklyn was affronted by his poor imagination. Couldn't his subconscious mind conjure a better fantasy? Simon Heath would use a cheesy line like that. Funny, now he came to think of it, it sounded like the gaffer talking. How annoying to be reminded of work when he was trying to sleep.

Slowly coming round, Brooklyn groaned.

He heard his sister scream.

"Vix!" Brooklyn yelled, instantly awake.

He jumped out of bed, yanking open the door to his room, stopping only to switch on the ceiling light. Who cared about alerting the neighbours? He had to rescue his sister.

152

Disorientated, expecting the lamp's glow to spill out into the corridor, he found it already lit. Two figures peered into Vix's bedroom. Brooklyn didn't recognise the tipsy girl in the low-cut blue ballgown. The man with her, at least twice her age, was someone he knew too well.

"What are you doing here, Brooklyn?" Simon Heath, red-faced and bursting out of a penguin suit, would have looked comical if he wasn't irate. "Count yourself lucky there's a lady present, or we'd be having words."

The gaffer staggered away from Vix's door. Beneath his black dinner jacket, a white shirt was half undone and stained with red wine. Both he and his friend stank of cigarettes and alcohol.

"He thinks I'm a lady." The girl giggled, simpering at Brooklyn. She tottered towards him on six-inch stilettos. "Aw, you're cute'n'all. Is he your son, Simon?"

While he longed to know who his father was, Brooklyn decided he'd slit his wrists if it turned out to be Simon. Surely even his mother had more sense than that?

Vix shouted, "Help."

"Vix, it's only Simon. It's okay," Brooklyn said, although it wasn't okay at all. This wouldn't end well. He almost knocked the girl over, barging into Simon in his haste to see Vix.

Simon grabbed his arm.

Vix sat up in bed, the leopard-print duvet curled around her. "Brooklyn?"

"Don't worry Vix," Brooklyn said.

"Oh no, she should be worried." Simon pulled him around so they were face to face. He eyeballed Brooklyn. "In fact, you should be very worried too, lad. Answer my question."

"I… we… " Brooklyn delved into his sleep-deprived brain for inspiration. "This is my sister, Victoria. Vix, um, it's my boss. Simon."

Her lip trembled. She was silent.

"We thought we should look after the place for you," Brooklyn continued. "As extra security."

"Did I ask you to?"

"No. Not exactly."

"'No' will be sufficient. I arrange my own security, thank you very much. Isn't that why I took it upon myself to visit the property at half past midnight?"

The barefaced lie took Brooklyn's breath away. He gawked at his boss.

"My wife didn't kit this apartment out for you to doss in it."

"I..." About to mention he'd assembled and moved the furniture, Brooklyn decided it was safer to stay quiet.

"I thought—" the girl began to say.

"Don't embarrass yourself, Karla." Simon pointed to Brooklyn and Vix in turn. "I want you both out of here in ten minutes. Take your things and go."

"Sorry, boss," Brooklyn said. "Come on, Vix. We'd better do as he says."

"Oh yes." Simon stood with his arms folded. "I'm watching you like a hawk. And you'll give me the keys, please, lad. God knows how you got them."

Bleary-eyed, Vix pulled on the school uniform she'd laid out for the morning and started filling cases and bags.

"Don't just stand there, Brooks," she complained.

"I'll get food and stuff from the kitchen, Vix. We'll stick it in the van."

"Out the back, is it?" Simon asked. "I thought I saw it there. You can move that too."

The girl, Karla, shivered. "It's cold. I want to go home."

"Get an Uber," Simon commanded.

She stared at him, lip curling.

"All right. I'll do it." Simon jabbed his phone. "What's the address?"

"Yelland Lane in Winford."

"That's out by the airport. Take me to the cleaners, why don't you?"

"Not my fault." Karla scowled. The romantic mood had soured.

"Um, do you need a lift home, boss?" Brooklyn asked. They might gain another night if Simon left.

"Are you telling me I'm drunk?" Simon demanded. "I'll be the judge of that."

"Not saying you are," Brooklyn mumbled. "Just wondered."

"For your information, I'm well capable of getting myself home. Dob me in to the police and you'll be in more trouble than you'd believe," Simon threatened.

He didn't know the half of it. "Okay. Sorry boss."

"Get moving."

Karla staggered off, fumbling for a cigarette and sparking up before she was out of sight. Simon gave her the evil eye before directing his glare onto Brooklyn.

Brooklyn took the hint. He packed his clothes in under two minutes. Karla's curses were clearly audible as she tried to find the way out. In spite of his situation, Brooklyn sniggered. Simon's luck had turned, and he deserved it.

Under the gaffer's stern gaze, Brooklyn moved to the kitchen, flinging possessions in a random order into any containers he found. Vix joined him.

Simon opened the back door, grabbed a couple of pieces of baggage and dumped them outside. "Thirty seconds left," he yelled.

"Okay, boss." Brooklyn dragged a suitcase into the car park. "Please – would you mind – it's quicker if you pass me a bag."

He'd been right in guessing Simon would do it. His boss's rage wouldn't fade until Brooklyn and Vix were gone. Possibly not even then.

They ended up in a relay: the trembling Vix handing their belongings to the gaffer, who gave them to Brooklyn, who stuffed them into his van.

He caught the sound of an unoiled hinge squeaking.

A head appeared from the window of the flat above.

"Mr Heath?" Juliet's plummy voice pierced the air like a knife. Only her messy grey hair proved that she'd just got out of bed.

Simon swore under his breath. "This isn't the right time to discuss your bathroom," he said.

"Too right. May I ask what you're doing here this late at night?"

"Evicting squatters."

"But that's your man, Brooklyn."

"Not anymore." Simon lost any remnants of patience. "You're sacked, lad. Don't bother turning up tomorrow. Apprentices are two a penny in Bristol. I'll get another like that." He snapped his fingers.

Vix pushed out her lower lip.

Brooklyn saw she was simmering, about to blow. "No, Vix," he said.

"Don't order me about, Brooks."

If it hadn't been so dark, he was sure he'd have seen a hot, angry flush spread across her cheeks.

"I'm sorry," she said to Simon, in a tone that sounded quite the opposite. "You're sacking my brother? He's your best apprentice."

Simon stepped back. He looked Vix up and down. "Why am I attracting angry women tonight?" he asked, an amused laugh turning into a belch.

Brooklyn clenched his fists. Simon's roving eye gave him the creeps. The gaffer appraised Vix like a piece of meat. That sort of provocation would push a mild-mannered man towards violence. But if he laid a finger on Simon, he'd be in an even worse mess. He stood still, grinding his teeth.

Vix rewarded Simon's interest with a filthy look. "I'm fourteen," she said. "Spotted the school uniform?"

Simon peered at her. "Then why aren't you over at Liz's?"

"There was a flood," Brooklyn said.

It was the first thing that came into his head, and such a blatant lie that he immediately regretted it. He still tried embroidering it. "The bath overflowed. Everything downstairs needs drying out. She's staying with a neighbour, but they didn't have room for us."

"I see."

It was hard to tell if Simon believed the tale. Brooklyn kept a straight face.

Lights flicked on in the apartment block and the neighbouring terraces. Simon glanced at them and scowled at Brooklyn. "I haven't changed my mind. Clear off, both of you. I don't need the drama."

"Come on, Vix," Brooklyn said. He got into the driver's seat and started the engine.

She didn't move.

He wound the window down. "Hurry up."

"Chop chop," Simon said.

"I'm not coming." She stood square, arms folded, lower lip jutting out.

"Vix, this is nuts." Brooklyn was too tired to be angry. "We'll have to sleep in the van, but tomorrow—"

He hadn't worked out what he'd do in the morning, with no home or job. Maybe they'd think up a solution once they'd had some rest. He could only hope so.

"I can't sleep in that." She pointed a thumb at his van.

Simon's eyes glittered. "Perhaps I can help?"

Brooklyn tensed up at the man's hypocrisy. First, Simon had bullied them out of the flat – to be fair, a flat they shouldn't have occupied – and now he pretended to be Vix's saviour.

What did he want?

Vix didn't fall for it. "No thanks. I'd rather camp under a tree."

"Vix…" Brooklyn jumped out of the van and grabbed her arm. There might be an army of spectators behind those windows lighting up all around. He didn't care.

"You're not safe on your own. Let's get out of here," he said.

She wriggled free. "Leave me alone."

As Simon approached, grinning, she turned and ran. It took only a second for her to vanish into the dark.

"Vix!" Brooklyn leaped after her.

"Not so fast." Simon moved to block him. "Give me the keys, or I'll call the police."

Brooklyn scrabbled through his pocket, dragging them out and lobbing them at Simon. "Let me go. I have to find my sister."

"Suit yourself," Simon said, as Brooklyn jumped back into his van. "I won't waste time looking, that's for sure."

Bleary-eyed and clammy with sweat, Brooklyn drove away from the apartment block. Seeing Aldworth Terrace deserted, he negotiated Cliftonwood's winding streets, driving up and down and along the Avon Gorge. Vix was nowhere in sight. He stopped to phone her, which he should have done in the first place.

The call went to voicemail.

You rang the police when someone went missing. Yet it was the very last thing he should do. Dialling 999 would open up a world of pain. Brooklyn stood to lose both his sister and his liberty.

He repeated his circuit through the tangled web of byways, stopping only when a large, low-slung animal dived across the road in front of him. Reactions dulled by fatigue, Brooklyn slammed on his brakes just in time. What had he seen? Its shape reminded him of an anteater. In Bristol, though? The old zoo in Clifton had been closed for years.

Distracted from his quest and dumbfounded, he sat behind the steering wheel. The stationary van's engine idled. Eventually, he decided he'd seen a badger.

He called her again.

Voicemail.

"Where are you, Vix?" he yelled into the phone.

His limbs heavy, Brooklyn drove once more into the crazy maze of crescents and terraces hugging the hillside. His eyes darted back and forth, seeking her out. There was no sign of her.

Shattered, he stopped, just for a moment. He yawned, slumping forward onto the steering wheel. His eyelids closed.

When he jolted awake, he saw from the dashboard that an hour had passed.

He also remembered Vix was missing.

Brooklyn's fists tightened as he imagined her cold and lost. Robbed. Hurt.

He phoned her.

She didn't pick up.

He turned on the ignition.

Chapter 35

October 2023

Vix

She'd never run so fast. It felt like flying, feet skimming the pavements and barely touching down. Still in a state of shock, Vix took no notice of her surroundings until a fox barked. The sudden, sharp sound startled her.

Once she stopped, the animal fell silent again. A low hum of traffic rumbled in the distance.

Where was she? In her desperation to escape a night in the van, she'd fled in a random direction. It had been downhill, though, towards the foot of the Avon Gorge. She reached the end of a steeply sloping road, ranks of tall houses looming darkly on either side. The street ended in a T-junction. Vix recognised a busy highway parallel to the harbour. Despite the late hour, she saw cars, taxis and lorries speeding past.

Her head buzzed with questions. So that was Simon? A bully and a creep, obviously. She'd never met him before, and Brooklyn hadn't said much about him. Her brother didn't say much about anything. His job must be terrible.

Despite her sympathy for Brooklyn, she didn't reach for her phone. She'd already ignored a few calls, undoubtedly from him, but she wasn't prepared to sleep in that cold van. Adrenaline wearing off, Vix shivered. Summer was well and truly over. The chilly night, although dry, didn't lend itself to rough sleeping. Where could she go?

Spike. He was her only chance. Subconsciously, she must have realised it and run towards the water. It was Spike's home. Vix needed shelter, and he had plenty of room on his boat. He was her friend, after all. And being gay, he wouldn't expect icky favours in return.

She sprinted to the main road and slunk past shuttered shops and apartment blocks to the closest crossing point. The rickety old swing bridge reminded her of war films, its grey metal structure out of place against the Georgian terraces nearby.

The traffic thundered away in a different direction. It was eerily quiet. She listened.

A drunk man stumbled across the bridge. He was in no danger himself – a rail protected him from the water – but did he pose a threat to her?

Vix hung back.

He spotted her. "You got a light?" he asked. A sour, beery smell wafted from him as he neared.

"No." Vix flinched, assessing her chances of running away. They were surprisingly good. She was fitter, a quarter of his age, and sober.

He hiccupped. "No worries. Have a good night."

Still edgy, she spun around and bolted, using the footpath on the opposite side of the bridge. Past a crescent of houses, she came to the road hugging the New Cut of the River Avon. It was an odd name: the waterway seemed older than time to her. The swiftly flowing river on her right, the wharves and houses on her left, barely tugged at the edge of her awareness. She watched instead for strangers. Thanks to the yellow streetlights, she'd spot pedestrians easily, but she also had no shadows to hide in. Next time, she might not be so lucky.

Vix didn't stop until a stitch sent a warning pain to her belly. When she'd calmed it with a few deep breaths, she started running again.

A police car approached, blue lights off, but its checkerboard markings sparked fear. She ducked into an alley beside a corner shop, emerging once the car had passed. Finally, she spotted a sign for the SS Great Britain. The marina must be close. She darted between factories and newbuilt flats until the harbour lay before her.

Not that getting into the marina was easy. The tall, heavy gate was locked. She should have known. Tears of frustration stung Vix's eyes.

She stared at the pontoons and the boats clustered around them, dim shapes like sleeping animals huddled together. If only there was some way to reach Spike and ask him to let her in. But she didn't have his number. Cody had forgotten to give it to her. He'd be sound asleep right now. Anyway, if she called him at stupid o'clock, he'd ask questions. She didn't need that.

Her gaze lit on the railings around the perimeter. It would be easy to slip through them, but then she faced a steep drop to the quayside below. Could she jump down? Possibly. At one end, the distance was less than her height.

She had no choice but to try.

Vix crept between the black metal bars and sat on the edge of the precipice, legs dangling. The wall was higher than she'd thought.

Still, she could make it. She must.

Vix took a deep breath and sprang downwards, landing with a thud. Although she'd braced herself, the impact jolted her whole body. Pain flooded through her ankle. Worried she'd twisted it, Vix gingerly

160

stretched and stood up. To her relief, the joint took her weight. She'd only jarred it. She limped to the central pontoon, making out the Green Man's stern face. Creeping towards the boat, she eased herself down onto its deck.

Her heart drummed against her ribcage. She rapped on the door, a harsh sound that echoed over the quiet black water. Vix cast a cautious eye around, grateful she hadn't disturbed the other vessels.

Unfortunately, Spike hadn't noticed either.

Did he have a bell?

She found a button to press. Maybe that would do it. It made no noise, though, so perhaps it wasn't working.

Ignoring a nagging sense of dread, she thumped on the door again.

She was rewarded with a familiar high-pitched bark. Yet, although Vix hissed, "Gaz! Wake Spike up," the animal's whimpering had no effect.

Gaz scrabbled at the inside of the door. Vix wondered if Spike was even there with him. She searched for another way to attract his attention.

Would knocking on the windows help? There was a skylight, and portholes along the side, accessible via a narrow ledge around the boat. Although barely roomy enough to tiptoe around, it was a better bet than climbing on the roof. That was covered in solar panels, which looked slippery.

Vix told herself she could do it. Wriggling past the safety rail, she planted both feet on the tiny ledge.

The boat wobbled fractionally, enough to remind her to be careful. Vix thrust her body forward against the wall, inching towards the first window. She gave it a smart tap, and listened.

Nothing.

Afraid to use too much strength — breaking the glass wouldn't get Spike onside — Vix tried again. Then, holding her breath, trying to ignore the water below, she moved on to the second.

Gaz howled.

"What is it, boy?" Spike's mumbled question was music to her ears.

"Let me in, Spike. It's Vix."

She heard him stumble through the boat and open the door.

"Where are you?" he said. "Don't play games."

"By the window."

161

His head appeared first, hedgehog hair messy and pale. He raised an eyebrow, then swivelled his torso towards her and extended a hand. "Hold on tight, Vix."

She didn't need telling. Gripping his hand, she edged back to the deck.

Spike bear-hugged her. "That was crazy," he scolded her. "You don't know the boat, or the weather, or anything. You might have got yourself killed."

"Sorry." Vix stared up to meet his eyes. Despite Spike's sharp words, his overwhelming emotion seemed to be relief.

"Well," Spike said, "what's so important that it made you risk your neck?"

Chapter 36

October 2023

Vix

The smell of freshly baked pastries wafted past her nostrils. "Mmm," Vix said. She snuggled under her blanket, still half asleep.

"Up and at 'em."

At the gruff voice, her eyes flicked open.

"Uh, Spike, what…"

"You and your brother were evicted, remember?" His eyes twinkled, and she wondered how much of her story he believed. Nevertheless, he'd let her stay. The ornate dining table converted into a surprisingly comfortable bed.

Vix nodded.

"Time to get up. A school day, right?"

Vix couldn't deny it. She'd slept in her uniform. Spike had offered clean pyjamas or a shirt, but both were miles too big.

"I tell you what," Spike said, "you grab a shower while I make coffee and put the table back together."

"Sure." She stretched, yawned, and stood up, almost falling down again as the boat's gentle rocking caught her unawares. Shimmying past Spike, she stubbed her toe on the dozing dog. Gaz yipped in protest before returning to his slumbers.

Spike chuckled. "I should have said beware of the dog. By the way, use any towel you can find."

A pile in rainbow colours sat on a shelf above the eco-friendly toilet. Vix chose sunny yellow. She locked the sliding doors that separated off the bedroom on one side and the dining room on the other. Stripping off, she stepped into the shower. A powerful jet of warm water washed away her sleepiness.

"How was that?" Spike asked when she returned.

"Lush. But you've got mildew on your grouting. Want me to sort it?"

He smiled. "You sweet talker. Yes, please. Do it after breakfast." He gestured to the velvet banquette.

Vix sat down. If she hadn't just slept on them, she'd never have guessed the cushions doubled up as a cosy mattress.

Spike pushed forward a plate of flaky pastries. "Help yourself. Coffee?" He pointed to a filter jug on a hotplate, the sort Keisha and Aleisha's mum liked.

"Got any tea? Please," Vix said, remembering her manners. She peered at the food. "What are these?"

"Croissants. A reminder of good times in gay Paree."

"Where?"

"You know, France. Paris."

Vix blushed at her ignorance. "You lived in France?" she asked, picking up a croissant and nibbling the edge. Crumbs fell everywhere, but it tasted delicious.

The dog suddenly appeared at her feet, bright and alert. Tail wagging, he licked the floor clean.

"I visited Paris often. Purely for business, but as I worked for my lover, pleasure intruded." The lines on Spike's forehead softened. "Paul and I designed jewellery. Or I should say, I created the pieces and he sold them. He had the contacts, the public school education and so on. I was a boy from Bristol with no GCSEs."

"Still living the dream." Vix finished her croissant and picked up another.

"That's a pain au chocolat."

"Who knew?" Vix laughed. "Next time I'm in Paris, I'll ask for one. A pain au chocolat, por favor."

"Good luck. That's Spanish."

Vix sighed. "Spike, I haven't even got a passport."

"Plenty of time to get one when you leave school. But first, here's my number one life hack. Listen to your teachers. Work hard. I didn't, and they threw me out. I have literally no qualifications."

Spike handed her a mug of tea.

"This is cute." She traced a finger over the bone china and its stylised pattern of leaves.

"Charles Rennie Mackintosh."

"Friend of yours?"

"Inspo," Spike said. He sat opposite her and devoured a pastry. "I'm surprised you didn't wake when I went out to get breakfast."

"Dog-tired." Vix sighed, then chuckled as Gaz pricked up his ears. She brushed crumbs off the table for him.

"It was late when you got here," Spike agreed. "You're lucky I didn't have company. I've hardly closeted myself away since Paul died."

Vix fidgeted, head suddenly dizzy, tears welling. Why did the mention of death have to bring back memories? She coughed to cover her embarrassment.

"Are you all right?"

"Swallowed the wrong way," she lied.

"You knew I was gay, right?" His eyes narrowed.

"Sure. I'm okay with it." She was more than okay. It made his place a safe haven.

"Not everyone is so enlightened," Spike said. "Or were. My parents couldn't hack it when they found out. I was your age—"

"Typical," Vix interrupted, righteously indignant. "Everyone thinks you're a kid, so obviously you're wrong about everything. You don't even know your own body."

"To be fair, I didn't want to come out to them. I'd planned to tell my sister-in-law. Epic fail. I thought I could trust her, but she shopped me to the police."

"They arrested you for being gay?"

"Not quite, but it got heavy. My school expelled me before I took a single GCSE exam. I ran away from home in a fit of pique. To London, where the streets were paved with gold."

"I guess they weren't." Vix gawked at him. She wondered what tragedy he'd describe next.

"They were paved with gold, actually." Spike chuckled. "Your eyes! Any wider, and they'll swallow me up. Listen, I lucked out. When I packed, I took my jewellery portfolio with me. I'd made bits from recycled materials, like this."

He pointed to the silvery balloon-shaped stud in his left ear.

"So I walked door to door in Hatton Garden until I met Paul. He liked what he saw, in every sense. I was a pretty boy."

Vix squinted at him, trying to imagine teenage Spike beneath the weatherbeaten face and alien hair. She gave up.

"He hit on you at fourteen? Seriously?"

"I was willing," Spike said. "Anyway, I was fifteen by then. And into older men, especially fit guys. You should have seen Paul's abs. We had fun, working together on eco-friendly pieces, travelling to fashion shows. We played hard too."

He waved around the room. "I've got Paul to thank for the boat. He bought it for me."

"You said he chose the decoration and all."

165

"Yeah." Spike grinned. "Over the top, isn't it? It kind of worked, back in London. We had it moored up in hipster Hackney. It was his bolthole. Paul was married, you see, so we couldn't be together all the time... Does that shock you?"

"I'm not judging you."

Polyamory wouldn't be Vix's choice, though. When she had time for a relationship, she wouldn't share with anyone else. Until then, she'd ignore the stirrings of her body. No boy would make a fool of her. She had goals to meet, a future she'd planned out. And it would happen, as long as nobody discovered her secret.

Vix clenched her fists. She couldn't afford to think about the impossibility of maintaining the lie. It would drive her mad.

"He called me his safety valve," Spike said. "It kept the marriage alive. His wife never knew, and that made it hard when he passed away."

So it wasn't polyamory, but cheating. Paul had used him.

Spike looked away, his voice quiet. "At his funeral, I sneaked into the back of the church, St Martin's in London. I didn't go to the wake afterwards, and nor did the rest of our team. She asked family and friends only. Plus the rich clients, Lord This and Lady That. We weren't invited."

"Hey." Vix squeezed his arm, as if simply touching him would remove the pain. Whatever Paul had been to Spike, the death had left scars.

"I blubbed like a baby. They must have thought it was because I'd lost my job."

"Did you?"

"Of course. It was Paul's business. He fronted it. So far as the clients were aware, he designed their bespoke jewels. They didn't know he was just a posh bloke with a big contact book.

"Anyway, it's not all bad news. When he died, it saved my life. I'd been overdoing the champagne and drugs, just like him. With Paul gone, the money dried up. I had to get clean."

"Isn't that tough?" Vix tried to avoid addicts, and they weren't difficult to recognise.

Spike shrugged. "What choice did I have? I nearly became homeless. Being broke, the first thing I did was give up the mooring at Hackney. I couldn't afford it. By selling my valuables, I scraped the cash together for a cruising licence, which is cheaper, and I brought the boat to Bristol."

He shook his head and laughed. "Navigating was a big adventure."

Vix nodded. She couldn't imagine even driving Brooklyn's van, let alone steering a boat.

"I scraped her side a couple of times," Spike said. "But I did it. And I'm settled now. I even make jewellery again. With recycled materials, you know? I don't have Paul's aristocratic clients, but I get by."

"I'd buy from you if I had any money," Vix said.

"That's what they all say." Spike eyed her half-drunk mug of tea. "Haven't you finished? You should be going off to school."

"Sure. I'll ring my brother."

"Your taxi service, is he? Well, I'm looking forward to meeting him."

Vix didn't share his enthusiasm. She was even less thrilled about phoning Brooklyn at all. He would be so mad at her for running off and ignoring his calls. Shoulders tense, she reached for her mobile. Before using it, she flashed her best smile. "Can I stay here tonight?" she asked.

Chapter 37

October 2023

Brooklyn

"Where are you?" Brooklyn growled. He'd driven the van, fallen asleep in it, driven, slept, driven, slept. Finally, her call had woken him.

"I'm at…"

He listened, but Vix's answer made no sense. He had to ask her to repeat herself.

"It's a boat?" he echoed stupidly.

"I already told you that, Brooks."

He heard a man's voice in the background, which didn't ease his anxiety. At least she was alive. "Okay, I'm coming," he said.

"Can you bring my backpack?" she asked.

"Yeah." Relief didn't stop him being irritated at her bossiness. Still, her school things were easy to find; they were in the van along with all her other possessions.

At half past seven, traffic was already buzzing around him. Brooklyn realised to his horror that he would pass through the city's clean air zone to collect Vix. That meant a hefty charge, which he'd need to pay quickly to avoid a fine. He'd have words with her.

It began to rain, a heavy downpour typical of Bristol. The sky seemed to have only an on-off switch, with nothing in between. Windscreen wipers struggling, he almost overshot the turn for the SS Great Britain. It would have sent him headlong through a bus gate and incurred another penalty. Simon frequently grumbled about the council placing obstacles in the way of Bristol's motorists. For once, Brooklyn felt sympathy for him. Luckily, he noticed a sign for the tourist attraction just in time, the van's tyres squealing as he swung the vehicle hard left. The large car park by the ship was almost empty; nothing was open yet, and it was too early for charges to apply. Brooklyn parked up and ran to the marina, not even stopping to admire Brunel's great ship on the way.

Vix stood outside a gate. She sheltered under an umbrella held by a tall man with turquoise hair. What had she done?

Brooklyn wasn't in the mood for small talk. "Who are you?" he asked.

Vix looked taken aback. Perhaps she feared a fight would break out. Brooklyn was hurt; she should know he wasn't violent. He couldn't speak for the other guy, of course.

"This is my friend, Spike. He's gay," Vix said.

"Hi." Spike smiled, displaying even white teeth. "You must be the famous Brooklyn."

"Infamous," Vix said, in a rare display of wit. Her facial muscles relaxed.

"I hear you've been evicted from your digs," Spike said.

"Um, yeah." If that was the story Vix had given him, Brooklyn would play along with it.

"Good of you to take her to school," Spike said, "although I don't see why she can't get the bus in future."

"We'll talk about it." Brooklyn's heart drummed against his ribcage. He took a step forward. "In future?" he challenged.

"I'm staying here tonight," Vix said. "Maybe longer."

"Longer?" One of Spike's eyebrows quirked up. "Nice of you to ask."

"I can, can't I?" She twisted her hands together, a sign of anxiety which Brooklyn knew well.

"For a while," Spike agreed. "Brooklyn, what are you planning to do? Vix said you slept in your van."

"Yeah."

"How soon can you get a new place for the two of you?"

He couldn't fault Spike for asking that question, with Vix inviting herself to stay forever. Still, it put Brooklyn on the defensive. "I'm looking," he said.

"We can't afford much," Vix said, which was the wrong comment at the wrong time in Brooklyn's opinion.

Spike seized on it. "Well, you're basically homeless right now. The council has a duty to help, especially as there's a minor involved. You need to ask the housing department. Or social services."

"I'll deal with it," Brooklyn said. He hoped Spike hadn't noticed Vix grow pale. The mention of social services had obviously freaked her out too. As far as social services were aware, they lived in a cosy bungalow in Henleaze with Nanna Lizzie.

"Good." Spike's eyes fixed his. "Now you'd better get her to school. Because whatever you're running away from, bunking off school will get people looking."

What had Vix told him?

"I'm not on the run," Brooklyn muttered.

"And I'm not bunking off," Vix said.

Spike saluted her. "See you later."

169

"Can I borrow the brolly?" she asked.

"Don't push it," Spike said. He handed it to her. "The answer is yes, but I want it back."

It was large and black, flapping like a giant bat above them as she walked with Brooklyn to his van.

"Who is that guy?" Brooklyn asked when they were out of earshot.

"I told you. Spike. He's a friend."

"Since when were you friends with an old man?" While Spike was hardly a pensioner, he must be close to Simon Heath's age.

"We met at the climate change rally." She bit her lip. Eyes wide, she asked, "Did I tell you I went?"

"No, and don't pretend you forgot. I'm not that dumb." They'd arrived at the van. He unlocked it. "If he so much as touches you—"

"He won't. Like I said, he's gay." She climbed in beside him.

Brooklyn started the engine. "So how much does Spike know?" he demanded.

"Nothing."

"Then why was he talking about social services?"

"Spike won't do anything stupid. I'll tell him not to. He's sound."

"But he knew we weren't living at home. It would be easier to go back there, Vix. I've had to pay the clean air charge."

Vix gasped, gawping at him as if he'd suggested she cut off a limb.

"Can we just not talk about this?" she said. She put in earphones and began tapping her fingers on the dashboard.

Brooklyn suspected she wasn't really listening to music, although she made a good show of it. He switched on the radio, hoping the beats would drown out his worries.

Dropping Vix at school without drawing another word from her, he drove to Henleaze. He was shattered, and now that Simon had sacked him, he didn't need to turn up for work. Upstairs in the dormer bungalow, there was a bed with his name on it. Would he prefer to sleep somewhere else? Yes, even though unlike Vix, he didn't believe in ghosts. But apart from fitful naps in his van, he had no alternative.

Chill air enveloped him when he entered the property. It seemed even colder inside than out. Brooklyn staggered to his room and curled up under the duvet. The bedlinen felt slightly damp. Within seconds, he was oblivious.

A sense of dread clutched at him when he awoke three hours later. He decided on a shower to refresh himself, but of course, there was no hot water. Brooklyn pummelled himself with freezing cold jets, which brought him right out the other side of sleepiness. The problems he'd tried to ignore crowded his head, buzzing like wasps for attention. Hunger headed the list, gnawing at his stomach. Ignoring the freezer, he rummaged through the kitchen for food he'd overlooked on previous visits. He found tinned mushy peas and corned beef. With no idea how to cook them, he spooned his meal straight from the cans.

His belly full, he turned to money. If it ran out, they'd starve. He needed to find employment, but how? There was the jobcentre, and agencies; Ricky claimed they had plenty of work, and at higher rates than Simon paid. If that was the case, though, why hadn't Ricky moved on? Anyway, Brooklyn had heard that employers wanted references, and he didn't expect Simon would be keen to give one. Perhaps he should go into business by himself. He could turn his hand to most tasks now, and if nothing else, he could market himself as an odd job man.

The doorbell rang. Brooklyn answered it to see Stan, dressed in a smart suit and tie.

"Yes?" Brooklyn asked, chest tightening as he braced himself for enquiries about Nanna Lizzie.

"How come you're not at work?" Stan asked.

"Um, day off," Brooklyn lied. Why was it any of the Pole's business?

"Oh, good." Stan beamed. "I've been waiting for the gas engineer, and he's late. Can you let him in, please? I have to go into the office."

Brooklyn envisaged a boring day at a desk. Who would take a job like that? Then he remembered that he no longer had any work at all, and therefore no money coming in. He scowled.

Stan's face fell. "It would really help," he said.

If he agreed, Stan would leave. "Yeah, I'll do it," Brooklyn said.

"Thanks." Stan handed over a front door key. "I'll come back for it in a while."

"I might be out."

"Liz will be here, won't she?" Stan peered at him suspiciously.

"She's lying down. Flu."

"I'll send Agata round with a cake later."

Didn't he have an office to go to? Brooklyn fumbled for an excuse. "Don't. She's off her food."

They agreed Brooklyn would leave the key under a plant pot when the engineer finished. At last, Stan ambled across to his car.

Brooklyn returned to the kitchen. He made himself tea – no milk, four sugars – and continued thinking about self-employment. Cards for gardeners, decorators and electricians were often shoved through the letterbox. Vix might design one, and a poster for display in the local shops too.

His phone's strident ringtone screamed at him. Brooklyn saw it was Simon's number. He didn't answer it.

Simon tried again. The gaffer must be really keen to talk. He wouldn't stop, would he?

Brooklyn took a sip of tea, scalding his tongue. He wondered whether to set his phone to silent mode. But if he did, he risked a visit from the boss later. Simon was clearly desperate. And he knew where Brooklyn lived.

Although the gaffer's house was five times the size of this one, and in a more favoured road, it wasn't far. Simon would swing by on his way back from work. Then he'd ask to speak to his old friend and customer, Lizzie.

Excrement would hit the fan.

Big time.

On Simon's third attempt, Brooklyn picked up the call. "Hello?"

"Brooklyn, my lad." Simon's breezy tone suggested the news wasn't that bad. "I may have been too hasty."

What did he mean? Brooklyn was lost for words. "Um, yeah," he managed.

"Can you come in now, do you think?"

Brooklyn flushed. He wished he lived in an alternative universe where he could tell Simon what to do with his job. But he needed money too badly. He nodded, before twigging that Simon wouldn't see him. "Yes boss."

"The manor, all right?"

"I'm on my way." His shoulders straightened, heart leaping as he cut the call. He punched the air. His elation subsided as he remembered all the other challenges in his life. However, Vix was sorted for a while, and he could stay in the bungalow. He shivered. Telling himself it was because the house was cold, he set the heating to come on in the evening.

Stan's engineer turned up then, so Brooklyn treated himself to another cup of tea. He retrieved food and clothing from the van, and disposed of Stan's key. On the hook for a clean air charge that day already, he took the quick route to Somerset, driving south on the A370 across the high swing bridge. With the rush hour long since over, he made good time.

The mansion remained as he'd left it the previous day, covered in scaffolding, the front door propped open. Simon's Merc and various vans sat on the sweeping gravel drive. The air resounded with familiar noises: rhythmic thumping, sawing and the whine of drills. Pop music occasionally intruded when the machines stopped for a second, but whoever had switched on the radio was fighting a losing battle.

Brooklyn entered the lobby, a huge space where a turned wooden staircase rose three floors high. The walls were in a rough state: worm-ridden panelling had been removed, ready to be replaced with new. It was an intricate task, which he'd hoped to work on.

Hearing Simon yelling over the cacophony, he followed the sound to a drawing room.

Simon spotted him and immediately stopped shouting at a hapless contractor.

"About time, Brooklyn. You can work with Ricky on the panelling. If you can find him. The moron's snuck off for a smoke, no doubt."

Brooklyn wouldn't have put it past Ricky to sneak off to the pub, had there been one nearby. "I'll find him," he promised.

"We'll forget about last night, eh, lad? You'll stay away from Clover House in future, mind."

"Thanks."

Uneasy at Simon's change of heart, Brooklyn didn't stick around to ask questions. It was a waste of time scouring the huge old pile for Ricky, too. He phoned him.

"You're back at the manor?" Ricky said. "Well, well, well."

"We're on panelling."

"Right. Give me ten and I'll see you round the front."

Brooklyn made himself tea, with more than a splash of milk. He should enjoy a cuppa while he could; he'd be working like a dog to compensate for Ricky's slacking. Sipping the sugary liquid, he stood outside, surveying the mansion and enjoying the air's sweetness. It had a grassy tang absent even from Clifton. The whole of Bristol smelled of exhaust fumes, clean air zone or no.

Ricky sidled around a wing of the building. On seeing Brooklyn, he spat a roll-up from his mouth. The cancer stick smouldered reproachfully amid the gravel.

"So you're back in business, Brook?" Ricky asked. Without waiting for an answer, he glanced left and right. "Our deadline's been brought forward a month. Mad, ennit?"

"Yeah." There was a dizzying amount of work to do.

"Simon's on a bonus, ennee?" Ricky said. "I put in a word for you, mate, I did. I said to my cuz, you wanna bring Brook back. Give 'emm a second chance, like."

"Thanks." He wouldn't have guessed Ricky was his ally.

"You owe me, Brook," Ricky whispered. "So when I can leave a few bits in your garage?"

Brooklyn paled. He should have known.

Chapter 38

November 1992

Jules

A rank aroma wafted through the dock. Rufus was sweating, his pale skin clammy with moisture.

The jury would return soon.

He obviously knew they'd send him down.

But what would happen to Jules?

Lucy Lillingstone had given a heart-warming closing speech. She reminded them that it was thanks to Jules that Steve's murderer was brought to justice. Without her, the police might never have solved the case. Jules had made mistakes, as many people did. But she was a dedicated teacher who had only ever wanted the best for her pupils. When she found out about Rufus's crimes, she was as horrified as the jury.

She'd suffered enough.

They should find her not guilty.

George occupied his favourite spot in the front row of the public gallery. The Purslow family and a host of keen young journalists sat forward, expectant. George just seemed annoyed, arms folded and blue eyes frosty. He'd been there every day. Was he in court to support her, or only to see justice done for Damien?

Penny hadn't been back since half term, but here she came, creeping into the room with a muffled apology to the usher. She must have taken the afternoon off. Having bagged a seat beside George, she made a comment to him. He perked up.

It was barely a year since Jules had arranged Penny's blind date with Rufus, although it felt like forever. With hindsight, no wonder they hadn't hit it off. But who would have guessed?

A door opened. The jury filed back into their seats.

"Jules," Rufus whispered, "you're going down. And don't think that's the end of it. As soon as I can, I'm coming for you."

He cackled. "You're a dead woman walking. Remember that."

The judge glared at him. "Mr Cameron and Mrs Sharples, please stand up."

As Jules rose to her feet, the judge asked the jury's foreman to do the same.

"Have you reached verdicts on all the counts put before you?" he asked.

"We have." The foreman's moustache quivered as he spoke. Sleek and smart in a suit, he was about the same age as her husband. He could easily have been one of George's Freemason buddies.

"And are you all agreed on them?"

"We are."

The elderly clerk took over, his powerful voice booming around the chamber.

"Do you find the defendant, Rufus St John Torrance Cameron, guilty or not guilty of the murder of Stephen Wayne Purslow?"

"Guilty."

Steve Purslow's sister shouted, "Yes!"

"Silence, please," the judge said.

There was no reaction from Rufus as the clerk went through every charge against him. The jury had found him guilty of each one.

Then it was Jules's turn.

"Do you find the defendant, Juliet Dawn Sharples, guilty or not guilty of aiding and abetting the indecent assault of Stephen Wayne Purslow?"

Jules stared at the foreman. Hoping.

He cleared his throat. "Guilty," he said.

The room appeared to shimmer.

Jules felt Rita clutch her arm, keeping her upright.

She heard Rufus hiss, "Don't forget."

As her vision began to clear, seeking out a friendly face, she focused on Penny.

Her best friend was holding George's hand.

Chapter 39

November 2023

Juliet

Hairs prickled on Juliet's neck. She stared at the TV, a knife and fork slipping out of her hands and onto the tray she'd placed on her lap. A ham omelette lay half-eaten on the plate. Her appetite had vanished.

An old photo dominated the screen, Rufus at the age of twenty-five, smiling under a mop of tawny curls. A mullet. The haircut, short at the front and long at the back, was ubiquitous in the late twentieth century. What was wrong with her, focusing on such a trivial detail while her heart raced with terror? If he came for her, she was in grave danger. And he would come. He'd said so.

"Cameron has been freed despite objections from Stephen Purslow's sister."

No-one had asked Juliet for her objections.

An image of the dead boy flashed up: little Steve at the seaside, his crooked smile captured by the camera. He was riding a donkey, the bridle held by an older child. Shirley Purslow. Freckled, pigtailed and tanned in the picture, she hadn't been in Juliet's classes, but it was impossible to forget her. The family had attended every day of the trial. It must have been hard on the young girl.

In the studio, the journalist sat on a couch beside a thin, neat woman with long flaxen hair, ends dyed in a rainbow of candy colours. She looked tiny and pixieish beside the burly interviewer.

"Mrs Shirley Wilks has fought long and hard to keep Rufus Cameron behind bars. Welcome, Shirley. Can you tell us how you're feeling at this news?"

"Gutted." Shirley dabbed at tears with a tissue. Close up, she seemed old and tired, her reddened eyes surrounded by wrinkles. "That man – I'm not going to say his name – is a monster."

Juliet couldn't agree more.

"What would you say to Rufus Cameron if you saw him today?"

"Say?" Shirley spluttered. "I'd punch his lights out."

The contrast between her fey appearance and fierce words was almost comical. Juliet found herself wishing Rufus would run into Shirley.

"I'd do that teacher, and all," Shirley said. "You know, his helper."

"Juliet Sharples, a teacher from Bristol, was sent to prison with Cameron," the interviewer supplied. "Unfortunately, we've been unable to reach her for comment."

They couldn't have tried very hard. It was a small mercy.

"So, do you have a message for the Parole Board?" the interviewer asked.

"He's fooled them, hasn't he? Rufus Cameron is still dangerous, whatever lies he's told them." Shirley wagged a pink-tipped finger. "And I've got a message for him. If he steps out of line for a second, if I hear he's got so much as a parking ticket, I'll be telling the probation service to stick him right back where he belongs."

"Well, that's all we have time for," the reporter said. "Thank you, Shirley Wilks. And now for the weather…"

Juliet saw her knuckles had turned white. Yet even if Shirley Wilks was serious in threatening violence, she'd have to find Juliet. And that wouldn't be easy. Juliet was no longer young and pretty. She had slipped into the invisibility of middle age.

It wouldn't protect her from Rufus, though. He was too clever, and utterly ruthless. If Rufus wanted something, he got it. The cheeky chappie image on the screen belied the fact that he was a murderer and child abuser. Perhaps his appearance now would better reflect his rotten, psychopathic core. Chillingly, it would disguise him too. Suppose he'd returned to Bristol already? She might have walked past him in Clifton Village without recognising him.

For three decades, she had lived under the sword of Damocles, not knowing what form his revenge would take, who or what would be his instrument. Now he was free to do as he pleased, and that sword was about to descend.

Chapter 40

November 2023

Rufus

He'd died and gone to heaven. Rufus closed his eyes, letting blissfully warm water pour down on his head and body. A drench shower. Who knew such a wonderful thing existed? His mother had installed three in her house: two in ensuites and one in the main bathroom. The latter also boasted a freestanding bathtub set on four clawed feet. It looked Victorian, but it was apparently the latest trend. That was typical of her. She read magazines such as 'House Beautiful', aiming to stay ahead of the neighbours with her renovations. Once, she'd been proud of the old powder-pink fittings. Not anymore. She'd laughed when he asked why they'd vanished.

It was a far cry from prison shower blocks, which produced tepid dribbles if you were lucky and an ambush by nonce-bashers if you weren't. You wouldn't see marble tiles and rose-scented shower gel either.

The tag on his ankle was a nuisance, but he could remove it when he really needed to. He'd always had thin hands and feet. Vaseline jelly worked wonders as well.

He soaped his body, shampooed his sparse hair and began humming a Smiths tune. Eventually, he switched off the stream of water and wrapped himself in a huge, fluffy towel. After a final approving look in the mirror, he left the ensuite and sprawled naked on his king-size bed. Rufus had the best guest room in the house. Once his oldest sister's bedroom, it had been redecorated beyond recognition.

His mother had really killed the fatted calf for him. In three days, she'd cooked his childhood favourites: roast beef with Yorkshires, chicken pie, cherry cake. He could look forward to a full English breakfast later. To his irritation, Rufus's body was stuck on jail time, up with the lark at 6am.

He sighed, swigged water from the bottle left out for him – not the Ritz, but it was close – and chose a shirt and chinos to wear. When his mother had realised his old clothes were outdated and ill-fitting, she'd chucked them out. Within a day of his release, she'd filled his wardrobe with an express delivery from Marks & Spencer. Rufus preferred the Gap, but she hadn't asked.

She peered at him constantly, eyes fond and tearful. If she'd hugged him once, she'd done it half a dozen times; embraces he forced himself to accept. For thirty years, he'd been conditioned to expect danger from human contact.

The love and attention lavished on him now was a step change from his childhood. Then, Rufus had been dumped on a series of au pairs, including Andreas from Germany. His parents liked to think they were progressive. No tired old stereotypes for them. Why should a mother's help be female? They even forgave the Germans for the war. Hence, Rufus was handed into Andreas's care, and the least said about that, the better. Still, with both his parents working in high-flying careers, they could afford this large Tudorbethan house in Surrey. His mother must be lonely, rattling around in it by herself since his father passed away.

His sisters had visited yesterday for a celebratory meal. They hadn't brought their families — it wasn't allowed — but they'd brought Argentinian Malbec. In a screwcap bottle, no less. He'd savoured three glasses of the fruity red. Not all supermarket wine was paint stripper nowadays. A new wide world lay ready for Rufus to explore.

He'd need money, though.

Everything cost a fortune. That delicious Argentinian wine was ten quid. As for petrol, food, rent — the numbers blew his mind.

Of course, he could sponge off the old girl, with her pensions and investments. He'd never have to work again. That wasn't the future he'd planned for himself, though. No, he wanted to return to game design. He loved it so much that it didn't feel like work. It stretched you creatively, and you met interesting people. Young people. Tasty people.

If only his skills were up to date. While a whizz at Assembly and C, his knowledge of the newer programming languages was theoretical at best. He'd done courses in C++ and JavaScript, both invented while he was inside, but he hadn't used them to a meaningful extent. And as for Unreal Engine 5.4, he hadn't a clue.

He had a lot of catching up to do. And he aimed to start with one person in particular. That reminded him. He hadn't heard from Beanie Man. What a timewaster.

His mother knocked on the door. "I've brought coffee."

How was that for service? She had a nifty little machine: you placed a capsule in it, pressed a button, and a top-notch espresso appeared. He loved the twenty-first century.

Rufus arched an eyebrow at the sight of the tray she carried. A brown paper package, the size and shape of a large book, sat alongside his usual porcelain cup and copy of the Times.

"What's that?"

"Oh, it arrived yesterday evening." Her voice seemed breathy. Anxious. "You'd gone to bed when the despatch rider brought it. It's from Andy Mayne."

She pointed to the Quicksilver logo printed on the address label.

"Thanks," Rufus said. How strange.

He waited until she'd gone. Revelling in the aroma of fresh beans, he took a sip, then tore open the wrapping. A folded sheet of A4 paper, a card in an opened envelope, and a boxed iPhone fell out onto the bed.

He examined the paper first, a letter from Andy Mayne. The lawyer explained he'd received a parcel for Rufus and felt obliged to check the contents. They appeared to be in order.

Heat rose up Rufus's throat and flushed his cheeks. As his lips curled into a snarl, he realised that Andy was only being cautious. What if the sender had included anthrax, excrement, or a bomb?

Instead, there was a bland card bearing a picture of a horseshoe on the front, and inside the printed words 'Read the message. Good luck.'

What message, and from whom? Rufus emptied the iPhone's box. In jail, he'd steered clear of mobiles. There were plenty around inside, but they were illegal, and used for transactions that didn't concern him. Now, he even struggled to switch on his new toy. The black mirror stared at him, unblinking. Rufus realised the battery was dead. He plugged in the charger provided with it, and the phone sprang into life.

A text waited for him.

Eagerly, Rufus tapped the screen. The design was so clever, with its touch-sensitive little symbols. 'Juliet Price's address is Flat 2, Clover House, Aldworth Terrace, Clifton, Bristol' he read.

Of course it was. Bristol, the one place he was forbidden to visit under his licence. Still, what the cops didn't know, wouldn't hurt them.

Rufus laughed, anticipating the surprise on Jules's face, the thrill of holding her in his power. The joy of seeing her dead.

Chapter 41

November 2023

Juliet

Juliet couldn't sleep. How long had it been now, since she discovered Rufus was out? Two days, perhaps, or three. Each night was the same. She tossed and turned, ears straining for the slightest noise. Eventually, fatigue overcame her insomnia. In the small hours, she crashed out.

Then the day would begin, with gallons of coffee and an attempt to lose herself in translations. She wasn't overburdened with work, but her sleepiness meant it took longer than usual. A couple of times, she'd found herself napping at the keyboard.

Waiting for Rufus to strike was like a slow death.

Lying in bed, she shivered. Winter's chill sent twinges through her joints, despite the blankets she'd piled on top of the duvet. She'd have to start using the central heating, an expense she'd hoped to avoid. Of course, she'd switch it on if a potential buyer visited.

There had been no viewings, even after Hayley took a flattering set of pictures. The smell of magnolia paint still lingered. Juliet had slathered it over the horrible wallpaper, and touched up the woodwork too. She'd cleared out more of the junk. The place actually looked presentable. Why hadn't a young professional snapped it up? Tomorrow, she'd ring Hayley.

What time was it, anyway? Juliet had lost track, caught in this strange limbo of worry, sleep, work and coffee. Nights were longer than usual in November, the light dim even during the day. Hayley might be at her desk soon. Maybe Juliet should get up and send her an email. Eat something. Mostly, she couldn't face food, but hunger always drew her to the kitchen eventually. She'd been snacking on the contents of Greg's tins, unwilling to leave the flat in case Rufus lurked outside.

Her stomach rumbled. Juliet checked her phone. 3am.

The noise grew louder, and a thud startled her. It wasn't her belly after all.

Was Rufus here, in her flat?

She leaped out of bed.

Teeth chattering, she switched on a light, dressed, looked for a weapon. There was nothing suitable. For a moment, she regretted throwing away Greg's junk.

She heard a crash from the flat below. Her frenzied breathing slowed. She was alone after all.

Still, nobody should be in Flat A at this time of the morning. Simon Heath wouldn't be working there now. Anyway, she hadn't seen him since he'd turned up in the middle of the night to argue with his man, Brooklyn. Simon's Transit and Brooklyn's Astra van had been absent from the car park ever since.

She took a peek out of the window. As expected, they weren't there.

Slamming and banging sounds continued percolating up through the building's flimsy structure. Whoever was downstairs, they were up to no good. And if it was Rufus, he'd realise eventually that he'd got the wrong apartment. He'd search the other flats. He'd come for her.

She didn't like the police. The police didn't like her. But she was entitled to their protection.

Juliet picked up her phone and punched in 999.

She hoped they'd get to Clover House in time.

Chapter 42

November 2023

Brooklyn

Brooklyn paused halfway up the stepladder, hammer in hand, and yawned. Insomnia was new to him. He resented it, fought it, but still it held him in its claws. While he preferred his bed to the van, he hadn't had an unbroken night's sleep since he returned to the bungalow. It had been two weeks now. He would lie awake for hours, missing Vix and Nanna Lizzie, chewing over his fears.

He didn't believe in ghosts. He never had. Yet he swore he heard the old woman's voice, a whisper urging him to take care of Vix, that Spike couldn't be trusted. That accorded with Brooklyn's view of Vix's new friend. There was something off about Spike.

Spike was like a brother to her. But she already had a big brother in Brooklyn, so why did she need another one? He hated the way Vix and Spike gazed at each other and giggled, as if sharing a private joke.

Brooklyn's brow furrowed. Vix shouldn't hide secrets. She shouldn't laugh at him either.

"Don't fall asleep up there."

Brooklyn jolted in surprise. He nearly fell off the ladder.

Ricky jerked a thumb towards the door. "Boss wants you."

"Why?"

"How should I know? 'Spect you've screwed up again." Ricky stumbled against the ladder. It wobbled alarmingly. "Oops, careless."

Brooklyn said nothing. Ricky had finally given up pestering him about Lizzie's garage, but he wouldn't put himself out for Brooklyn again. Brooklyn wondered if there was more to it than a grudge, though. Ricky seemed on edge, his hands shaking.

"Goin' for a ciggie," Ricky said, turning his back and stomping off.

That suited Brooklyn. He would be happy to spend the rest of his life in a Ricky-free zone. He locked his tools in their box. They were easily mislaid otherwise. He'd also lost expensive kit to light-fingered colleagues. No prizes for guessing the prime suspect.

It took a while to find Simon. Eventually, Brooklyn tracked him down to the orangery. This was a huge, elaborate greenhouse, with not a citrus fruit in sight. Simon's voice could be heard from fifty paces as he harangued a hapless glazier.

"Boss? You wanted me."

Simon stopped listing items to be placed where the sun didn't shine, including the contractor's last bill.

"Ah, Brooklyn, lad. Let's talk outside."

Brooklyn followed him into the manor's extensive grounds. Ricky had found a sheltered spot in which to skulk, multi-tasking with a roll-up in one hand and mobile phone in the other. Brooklyn heard him say, "Okay, I'll go back and look. But how d'ya know they ain't watchin' it?"

"There." Simon pointed to an overgrown rose garden, well away from Ricky. "Because walls have ears."

Brooklyn began to feel more optimistic. Maybe this wasn't bad news. When he made mistakes, Simon wouldn't hesitate to bawl him out in front of his workmates. "How can I help, boss?" he asked.

"Aldworth Terrace. Flat A is back on," Simon said.

"You want me to start work on it again?"

"Yes, but I need you here too. I'm under the cosh on both developments."

Simon lowered his voice to a whisper. "Between you and me, the owner of Flat A wants rid of it. It was burgled last week, can you believe?"

An icy chill gripped Brooklyn. He gawked at Simon. "I didn't... I mean, I gave you the keys back."

"I never said it was down to you." Simon's tone was grim. "I have my suspicions. Anyhow, they left the flat in a right state. Turned it over. That nice rug is missing, and goodness knows what else."

"Um," Brooklyn fidgeted. He wondered if his suspicions matched Simon's.

"I've been thinking. I can understand why a lad your age wants to live away from his elders. A bit of freedom to see who he wants to see. Especially girls, right?"

"Could be." He struggled to make out Simon's angle. Still, it never hurt to agree with the boss.

"I'll square it with the client for you to stay in Flat A for a couple of weeks. Keep an eye on things. What do you say?"

Brooklyn's jaw dropped. Had Simon really offered to let him return to Clover House?

Simon folded his arms. "That's not an excuse to live it up. No parties. Bring a girl round occasionally, but that's all, you understand?"

Brooklyn nodded. He might stretch the definition of 'occasionally'. While he'd enjoy bringing Marley to the flat, he'd much prefer to prise Vix away from Spike. If they were legit, his sister could even switch on the light to do her homework. He chuckled.

Simon leered. "Thought that would appeal to you. You can show your gratitude by tidying the place up. Oh, and there's the finishing off as well. Can you patch that ceiling, for starters?"

"What about the lady upstairs, Juliet? Doesn't she need to sort out her bathroom first?"

"I've got an idea about that," Simon said. "Leave it with me."

"Any other jobs to do there?"

"You can put in shelves, I suppose. Don't knock yourself out. I need you fresh for work over here every morning. Clover House is strictly in your spare time, right?"

At last, Brooklyn figured out the point of Simon's offer. The gaffer expected free labour. He had no doubt the client would end up paying, even so. It was worth it, though. As he messaged Vix, he hoped she would agree.

Chapter 43

November 2023

Juliet

Was that a scuffling sound downstairs? Juliet, in the middle of a translation project, strained to listen. The arrival of the blues and twos last night would surely have deterred burglars, but not Rufus. And the police hadn't caught anyone yet.

Rufus would have learned how to break into a building, and how to hide from cops. Prison was a training ground for criminals. They shared skills with each other. How stupid of her to return to Bristol, the first place he'd seek her out. Juliet had placed herself in danger like a fly walking into a spider's web.

A bead of sweat formed on her upper lip. She imagined what Rufus would do. How far he'd go. The walls of the lounge pressed in on her. Despite fresh magnolia paint, it felt dark. Claustrophobic.

Someone knocked on the door, three times, loudly.

Juliet cowered on the sofa. Why hadn't she installed one of those modern doorbells, with a camera trained on visitors? The answer, naturally, was money. She'd been a fool. If she'd cut back on food for a few days, or worked harder, she'd have found the funds. It was too late now.

Then again, Rufus wouldn't knock politely. She might be grasping at straws, but it was more likely to be young Brooklyn, or James Sharples with his canvassing, or a Jehovah's Witness. In her old life, she would have pretended to be out when the Witnesses called. Right now, she'd be over the moon to see them. She'd welcome them in for a cup of tea and a chat about scriptures.

She crept to the door.

"Who is it?" Her voice trembled. If it was Rufus, she'd easily tell from his bass rumble. His face would have changed, but not the sound of him.

"Juliet? It's Simon."

"What do you want?" Simon Heath surely wouldn't be in cahoots with Rufus. Still, stranger things happened.

"I wanted to say thank you for calling the police."

"Don't mention it."

"Well, I appreciate it. They stopped a burglary, and I'm grateful. You know, I've been thinking, and I bet I can help you out. May I come in?"

She opened the door a fraction. Simon stood by himself on the landing. For once, he had dressed in what she would consider building clothes: a paint-spattered boilersuit and trainers.

He handed over a box of Milk Tray chocolates. "For you."

Her heart stopped racing. She felt a tear form in one eye. "That's really kind of you."

"My pleasure," Simon purred. "And I meant what I said. I'm sure I can help."

"Sorry," she said. "I assume you're talking about the bathroom? I can't afford your rates, as I told you before."

Simon smiled. "I suppose it's indirectly about the bathroom. I want to take that worry away from you. Am I right in thinking you'd like to sell?" His voice was smooth as silk.

"Have you been talking to Hayley?" The estate agent should have called first if she was sending Simon around.

"That would be Hayley Jones?" Simon said. "An enthusiastic young lady, isn't she?"

If it was an attempt at innuendo, she'd ignore it. She was too old to play games with Simon. "Yes, that's her," Juliet said.

"I haven't spoken to Hayley about your flat." Simon tapped the side of his nose. "I think young Brooklyn mentioned it, actually. We can keep this between us if you like, keep it free of commission if you get my meaning?"

"You want to buy the flat?" This could be the answer to all her problems.

"I'd like to take a look around."

"Come in."

Simon stepped inside, his gait confident. He strode past her into the tidy, restyled lounge. "Magnolia."

"Hayley suggested I freshen it up. She thought neutral colours worked best." Juliet twisted her hands together. Didn't he like it?

"Typical estate agent. They think a quick paint job solves everything." Simon sniffed at the air. "I'll see the bathroom next, I think."

He marched off. Trailing after him, Juliet's hope began to fade. She took long, slow breaths.

"I thought so. There's a mouldy smell in here," Simon announced. "I suspect it's coming from under the bath. Mind if I check?"

She was damned if she agreed, and damned if she didn't. "The panel is quite hard to remove," Juliet said.

"Oh, I don't think it will be." Without asking further, Simon fished a screwdriver from his pocket and knelt down beside the bath. Within seconds, the panel was off.

"Easy if you know how," Simon said. He stared at Brooklyn's repairs. "Dearie me. Someone's done a botch job here."

A knot tightened in the pit of Juliet's stomach.

"I suspected a structural issue, given the condition of the ceiling downstairs," Simon said. "Obviously, you have an obligation to my client—"

"Is that really why you came here?" Juliet interrupted. Her eyes grew hot, and she rubbed them. She wasn't about to lose her dignity by crying. "If you just wanted access, Mr Heath, you could have asked."

"Call me Simon. And I am absolutely serious about buying, don't you worry."

He simpered, his voice oily again, evidently trying to get back into her good graces.

"I can pay cash," Simon added. "How does that sound?"

It sounded too good to be true. Nevertheless, Juliet exhaled. Some of the tension left her body.

"No mortgage, no chain, no drawn-out legals. You won't get a better deal." Simon sucked his teeth. "It's a fixer-upper, though, no doubt about it. You've got a liability right here in your bathroom. How much did Hayley say it was worth?"

She'd received an email from the estate agent and had even printed a copy. "I can show you in black and white," she said. "Look."

Simon examined the stapled A4 sheets. He grimaced. "She's having a laugh."

The builder had always intended to lowball, Juliet realised. "So how much would you pay?" she stammered.

"Twenty grand less," Simon said. "Cash on the nail."

"Sorry, I…" Juliet shook her head. She'd barely make ends meet if she took his offer. Still, how could she afford to stay in Bristol with Rufus on the loose? He was a ticking time bomb.

Simon shrugged. "Cash is king, right?"

"I should talk to Hayley. See if she has a buyer lined up."

"It's up to you," Simon said. "I think she's spinning you a line to win the business. A couple of months, no interest, and she'll have you dropping the price. And what if she does find a buyer one day? The minute their survey comes back, they'll pull out. So good luck with that."

He strolled to the front door. "My offer's on the table for twenty-four hours. A quick sale for cash. Call me, but don't wait too long."

Chapter 44

November 2023

Vix

Vix's mouth fell open. Packaging lay scattered all over Flat A's front lounge. When they'd first inspected the boxes, she and Brooklyn had left most of them undisturbed. They'd taken the minimum they needed for comfort. In contrast, the burglars had opened everything.

"What a mess," she said.

Brooklyn seemed unfazed. Still, his boss had warned him about the chaos.

"Can I do my homework before clearing up?"

She didn't wait for an answer, carrying her backpack into the dining room. The void in the ceiling yawned above her. She scowled at it. "Can't you repair that?"

"All right." Brooklyn winced. "It's not just woodwork, though. There's plastering. I did a day of it in college, so I guess I'll be okay."

"You'll be more than that," Vix said. "You're good at building. Simon Heath takes advantage of you."

Brooklyn grunted non-committally. "What about dinner?" he asked.

Vix sighed. Did he ever stop thinking about his stomach? "I'll go out and buy food if you tidy the kitchen," she said.

"Yeah, okay," Brooklyn said, to her surprise.

Pleased to have the best of the bargain, Vix extracted twenty pounds from his wallet and slipped outside. A bracing breeze rattled her teeth. While she'd been away, autumn had tightened its grip on Aldworth Terrace. A scattering of diehard leaves clung to the tall trees lining the road. The rest had fallen, creating a slushy brown mulch on the ground. She picked her way through, stopping only to help an old dear who had slipped over on the pavement.

Vix reached out a hand. "Here, grab hold of me."

"Thanks." The grey-haired woman took up Vix's offer. She was heavier than she looked; Vix almost reeled backward.

Vix realised it was Juliet just as the older woman's eyes widened.

"Are you trespassing again?" Juliet rasped. "I'll tell Simon Heath."

Vix snatched her hand back. "Good luck with that."

"Wait." Juliet's tone softened. "You seem awfully young. If anyone's making you do anything you don't want to do—"

"You're mad," Vix snapped, stalking off. She didn't need to listen to this rubbish.

Her body shook with fury as she marched uphill to Clifton Village. How dare Juliet accuse her of a crime simply for walking down the street? Of course, that wasn't exactly what the old lady meant. She'd worked out Vix was back in the ground floor flat. Well, Vix had every right to be there, because Brooklyn had squared it with Simon Heath. He had, hadn't he?

Vix took a deep breath to banish the doubts worming their way into her mind. Her brother wouldn't lie. Anyway, if it all went wrong again — and it might, as that was her life, wasn't it? — she could go back to Spike's boat.

He'd sounded relieved when she phoned to say Brooklyn had found a flat. Her presence affected his love life – Spike had pointedly spent a couple of nights away with 'a friend'. She hoped he'd enjoyed her company, though.

He hadn't opened up to her again. Vix hadn't encouraged him to, either. If she'd asked questions, he might have reciprocated. She'd have been forced to lie, a rabbit hole best avoided. Once a deception began, there was a constant pressure to maintain it. You could never relax.

She realised how much she'd been hiding from Spike. How tense she'd been.

By the time she reached the shops, Vix had calmed down. She made her purchases and returned to Clover House. Her brother had kept his word; the kitchen was clean and tidy.

"What are you cooking?" Brooklyn asked.

"Veggie chilli and cornbread. Spike taught me how to make it."

He gaped at her. "Where's the meat?"

"It's vegan and better for the planet." She relented. "I bought you some value sausages, though. You can have them on the side."

"Thanks," he said, without much enthusiasm. "Um, I have to measure up for the ceiling repair."

"Who's paying for it?" Vix asked. "Don't you need materials?"

"Yeah. I'll tell Simon."

Her misgivings returned. "What exactly did you agree with him?"

"I can stay here for security. I'll sort out the ceiling, and the finishing. Get the place in order. All in my spare time." He shrugged. "Yeah, he's ripping me off. It's better than paying rent, though. And we can put the lights on now."

She heard a distant BBC jingle. "I think that's Juliet watching telly. Listen Brooks, she was going to phone Simon about us being here."

"When – today? I'll tell her he said it's okay."

"Rather you than me."

While he carried out his mission, Vix switched on the oven and chopped vegetables. The aroma of frying onions mingled with a burning odour. That was odd. She opened the oven, spotting a large jiffy bag inside. Even odder. Gingerly, Vix lifted it out with a couple of forks. She dumped it in the sink. Already blackened at the corners, the envelope might have burst into flames at any minute.

She stopped work and stared at it, heart thumping as she realised how close she'd been to setting the building on fire. It seemed like hours before Brooklyn returned.

"Hey, Brooks, come and see this," she yelled.

He dashed into the kitchen, wrinkling his nose at the smell. "What is it?"

"You tell me." Vix pointed a finger at the smouldering object.

"I don't know. It stinks."

Brooklyn wasn't a good liar, and Vix was 99% sure the surprise on his face was genuine. "Simon's paperwork?" she suggested.

"That's not just paper," he said, sniffing. "Might be what the burglars were looking for."

He tested the envelope with his finger. "It's cool enough to open."

"Do it."

Vix held her breath as her brother ran a kitchen knife across the seam. He tipped the envelope upside down.

A bundle of charred notes fell out.

"Money," she gasped. "We could use that, Brooks."

Brooklyn stared both at the notes and the bulge that remained in the envelope. His expression suggested he'd seen a bomb. "Leave it. You don't know whose it is," he said.

Vix eased a couple of fifty pound notes out of the rubber band that bound them together. "They've got the same serial number."

Brooklyn snatched them from her and stuffed all the counterfeit cash back in the envelope. "I'm chucking it in the bin outside. Make it someone else's problem."

He took the envelope out to the car park, switching on the kitchen's extractor hood when he returned. "Get rid of the stench."

Vix shuddered. Brooklyn was right. They shouldn't take the fake money. It belonged to someone. But wouldn't they want it back? Throwing it away didn't solve anything.

"Hey," Brooklyn interrupted her train of thought. "Juliet is cool with us living here."

Vix pulled a face. "How come you charmed her so easily?"

"She made me call Simon," Brooklyn admitted. "He told her. Guess what? She's selling her flat to him."

"It needs big repairs, doesn't it? You'll end up doing them. I bet he's pushed her price right down, and all."

"Yeah," Brooklyn said, confirming her impression that Simon underpaid everyone. He retreated to the front room to continue unjumbling it.

Vix placed a bubbling casserole pot of chilli in the oven, followed by the cornbread. She'd pressed a frying pan into service for the latter, as she couldn't find a cake tin. It was probably still in Brooklyn's van, or perhaps it had never left the bungalow at all. As long as she was careful not to touch the metal handle without oven gloves, the pan should work for this recipe. Trying to ignore her worries, she opened her laptop on the kitchen island. Soon, she was absorbed in her homework.

She heard the sound of a key in the lock before the kitchen door opened.

Vix jumped to her feet. "What the—. Who are you?"

"I should ask you the same, me babber." The baby-faced youth lounged against the counter. "I'll be collecting something I left 'ere, then I'll be on my way."

"Brooklyn," Vix shouted, her yell turning into a scream. She stood up, shrinking back from the intruder.

He smirked. "Brooklyn? I should have known. 'Ee can't resist a cosy little love nest. Well I won't cramp 'is style."

A grin revealed yellowed teeth. Vix saw he was older than she'd first imagined. The boyish face was deceptive.

He opened the oven, recoiling and slamming it shut again as hot air blasted out. "What have you done with my stuff?" he hissed, turning to glare at Vix.

Brooklyn was standing beside her now. "Ricky? What's going on, mate?"

Finally, it made sense. Her brother had told Vix about Ricky, how he'd badgered Brooklyn to hide something for him. Now she knew what.

194

They all stared at each other, the stand-off broken when Vix said, "How many people have keys for this flat, Brooks?"

"Who knows?" Brooklyn scowled. "You're out of order, Ricky. Get out."

"Me? You've taken something that belongs to me." Ricky picked up one of the kitchen knives that Vix had left on the counter. He swaggered over to Brooklyn.

Vix noticed that Ricky was short for a man. He had to look upwards to eyeball Brooklyn. If she hadn't been terrified, she'd have found it comical.

The men were both ignoring her. More fool them. She slipped past them, easing on heatproof gloves and opening the oven. Briefly, she considered which pot to choose, and settled on the casserole. The frying pan would be easier to control, but hot stew threatened more carnage.

There were handles on each side. Vix gripped with both hands. "Stop," she shrieked, brandishing the vessel. She hoped she looked menacing.

"I don't plan on stayin' for dinner," Ricky said.

Vix swung it towards him. "I'm not asking you to. Get out of my kitchen, or I'm tipping it all over you."

"I meant to say, your envelope's in the bin outside," Brooklyn said.

Ricky cursed. "Where's it to, did you say?"

"General waste. The wheelie bin nearest the wall."

Ricky whistled. "Okay. I'll go look. Perfect timing, boy. You've got a little firecracker on your hands. I didn't think you had it in you."

"I'm not—" Vix stopped when Brooklyn put a finger to his lips.

"It'd better be there, mind," Ricky warned, "or I'll be back."

Vix bolted the door after him. "I'd like to see him try." She was trembling.

Brooklyn gathered her in a hug. "I'll ask Simon to change the locks. Not ratting on Ricky, though."

Ricky knocked on the window, holding the battered envelope up in one hand. He made a thumbs-up sign with the other.

Vix gave him a filthy look. "He thinks I'm Marley."

"Well, he's never met her," Brooklyn pointed out. "And I'm keeping it that way."

He sniffed at the savoury smell infusing the kitchen. "Can we eat now?"

195

It was good timing, with the cornbread just blackening at the edges. Vix doled the food onto plates. They sat at the island opposite each other, devouring the tasty meal. The anger and fear that had surged within her were gone. She yawned.

"I'm tired too," Brooklyn confessed. "Feeling meh."

"When I've finished my homework, I'll go to bed. Sorry, I forgot to cook sausages."

"Aw, I'm full now, anyway." He caught her eye. "Would you really have thrown our dinner over Ricky?"

She nodded. "It would have done some damage."

"You might have killed him. Death by chilli." He sniggered.

Vix's face burned. Another death on her conscience. Great.

"Not funny," she snapped.

Brooklyn's brows knitted together. "Hey, I didn't mean to upset you."

"Forget it." She picked up the emptied dishes and turned away. Tears filled her eyes. When she was down, Nanna Lizzie always had a hug and words of comfort. But Nanna Lizzie would never be there for Vix again, and it was all her fault.

"Vix?" Brooklyn was standing behind her. The hairs on her arm prickled, warning her of his closeness. She noticed a smell of sweat and sawdust. He hadn't even had time for a shower.

"Go away." Her voice trembled.

"Vix, don't spare any sympathy for Ricky."

"I'm not. Leave me alone."

He wouldn't stop badgering her. She hunched over the sink and began washing up, refusing to look around. The hot water scalded her hands, but it would never wash her clean. It couldn't.

Brooklyn gripped an arm. "Talk to me, Vix. What's the matter?"

She shook his hand away. "You still haven't worked it out, have you?"

"Worked what out?"

"I did it," she said. "I killed her."

Brooklyn gulped.

Vix stared down at the sink, continuing to scrub the dishes. "You hate me, don't you?" she said.

"I don't know what you're talking about."

Finally, she spun around to face him. "I killed Nanna Lizzie," she muttered.

Brooklyn's jaw dropped. He blinked. "Say again. How? She was dead when you came home from school… Oh. She wasn't."

He didn't phrase the last part as a question, but Vix answered it. "No," she said, screwing up her eyes in a futile attempt to hold back tears.

Brooklyn stood completely still, eyes flinty. "So what happened?"

Vix sniffed. "She didn't want me to go to the climate change rally. Said I had too much homework."

'Save the earth when you've done all your exams,' Lizzie had admonished her. 'Get those qualifications that are so important to you.' Voice quavering, hand clasped to her forehead, the old lady came across as a drama queen. And Vix had gone into meltdown. After all, she hated how her elders had trashed the world. Also, she'd promised Cody she'd go. She was looking forward to it.

"I shouted that global warming was all her fault," Vix told Brooklyn. "She was sitting in her armchair, wrapped in a blanket. I should have realised that was strange, but I didn't think about her. When she said I was grounded, I ran upstairs and listened to music in my bedroom. She called my name."

Vix paused.

"What then?" Brooklyn asked.

"Nothing," Vix said miserably. "I was too cross to bother going downstairs to find out. And when I did, it was too late."

It had taken two hours for her seething rage to fizzle out. By then, Nanna Lizzie's soul had departed to the heaven she so firmly believed in. Vix wanted heaven to exist for Nanna Lizzie, even if that meant hell existed too and she was going there one day.

Tears flooded out. Vix remembered Nanna Lizzie's cold hand.

Feeling for a pulse.

Knowing she wouldn't find it.

Trying all the same.

Hoping.

Despairing.

"You didn't kill her." A corner of Brooklyn's mouth twitched.

"I might have saved her." Vix scrabbled around in her pockets. They were empty of tissues or anything else to blow her nose. She used a tea towel and flung it in the washing machine.

Brooklyn swallowed. "Vix? I don't think you could have done."

"I'd have called an ambulance if I'd found her in time."

"No, Vix. It wouldn't have made a difference. Stan told me she was ill. I'm guessing she didn't want us to know. Didn't want us worrying."

"You really think so?" Vix's tears stopped. "What about social services?"

"Bet she didn't tell them. Because they'd have taken you away."

"And shipped me to Blackpool. Or somewhere worse." She imagined herself, an unwanted parcel, despatched to a bleak town full of strangers.

"Yeah. That's why I put her in the freezer." Brooklyn clenched his fists. Now he was crying too, and that was worse. Brooklyn never blubbered.

"I had to," he sobbed. "We had to pretend. Because if social services find out... But I shouldn't have done it. She deserves a proper funeral at a church. A big party where we all say nice things about her. I loved her, Vix."

"Me too." If only she could turn the clock back and tell Nanna Lizzie. But who ever said those words to each other, except in films? Perhaps now was the time. "She loved us, Brooks. And I love you."

"Love you too, Vix."

Brooklyn hugged her.

"You know what I think?" Brooklyn said. "Nanna Lizzie wouldn't want you to be sent away. She'd swap the party for a chance to make you happy."

Chapter 45

November 2023

Rufus

At last, the old dear had gone away on a mini-break. Not a moment too soon, either: Rufus hadn't taken long to tire of his mother's company. She adored a natter about the neighbourhood and her friends, about whom he knew nothing and cared even less. None of her chums ever popped over for a coffee, but perhaps that was only since his release. It was convenient that one of them had organised a girls' weekend at a spa. Girls! The youngest was seventy-five.

He'd made sure to raid her medicine cabinet before she left. It contained an interesting selection of drugs. Rufus envisaged her taking an accidental overdose, allowing him to get his hands on her investments sooner rather than later. He needed to find out what provision she'd made for him in her will. And do a trial run.

He relaxed in her spacious drawing room, eating a Marks & Spencer's chicken kyiv. She had stocked up with an Ocado delivery to tide him over while she was away. Rufus should build up his strength again, she said. She recommended this particular ready meal as charmingly retro. He didn't remember the dish at all. It must have gone in and out of fashion while he was inside.

Rufus followed it with a helping of trifle. Not too much. Perhaps he was overthinking it, but he tried to avoid putting on weight. His feet and ankles, at least, must remain slim.

He had been watching the TV news, the usual boring stuff: wars, atrocities in the Middle East, and the government losing a by-election. Some things never changed. He switched to wi-fi, and watched an hour of porn instead. It was a pastime he indulged with his phone last thing at night, but he preferred the large television screen. His new favourite toy, the internet amazed him. He would never grow weary of this box of delights. If only it had been available to him as a young man, his life might have taken a different course.

He'd discovered another of the worldwide web's uses when he stumbled upon an estate agent's site. Flat 2, Clover House was up for sale. Rufus had browsed photographs and a short video. The soundtrack, an upbeat jingle, annoyed him so much that he switched it off. Nevertheless, he now knew the layout of Juliet's apartment. It was compact. The entrance lobby led to a bedroom, bathroom and lounge, with the kitchenette off it. She couldn't have stung George Sharples for much in the divorce if she'd ended up in a place like that. Cliftonwood, too: frayed at the edges, full of students and hardly desirable.

Did she live there alone? It was likely, given the cramped conditions. Although he'd texted and tried to phone the sender of the message on his phone — Beanie Man, he assumed —there had been no reply. The next step was to arrange a viewing with the estate agent. With some reluctance, he tabbed away from a red hot scene. The porn would still be there later.

To his dismay, Flat 2 no longer displayed on the agent's website. Rufus phoned them up.

"Hello, I'd like to book a slot with you to see the flat in Clover House."

"That's one of Hayley's – hang on." Several beeps sounded as the man transferred the call.

"Hello, this is Hayley. I'm sorry, the Clover House property isn't on the market, but—"

Rufus interrupted her. "It was on your website yesterday. Have you agreed a sale? I can offer ten thousand pounds more. Do tell your client. I'm very keen."

He hadn't lost the ability to lay on the charm. She was sure to respond, especially as she'd earn more money from a sale at a higher price.

Hayley sighed. "I'm sorry, the client has withdrawn her instructions and agreed a private sale. Nothing to do with us." Her voice was strained.

"That's a pity," Rufus sympathised, reassured to hear the owner was female. He'd been wondering whether he'd been given duff information, or was even being lured towards a trap.

"I will phone her, of course," Hayley said, "but without evidence you're proceedable, I suspect she'll say no. It's a cash buyer, I understand. What's your situation?"

Rufus ignored the question. He was in no position to pay anything, let alone a ridiculous amount of cash. "Make that twenty thousand pounds over the asking price. Perhaps her husband can be persuaded?"

Hayley tutted. "No husband on the scene, as far as I know. It's her late brother's flat."

That was interesting. "Well, thank you for your time."

"Wait," Hayley said. "Mr, er?"

"Armstrong. Neil Armstrong." The name sprang to his lips before he had time to think. Rufus cursed his stupidity. Even Hayley would recognise it as the first man to walk on the moon, wouldn't she?

Apparently not.

"Neil," she reflected his ingratiating tone back at him, "we have a number of other properties in Cliftonwood, and I'm sure you'd be impressed by one apartment in particular. It's around the corner from Aldworth Terrace, in a lovely situation, and it's immaculate. Would you like to book—"

"I'm sorry, but no thank you. Clover House is… special."

He hung up. There was no point wasting time on social niceties with her. He had what he needed.

Fizzing with excitement, Rufus slung a few items into a satchel. He removed his tag with a degree of difficulty and pain, but the strap stayed intact. So did his ankle. He counted that as a win.

Once he'd tucked the tag up in his bed, he hunted for keys to his mother's Range Rover. While he didn't possess a current driving licence and had never driven an automatic car before, how hard could it be? A warm glow spread through him.

Chapter 46

November 2023

Vix

Vix stared out of the window at Aldworth Terrace, dark and quiet as the clock ticked towards midnight. She stood roughly where customers would have entered back in the day, when the ground floor was a shop. Thousands of folk must have passed through its doors. If their ghosts returned, what would they think of the luxury flats and cars?

Spike had invited her to deflate tyres tonight. The group planned to meet on Cliftonwood Road, practically on her doorstep. A queasy sensation danced around her stomach, as if she'd drunk a milkshake too fast. She ought to grab some sleep before they started, but she was too excited.

Brooklyn was in his bedroom, playing games on her laptop. Vix had lent it to him because Marley had cried off their date. She'd pulled an extra Friday night shift at her local supermarket. Apparently, it didn't pay to refuse. They wouldn't ask her again.

Vix had felt sorry for her brother. Now, she was starting to regret her kindness. She didn't enjoy watching TV on her phone. If she asked for the laptop back, he'd want to know why she was still awake. Bored, she observed spots of rain make ragged shapes on the glass. Thunder sounded in the distance. She hoped it would stop before she went out.

A black SUV drove at speed into Aldworth Terrace, pulling up abruptly outside the flats.

It gleamed like a sinister beetle in the pale lamplight. Why were so many cars the colour of night and funerals? The shade certainly suited this beast, which was killing the planet by its mere existence. Her fingers itched to teach its owner a lesson.

The driver, an old man in a flat cap, stayed inside his vehicle. It would be too risky to let down the tyres until he was gone, but he showed no sign of moving.

Who, or what, was he waiting for?

Chapter 47

November 2023

Brooklyn

Friday night's TV schedule didn't attract Brooklyn. He downloaded Call of Duty Warzone onto Vix's laptop. She didn't own the quickest machine, but he was able to get it working.

His phone rang.

Marley.

"Hey," Brooklyn said, warmth infusing his body. "I missed you. How was your shift?"

"Fine." She sounded breathless. Worried. "Brooklyn, are you okay?"

"Why wouldn't I be?"

"There's been…" She paused. "Is your sister all right too? And your carer? Lizzie."

His stomach churned. "They're fine," he lied. "What are you talking about?"

"It's just… Dad rang. He wanted to know where you were. He'd just started a late shift. Got a briefing. He says the police have been looking for you all day."

"For me? Why?"

He knew perfectly well. But he couldn't tell her.

"Not sure," Marley said. "Something happened in Henleaze. It must be bad because he told me not to approach you."

"He said that?" Brooklyn's skin prickled. He noticed he was sweating.

Marley was wrong.

It wasn't just bad.

It had to be really bad.

They must have found Nanna Lizzie.

"Where are you, anyway? At home?"

"At a friend's." He cycled through his football team. "Alex's house."

"Who's she?"

Brooklyn cursed himself. He could have said Tom, Ben or Matthew, but no, he'd gone for a name that might have been a girl's. "Alex is a guy," he said.

There was silence. He couldn't tell if she believed him or not.

"I'm going home now," he said, another falsehood. It was the last place he'd go.

Life as he knew it was about to end. He'd probably never see Marley again. "I love you," he said.

Chapter 48

November 2023

Vix

With nothing better to do, she was still staring at the motorist when Brooklyn dashed into the front room.

"What are you doing here?" he demanded.

"Chilling." It was as good a description as any. Something in his tone made her squint at him, clocking his flapping hands and the sheen of sweat on his brow. "What's the matter?"

Brooklyn gulped. "Marley phoned."

"So?" Vix's chest tightened. "Is she pregnant?"

"No. Worse. Vix, the police are looking for us."

"What do you mean?"

"They've been searching all day. Her dad asked her where I was."

The fluttering in her stomach turned into seasickness. Vix swallowed a mouthful of bile. "But why?" she asked, adding, "They don't know we live here. You didn't tell Marley, did you?"

"No way." He reddened. "Her dad told her not to approach me. They only say that when—"

"—it's murder," she finished. "How did the police find out?" She closed her eyes, taking panting breaths. The impossible problem remained. "I'm Googling it," she said, opening her eyes and removing her phone from her pocket.

She tried 'brooklyn barber', then 'henleaze'.

"Oh my God," she said, showing him the tiny screen.

"Read it out, Vix."

Poor Brooklyn. He struggled with text. Voice faltering, she began. "Human remains were found in a bungalow in Henleaze. Police were called by neighbours concerned that an elderly woman had gone missing. They are keen to talk to a 19-year-old man and a child believed to have information."

Brooklyn's gaze fixed hers. "Grab your stuff, Vix. We have to get away. Like, now."

She slumped against the window, feeling the room would start spinning at any minute. "Where are we going?" she asked.

"I don't care. Anywhere but here."

Chapter 49

November 2023

Rufus

A professional burglar would dress in black, wear a ski mask and a head torch. Rufus, however, was no robber. He wouldn't risk innocent bystanders imagining he might be. That was the quickest way to ensure they dialled 999. In a flash, the boys in blue would surround him, bad news for a man who had breached his licence conditions. He'd flouted both his curfew and the restrictions on his location. Before you could say 'pigs', he'd be straight back inside.

He'd chosen to disguise himself in other ways. The bald pate was covered with a flat cap. For good measure, a black wig straggled out below it. Luckily, his mother had been treated for cancer a few years ago. She hadn't chucked out all her hairpieces, and he'd butchered this one to fit him. He'd treated himself to a fake tan as well.

Then there were the number plates. He'd made enough friends among the losers in prison to learn about OCR cameras, and the possibilities for nicking and swapping plates. These he had borrowed from a neighbour who was away on holiday. His mother's tedious prattle had its uses after all.

Ordering a lock-picking kit was too dicey, so Rufus had made his own. He hadn't rotted in hell for thirty-one years without learning the devil's tricks. The hairpins had worked well when he'd tried them at home, and he carried a few more items just in case. He was all set. Frowning impatiently, he waited for the lights of Clover House to go out, one by one.

The downstairs flat remained illuminated, but at least no-one was looking out of the window anymore. Rufus decided to take his chances.

Carrying his satchel, he left the car and approached the apartment block's front door. A keypad sat beside it. Numbers would be punched into this, but Rufus bypassed it by applying a powerful magnet to the door latch. This broke the weak closure.

He entered the lobby.

It was all about acting confidently. Looking the part. As if a legitimate visitor, he swaggered up the stairs to the first floor. Flat 2 was at the back on the left. A potted orchid adorned a small table by the door. Rufus cupped his ear and listened.

Nothing.

He released the breath he'd been holding. A quick glance told him he was alone.

He placed the satchel down on the linoleum floor. Removing two straightened hairpins from a pocket, he inserted one into the door lock, turning it to one side and holding it in place. Carefully, he used the other pin to jiggle the levers within the mechanism. With a click, the door opened.

Rufus listened again.

He replaced the picks in his pocket, stuffed the hat in his satchel and strapped on a head torch. With a knife in one hand and handcuffs in another, he crept inside.

The fitted carpet muffled his footsteps. He heard soft snores behind the door leading to the bedroom. To make sure he'd found the right female, Rufus slipped into the lounge, his torch lighting up the bland space. Just as the estate agent's photos suggested, there was a desk squeezed into a corner. Rufus homed in on it, flicking through a neat pile of documents.

There it was. Juliet Price. Her maiden name. As another snore cut through the still air, Rufus wanted to laugh. But he didn't.

Not yet.

Chapter 50

November 2023

Juliet

A clicking noise. The gentle rush of air as a door opened. Startled within her dream, Juliet rolled over.

"Wakey, wakey."

She opened her eyes. Dazzling, blinding light flooded her struggling consciousness.

"What—"

A deep voice boomed. "Stop. Don't move, Jules, darling. Don't make a sound. There's a knife at your throat."

She recognised that voice.

Rufus.

He was out of prison and inside her flat, his weapon cold against her skin. But she was asleep, and it was just a nightmare.

"Go away," she mumbled.

The metal pressed into her. Pinpoints of pain suggested a breadknife.

"It's been a long time. I thought you might give me a warmer welcome."

This was real. Juliet froze.

What did he want?

He had a knife.

She was going to die, wasn't she?

He would get off on her terror. Well, she'd deny him that satisfaction, if it was the last thing she did.

"Hello, Rufus." Her voice hadn't wobbled. Good.

"What did I say, darling? No sound. Not even a teensy weensy one." He jiggled the knife a fraction, not enough to slice, but sufficient to send warning twinges.

She took a calculated risk and opened her mouth again. "Can I get you a cup of tea? I'm sure we have a lot to talk about."

Rufus cackled. "What makes you think I'm interested in anything you say? And forget the tea. Guess what? I've brought champagne, so we'll have a glass together. You love your bubbly, don't you? It'll be just like old times."

She felt metal against her left wrist. A snapping noise echoed. Then the blade at her throat was removed as Rufus stepped back, his torch now casting a wide beam across the whole room. Monstrous shadows lurked around him, but the real monster lived behind those glinting, animal eyes.

Rufus otherwise looked unremarkable. As with her, middle age camouflaged him. She might have passed him in the street without a second glance.

She'd never forget that voice, though.

"Sit up," Rufus commanded, waving the knife. It gleamed in the torchlight. "And don't even think about screaming. I'll slit your throat if you try."

Her left hand cuffed to the bedpost, Juliet wriggled into an upright position, joints creaking. An explosion of light filled her vision, blinding her once more, as he switched on the ceiling lamp. Spots of colour swam before her eyes. They cleared to reveal Rufus's smirk.

"Shabby little place," he jeered. "Shame you can't do better, Jules. And you've let yourself go."

Rufus didn't look too great himself. He wore a ridiculous black wig and a head torch, both of which he discarded. So, he was bald. Not one of his wild red curls remained. His sharp cheekbones and chin had sunk into jowls, hip T-shirts and jeans replaced by bland middle-aged clothing.

She wouldn't tell him. Better a coward than dead.

"Where do you keep your wine glasses?" Rufus asked. "Point, and I'll fetch them."

She gestured in the direction of the kitchen.

"Thanks."

His gaze lit on the mobile phone sitting on a bedside table. He scooped it up and stuck it in a pocket.

Once he'd left the room, Juliet scanned it for a weapon. Even her handbag might do, if wielded with enough force. But however much she stretched, nothing was within reach of her right hand. She tried squirming out of the cuff, left wrist chafing against the metal. No chance. Her breath emerged in ragged, sobbing gasps.

Thuds and muffled curses suggested Rufus wasn't having fun exploring the kitchen. Eventually, he returned with a tray. His knife lay upon it, along with two champagne flutes, a bottle of Moët et Chandon, and a kitchen towel.

Of course he'd choose Moët. It was Malcolm's favourite. Rufus would know; he'd stalked her back then. Watching her trysts. Scheming.

Juliet contemplated the heavy green glass. She imagined swinging it against the wall, slashing his throat with the jagged edge.

As if aware of her thoughts, Rufus followed her gaze. "It's your last drink, Jules baby. We won't stint ourselves."

"Here, let me open it." She offered her free hand.

Rufus laughed. "I don't think so."

He set the tray down on a chest of drawers, out of her reach, then picked up the bottle. Holding the towel over the cork, he removed the latter with a loud pop. Bubbles rushed out like birds released from a cage. Rufus filled the glasses, handing one to her. "To freedom!"

Juliet took a sip. She gagged. Once, she'd enjoyed the dry, biscuity fizz. It was the taste of celebration and romance. Yet now, there was nothing to celebrate. And her romance with Malcolm, so long ago, had been based on lies.

She'd rather drink vinegar.

Rufus's eyes glittered as he watched. A smile played on his lips. "More," he commanded, draining his glass.

Juliet forced herself to knock back the rest, coughing as bubbles prickled her throat.

"Good one, Jules. We're in the mood. So, now I want you to take a little something with the next one." From the pocket of his boring grey trousers, Rufus retrieved a small cardboard box, the sort that contained tablets. He removed two silvery blister packs from it. "A few pills."

Juliet squinted at the packet. "Valium?" she whispered, horrified. "Isn't it dangerous mixed with alcohol?"

Rufus placed the blister packs on the tray. He picked up his knife. "Well, that's the point," he purred. "Darling, we can do this the hard way or the easy way. I can carve you up and leave you to die slowly and painfully. Or you can slip off into sweet dreams with another glass of champagne."

He shrugged. "It's up to you, Jules baby."

"Or you could leave," she said, "and we'll both pretend this never happened."

Rufus tutted. "Sorry, Jules, two options only. Pain or pills."

If he used the knife, he'd revel in her agony. She had only one realistic choice, the lesser of two evils.

"Give me the pills," she said.

Rufus beamed. "Smart girl. Wait, though. I have a little extra task for you first."

He put gloves on. Juliet smelled the leather; they must be brand new.

"Tell me where I can find a pen and paper," Rufus said. "You'll be writing such a sad, sad note. And if I say so myself, the words will be exquisite. I've had plenty of time to choose them for you."

Chapter 51

November 2023

Juliet

"Are you going now?" Juliet wasn't slurring her words yet, but she had trouble finding the right ones. That half bottle of champagne had gone straight to her head. Mixing it with those blue tablets wouldn't have helped.

How many had she taken? More than twenty before she lost count. Rufus had brought two packets. He'd watched intently to ensure she didn't spit them out. Then he'd cuffed her free hand too, so she wouldn't make herself vomit by sticking fingers down her throat.

This was the end.

Maybe it wasn't. If he'd only leave, she'd have a shot at survival. Once he was gone, she could scream. Her neighbours might hear. They might not either, but there was a chance.

She squared her shoulders, trying to sit bolt upright. Whatever happened, she must stay awake. Falling asleep would be permanent.

"I'll be off in a jiffy, Jules baby." Rufus slouched back against the wall, looking down at her. "Once I'm certain you've drifted off to the Land of Nod. I can't leave the cuffs behind, can I, but I'd be mad to release you too soon. Who knows what you'd do? One of us might get hurt."

The flat's doorbell rang. Rufus jumped. His incredulous expression mirrored Juliet's surprise.

"Who the hell is that?" he spluttered.

"My boyfriend."

Where had that come from? Despite her peril, she was quietly proud that the lie drew a scowl from Rufus. She'd rattled him.

"He doesn't have a key?" Rufus muttered, eyes scanning the room.

He shook his head. "I don't believe you. There's no sign of a man about the place, and you seem as stunned as I am. Probably a drunk who got the floor wrong."

It rang again.

"Ignore it," Rufus said.

The visitor thumped on the front door.

Hope fluttered in Juliet's stomach. Could it be the police? She glanced at the knife on the tray, wondering whether to risk shouting for help.

When she noticed Rufus's gaze flick in the same direction, she knew it was no use.

The blows continued, louder and more insistent. The caller was going to break his hand at this rate. Rufus's frown deepened. "Not a word," he hissed.

"I know you're in there, Rufus Cameron," a man shouted.

"How?" Rufus muttered.

As a grinding, splintering noise suggested the door was being kicked in, he dived to grab the knife.

He must be about to stick it through her heart. Suicide note or no, he'd stab her before the police came to the rescue. Rufus's pent-up hatred consumed him and he wouldn't let her live. Desperately, Juliet tugged at the bedpost. The solid, old-fashioned piece of furniture wouldn't budge.

But to her relief, Rufus didn't attack her. He raced out of the bedroom, knife in hand.

She heard the door open. Rufus snarled, "Yes?"

"That's not very grateful, is it? After I sent you an iPhone," a man replied. His voice was rich and mellifluous. Juliet was sure she'd heard it before, but she couldn't place it.

"Thanks," Rufus replied, his tone anything but grateful. "I don't need your help anymore."

"So you've met Jules again?"

"What do you want?" Rufus barked.

"You don't recognise me," the man said.

"Sure I do. You were in the pub," Rufus replied. "So what?"

Taking advantage of his absence, Juliet smashed the edge of her champagne glass against the wall. Perhaps she could fend him off with that. Yet her movements were painfully slow. He'd have the upper hand.

"You should know me better than that," the visitor said. "It's Damien."

"No way," Rufus said, his scepticism loud and clear.

Could it really be Damien, George's kid brother? His voice had changed. It had yo-yoed between high and deep tones at fourteen, when he gave evidence against her and Rufus. She'd got on well with Damien before Rufus committed his dreadful crimes. Would he save her?

Why was she so sure she'd heard him speak more recently?

"I'm your number one fan," Damien said. "I asked the Parole Board to release you from your sentence."

"Damien did, for sure," Rufus acknowledged. "But how do I know you're really him? You didn't tell me back in the pub."

"It was too risky there. Remember this? You always used to like it."

Whatever Damien did, it produced a moan from Rufus.

"You steered me to adulthood," Damien said, "and gave me a chance to find myself. I wanted to thank you."

"You went to the police."

"In 1992, when I was a kid. She made me do it," Damien said. "Ruining things for both of us."

"True enough," Rufus said, his voice considerably friendlier. "Well, guess what? Jules is on the way out. The silly girl overdosed. She's written a delicious suicide note. Heart-rending."

"It couldn't be better," Damien replied.

"I'll read it out to you." Rufus chuckled. "Come on through."

Juliet stared at the aqua-coloured hair as Damien strode into the bedroom behind Rufus. She'd seen him at the climate change rally. He'd struck a chord in her memory then. Would she have tried to talk to him if she'd recognised him? Probably not. She'd have been too afraid of his reaction.

Yet only he could help her. However much he appeared to worship Rufus, her former brother-in-law wasn't a psychopath.

"Damien—" she began.

"Shut up," Rufus ordered. He held out the knife for Damien to admire. "I thought about carving her up, but this way is cleaner. No trouble from the law."

"Oh yes," Damien agreed.

"You'll love the note." Rufus placed the knife on the chest of drawers. He picked up the piece of paper he'd laid there: a short message drafted on one of the nine A4 notepads Greg had left behind.

"Dear Aunt Annie," Rufus proclaimed. "You're my only surviving relative."

He stopped. "What a shame. Her parents must be dead. Poor little Jules, an orphan."

Damien's eyes turned flinty.

"I'll carry on," Rufus said. "I miss Mum, Dad and Greg, and I just can't live with my guilt anymore. I've done all I can to atone for my sins, and I hope to see them all on the other side, God willing. Yours with love. Sorry. Jules."

"All that talk of guilt is rather Roman Catholic," Damien said serenely. "Don't they believe suicide is a mortal sin? If you top yourself, you go straight down to hell."

"Who cares?" Rufus sneered. "It's not really suicide, is it? Anyway, she deserves to rot in hell."

"She's not the only one." Damien began to toy with the knife, testing the weight of the handle in his palm, touching the blade with a finger.

"Leave that alone, man, it's sharp."

"All right." Damien put it down. He addressed Rufus calmly. "You don't get it, do you? I'm not here for her. I came for you."

Rufus stiffened. "You're talking in riddles, man."

"Am I?" Damien said. "Well, puzzle this out, then."

With a swift, co-ordinated movement, he punched Rufus in the stomach, following up with a blow to the jaw.

Rufus didn't even have time to look surprised. He keeled over immediately. With a crunch, the back of his head hit a corner of the chest of drawers.

Damien retrieved the knife.

"Worked it now?" he asked Rufus. "There was a tracker on your phone. As soon as you hit the M4, I knew you were on the way."

Rufus didn't reply. He lay on the floor, body twisted, blood seeping onto the swirly carpet.

Juliet gaped at the scene, almost too stunned to process it.

"I think he's dead," she gasped. Her words echoed inside her head, throbbing with the beat of her heart.

Damien's eyes flashed. He knelt down, angling himself to avoid the crimson liquid, and checked Rufus's pulse.

"You're right. Saves me the trouble of sticking one in the ribs. I'd better wipe my prints off the knife, I guess. Can't be too careful."

His voice seemed distant, as if heard through a glass of water. A trickle of sweat clung to his forehead. Despite his apparent nonchalance, he must be as shocked as she was. Surely he hadn't expected to kill Rufus?

She rattled her cuffs, an action that was slow and laborious. The air felt thick, pushing back against her when she tried to move or speak. "Help me, Damien. Please. He made me take Valium. I've got to make myself throw up. Can you find the keys?"

"Why would I do that?"

Her jaw dropped. "To save my life?"

215

"Your life means nothing to me," Damien said. "You changed mine forever when you sent me to Rufus—"

"I didn't know he was a monster."

He scowled. "Did you care? You betrayed me, Jules. You knew I was gay—"

That was news. "I didn't, Damien. You were so young."

Damien rounded on her. "Exactly. Fresh meat for your friend. How stupid was I? You were the only family member I trusted. I was going to come out to you. I thought you'd understand, help me explain it to Dad. As if."

"But I was stupid too," Juliet said. "I had no idea that Rufus—"

"So you keep saying," Damien replied bitterly. "But he was your friend. So you must have known. And not only that. Thanks to you, I was forced to testify. I came out of the closet much too soon. My parents disowned me."

As hers had done to Juliet. 'You've made your bed my girl, and you must lie on it,' her mother had said.

"Don't leave me to die," she pleaded. "That makes you no different to Rufus. You can be better than him."

Damien twisted his mouth to one side. "But this is so perfect. A murder-suicide. No witnesses."

Juliet screamed.

Then, as he stared at her, before he moved to stop her, she drew in more breath. And screamed again.

Chapter 52

November 2023

Brooklyn

Brooklyn didn't have a plan, just a half-formed idea. They would drive to Scotland. He'd never been further north than Cheltenham, and nor had Vix. No-one would expect them to go so far. He suddenly remembered about traffic cameras. Before they left, he'd have to rub dirt on the number plates.

His clothes were packed now. "Hurry up, Vix," he called out, shoving foodstuffs into carrier bags.

He heard a scream. Juliet. It must be. That was her voice. And noise travelled easily from her flat, at least in the back lounge adjacent to the kitchen. He'd started patching up the ceiling, but it wasn't properly repaired yet.

He was tempted to ignore it.

Then Juliet wailed again, loud and desperate, just as Vix came through with her suitcase.

"Did you hear that?" he asked.

Vix pursed her lips. "She's mad. You said so yourself. Probably having a nightmare."

It had seemed more real than that. Brooklyn had gone hostelling with a youth club once; another boy had talked in his sleep, but it was only a soft mumble. You couldn't make out any words.

"I'm checking up on her," he said.

"Do you have to? Oh, whatever. I'm coming with you. But we'd better be quick. You said if the cops got hold of Simon…"

"Yeah. We're toast."

He dashed up to the first floor, Vix following. The damage to the door was obvious.

"Burglary," he said.

"They might still be there."

"Don't care. She screamed."

Brooklyn felt in his pockets. His only weapon was a set of keys. He arranged them, spikes outward, through his fist.

"I'm going in. You stay here, Vix."

"No way."

He glared at her. When he crept into the hall, she still followed. Hairs on his neck prickled. He immediately noticed the absence of junk. Had the thieves taken it?

Light spilled through an open door. As Brooklyn made for it, another cry echoed from within the room.

He stopped at the threshold.

Pale in a long white nightgown, Juliet sat on a bed, her hands cuffed to a corner post.

A man towered over her, a heap of clothes at his feet. Not hers, though. Men's things.

At Brooklyn's approach, he spun around.

"Spike!" Vix exclaimed, just as Brooklyn realised who it was.

Whatever was going on, at least Spike wouldn't hurt them. He was Vix's friend. Brooklyn pocketed his keys again. Then he caught a whiff of blood, and his stomach turned.

That bundle on the floor...

The man lay completely still. He was old. Smartly dressed. The sort of person Simon worked for, clients who expected you to bow to them. Now, he was a mess. Head smashed up, jacket and shirt stained crimson along with the carpet, it looked serious.

"Vix," he said, "You've done first aid."

Last time was when Nanna Lizzie died. That hadn't ended well. Could she handle it again?

He didn't need to ask. Vix pushed past him. She knelt beside the man.

"Don't waste your time," Spike said. "He's dead."

"What happened?" Brooklyn asked, his chest tightening.

He had difficulty making out Juliet's reply, delivered in an odd slurring monotone. "He broke in... Forced me to take... overdose. But Damien killed him," she said.

"She calls me Damien," Spike said. "In case you can't guess."

Vix looked up from her position crouched beside the fallen man. Her eyes held no hope.

"There's no pulse," she said. "See that head wound—"

It was impossible not to.

"—well, he's bled out. Dead, all right."

Spike smirked. "As he deserves."

"Pardon?" Vix said.

"I've waited a long time," Spike replied.

That didn't tell them anything.

Vix ignored him. "Juliet, what did you overdose on?" she asked. "I can see a Valium packet, but that's a champagne bottle. Did you drink that too?"

Juliet nodded.

"Then you need to go to hospital," Vix said.

"Don't interfere."

Brooklyn's spine prickled at Spike's tone. "You heard Vix. I'll get an ambulance." He took out his phone.

"Don't do that," Spike warned.

The knife gleamed on top of a dresser. Spike reached out and grabbed it.

"Hey." Vix flinched from him. "Spike, stop waving that thing at my brother."

"Put the phone down," Spike said. "Now."

"I don't understand," Vix said. "Let him help her."

"No."

Brooklyn held his breath. He'd let Vix stay with this madman. What had he been thinking? How could they protect Juliet, or even get away?

"Come on, Spike," Vix said. "Juliet's a bit crazy, but she's harmless."

Not like the blue-haired man. Vix was too close to that knife. So was Brooklyn. They couldn't fight Spike and win.

"Please, Spike," Brooklyn tried.

Spike's lip curled. "She deserves all she gets," he said.

"Spike?" Vix said.

"She ruined my life."

Vix's eyes widened. "What?"

"Google Juliet Sharples," Spike said. "I was Boy A. This piece of trash is Rufus Cameron. He used me. And it was because of her."

"No," Juliet mumbled. "I thought he wanted you to test... games..."

"Same old lies," Spike said. "She'll say them over and over. Tried them on the jury, but they saw through you, huh, Jules?"

A flush stole across Juliet's wan face. "I was ill.... Couldn't defend... court... Didn't know."

She made an unintelligible sound. Reddening further, each word an effort, she said, "Worked it out... Steve's body... harbour. Went to... police."

"And told the cops about me. Do you realise what that meant?" Spike's face was pinched, hawk-like. The small, angry eyes seemed to contain nothing human.

219

"My parents found out I was gay," Spike said. "Oh, I'm out and I'm proud, now. But it was different at fourteen. Dad was hardcore homophobic. Sure, he blamed Rufus for it, but he was wrong.

"I've always been gay. I wanted to choose when to come out. Wanted her to help." Spike pointed to Juliet. "Guess what happened instead? My dickhead brother got my parents to pay for conversion therapy. Like that would work. I ran away, and six months later, they were dead."

Brooklyn stiffened. "You... killed them?" he stuttered.

"No." Spike glowered. "Were you even listening? I'd left home. Gone. Vamoosed. What do you think I am?"

A lunatic with a knife. "Sorry," Brooklyn said.

"I never saw them again," Spike said. "No reunion in glorious technicolour. No violins. No way to make it right."

Vix's eyes glistened with moisture.

"Juliet wasn't to blame for your parents' deaths," she said. "Nor were you. How would you know they'd be gone so fast?"

Her tone was soft and kind. Brooklyn was as proud of her as he'd ever been.

"The stress got to them," Spike said. "It was a boating accident. If I hadn't... If he hadn't... If she hadn't..." He clamped his mouth shut.

"Spike, don't torture yourself," Vix said.

"Dad couldn't love me as I was."

"I love you, Spike," Vix said. "Hug?"

She held out her arms.

Brooklyn's heart stopped. "The knife, Vix."

Spike let the knife clatter to the floor. He clasped Vix in a bear-like embrace.

"It's not Juliet's fault, it's Rufus's," Vix said, her voice muffled by Spike's chest.

"No," Spike protested. He didn't appear to notice Vix kicking the knife towards her brother, or that Brooklyn made sure it ended up under the bed.

"Sleepy," Juliet said, her voice weary. "So... sleepy."

They'd have to call an ambulance. Brooklyn wanted to ring 999 and run, but what would Spike do then?

Right now, Spike wouldn't hurt Vix. Maybe, while the pair were clinging to each other, Spike wouldn't notice Brooklyn leaving the room. He sidled towards the hall.

Spike heard him. "Where are you going?"

"Um… taking a leak," Brooklyn lied.

"Hold it in."

Vix pulled away from Spike, fixing her eyes on his. "Spike, I have an idea."

"Okay…" Spike sounded sceptical. "Hit me with it."

"You killed Rufus. Maybe you'll tell the cops it was an accident, but why should they believe you? Especially if you let Juliet die. You'll go to prison. Even if you murder me and Brooklyn, on account of us being witnesses. But I don't think you will, because we're your mates."

Spike no longer had a weapon. But why would Vix even hint at more violence? Brooklyn's tension rose a notch. Pain hammered his brows like a wild animal trying to escape.

Frowning, Spike tilted his head. "So what's your bright idea?"

"Listen," Vix hissed. "You can get away with Rufus's death, but only if Juliet lives. And she has to agree. If she tells the police she hit Rufus in self-defence, and doesn't say you were here, they'll never know."

"Why would I trust her?" Spike asked.

"Because we'll back you up, won't we, Brooks? We'll say when we got here, Juliet was by herself, except for the…" she faltered, "…except for the corpse."

A tear crept down her cheek. Brooklyn guessed it wasn't for Rufus. Vix must be recalling another moment, a dead body sitting in an armchair, eyes focused on a TV they would never watch again. He wanted to rush to his sister's side and comfort her, but fear had closed his vocal cords and glued his feet to the floor.

Vix was trying to trade Spike's freedom for Juliet's life. But where did that leave Brooklyn and Vix? They should have fled when they had the chance.

The silent air seemed charged with electricity. A storm threatened to overwhelm them.

Brooklyn glanced at both Spike and Juliet, wondering which would blink first.

Neither spoke.

Vix cut through the silence. "Will you do that, Juliet?" she asked. "Say it was you who killed Rufus?"

Juliet nodded. Slowly, each syllable an effort, she said, "Rufus drugged… me. I… fought… back."

"Spike?" Vix pressed.

221

"Okay." From the twisting of his lips, it was obvious Spike had reservations.

"Shake on it?" Vix asked.

He took her hand. "I'm doing it for you, Vix."

"Do it for yourself." Vix began to sob. "You don't want to get mixed up in death, Spike, trust me. Get away. Go as far as you can."

Spike released her hand. With a finger, he wiped the tears from her face.

Brooklyn felt heat rise within him. Had Spike and Vix played him for a fool all along?

"Leave her alone," he barked.

"Okay, mate." Spike stepped back. "No offence meant."

"He was only—" Vix said. "Never mind." She pointed to Juliet's fettered wrists. "Do you have the keys, Spike?"

"No." Spike turned his back on Juliet, bending to retrieve the knife. "I saw where you put this."

He wiped both handle and blade with a towel conveniently lying on the dresser. Pointedly ignoring Brooklyn, he said, "Goodbye, Vix. Don't come looking for me. I'll be gone."

He marched out of the flat. His footsteps resounded on the stairs.

Juliet, glassy-eyed, slumped forward. Could she be saved? If not, it was all for nothing. And they'd have even more explaining to do.

A shiver crept up Brooklyn's spine.

"Ambulance," Vix snapped.

"Yeah." Brooklyn took out his phone and thumbed 999.

Chapter 53

November 2023

Vix

Vix couldn't stop shaking. She'd done it. Spike had gone. She would never see him again. As adrenaline ebbed away, she felt like a hollow, trembling shell of herself. Yet she had to focus. Juliet still wasn't safe. Rufus had made her take sedatives and alcohol. If her stomach didn't get pumped out soon, Juliet would die.

She hardly listened as Brooklyn phoned 999.

"Ambulance, please," she heard him say, then, "Overdose. Come quick."

They were near the hospital, weren't they? It was little more than a mile away. But every minute counted.

Meanwhile, shouldn't Juliet vomit? Vix flashed Brooklyn a filthy look. He was in the process of giving a fake name and address. She wished she'd made him rifle through Rufus's pockets instead. How hard was it to call the emergency services – she could have done that. She wouldn't have had the presence of mind to lie about her identity, though.

She must find the keys for Juliet's cuffs. Vix crouched down by the corpse, trying to avoid getting blood on her clothes. She'd seen a towel, hadn't she?

There it was: on the dresser, with the knife that Spike had wiped free of prints.

Should he have done that?

It was all very well Spike destroying evidence, but wouldn't a clean weapon make the police suspicious?

Somebody's prints needed to be found on it.

They weren't going to be hers.

Rufus's, of course.

Vix used the towel to grab the knife and place the dead man's fingers around the handle. Then she flung the fabric square on the carpet, knelt down on it, and began checking his pockets.

From the jacket, she retrieved only a handkerchief. Next, she tried a trouser pocket, gasping with relief when her fingers touched cold metal. She pulled out a jingling bunch of keys.

Which would open the cuffs? Vix tried the smallest. Her hands quivered as she unlocked Juliet's manacles.

Juliet twitched and whimpered. She stayed on the bed, head bowed.

Vix sucked in her breath. "Juliet, can you hear me?" she asked.

Juliet said nothing. Her eyes flickered.

The first aid course hadn't prepared Vix for this. They told you to phone for help. But what if your patient died before help arrived?

"Juliet, can you throw up?"

There was no answer.

"Juliet!" Vix shook the old woman's shoulders.

No reaction.

Desperately, Vix glanced at Brooklyn.

"Okay, thanks," Brooklyn said, finishing his phone call. "The ambulance is coming."

"How long?" Vix pointed to Juliet. "Get a bowl or something. I'm making her vomit."

"Are you supposed to do that? Ricky said when his mate had an overdose—"

"Sure, Ricky told you. And you're always saying Ricky's a moron." Vix clutched Brooklyn's arm. "I'm scared she'll die."

"Yeah. I know." He pursed his lips. "You can't do more for her. We should go."

Vix's mouth fell open. "Why?"

"I've been thinking. We need to get away, whatever you promised Spike."

Surprise almost froze her to the spot. "Brooks, no. We're witnesses. It was just Juliet and Rufus, remember? Spike wasn't here, and he needs us to say."

Brooklyn grabbed her hand. "It's our only chance, Vix."

She shook herself free. "It's no use. The cops know, don't they – about Nanna Lizzie? Wherever we go, they'll find us. May as well face up to it."

His shoulders slumped and his eyes dulled. "Yeah."

Starting to tear up again, Vix sat next to Juliet. She placed an arm around the old woman's shoulders, shaking her gently. Juliet remained seated, but only just. Her eyes twitched, as if halfway between sleep and wakefulness. At least focusing on her stopped Vix from worrying about herself. A one-way trip to Blackpool was the least of it. Would she and Brooklyn go to prison?

He paced back and forth, as if preparing to bolt.

"Listen," he said.

Footsteps sounded on the staircase.

They grew louder.

Brooklyn's expression darkened. "They're here."

"We'll have to tell them everything, Brooks. About Rufus and Juliet."

"And us. And then what?"

"It'll be okay."

Vix knew it wouldn't be, though.

The first paramedic to arrive, a youth little older than Brooklyn, stopped at the threshold.

"Chris, look but don't come in yet," he said to his colleague, who was out of Vix's line of sight. To Vix and Brooklyn, he said, "Hi, I'm Matthew. I'll just check this fellow's vital signs."

"There aren't any," Brooklyn stated baldly.

"He phoned about Juliet. That man made her take an overdose." Vix realised she was squeaking, her voice unnaturally shrill. "Valium. With alcohol."

She added, "But then Juliet fought him. He tried to kill her, but she's alive. You have to save her."

"When was this?" Matthew asked. He was already down beside Rufus, checking his wrist for a pulse and tilting his chin to open the airway.

"Thirty minutes?" Vix glanced at Brooklyn.

"Yeah," Brooklyn said. "Think so. When she screamed."

"Okay. Me or Chris will be with her in a second." Matthew shone a light in Rufus's sightless eyes.

Couldn't he see it was hopeless? Rufus was already dead, and good riddance.

Finally, Matthew stood up, his face dour. "Nothing I can do for him," he announced.

Tell them something they didn't already know.

"This lady took an overdose, you say?" He went to Juliet's side.

"Valium," Vix said. "Two packets of Valium. Look, here are the empties. And champagne."

There was a commotion in the hallway. A tall policeman, dark-skinned and grey-bearded, strode into the bedroom. His eyes widened.

"Brooklyn? We've been looking for you."

His tone was not unfriendly, nor was it full of delight. Vix's gaze flicked between the pair as Brooklyn stared at the newcomer.

Eventually, Brooklyn said, "Errol. I thought you were on Traffic."

Errol? So this was Marley's dad.

The police officer's mouth quirked up at the corners.

"You thought right, Brooklyn. We were in the nearest car when we got the call. Big bash on in Clifton. Idiots who think they can drink and drive." Errol sighed. "It's their lucky night. So, is there another room in here, where we can sit down? You can tell me what happened."

"There's a lounge," Brooklyn said, as Vix interrupted, "That's Rufus Cameron."

She pointed to the corpse. "He's a sex offender. He broke into Juliet's flat, and drugged her. She fought back, and that's how he got hurt. That's right, isn't it, Juliet?"

"She's not responsive," Matthew said. "I'm taking her in."

"You do that," Errol said. "We'll get out of your way, then I'll secure the scene once you're gone. Brooklyn, would you mind following me, please? And – your name is?"

"Vix. Victoria Barber."

"Little Victoria." Errol smiled. "Come on through."

Vix noticed another paramedic and a female police officer in the hall as they passed. Errol nodded to both of them, as if to say, 'I've got this.'

The policeman switched on the living room light. "Sit yourselves down." He gestured to a sofa, its battered edges sticking out beneath a cream throw.

Vix perched beside Brooklyn, while Errol took an office chair opposite.

"My colleagues will take statements from you later," he said. "I'm afraid it will be a long night for you. Possibly a long day afterwards too. Was anyone else involved in the home invasion?"

Vix shook her head.

"No," Brooklyn said. "We heard Juliet scream. Came up."

"She was fighting that man. Rufus," Vix said. "Fighting for her life."

"He's a piece of work," Errol said unexpectedly. "I remember the case. The boy in the Floating Harbour."

He tutted. "It wasn't just the one boy, either. There will be dozens dancing on his grave. They'll thank that lady for doing them all a favour."

Little did he know. Vix thought of Spike and the Green Man bobbing on the harbour. He'd be gone soon. Like a ghost. A dream. She had a story to tell, and it didn't include him.

She hoped they'd believe her.

The female police officer stuck her head around the door. "Another car's here, Errol. We'll be taking this pair to the station. The DI dealing with the incident in Henleaze has been informed."

Vix chewed her lip. There was no escape.

"Am I in trouble?" Brooklyn asked, Adam's apple wobbling.

Errol's brow furrowed, although his eyes were kind. Vix suspected he was going to give bad news, and he didn't like doing it.

"I can't pretend you're in the clear," Errol said. "It depends what you've done."

Chapter 54

November 2023

Juliet

Juliet ran a damp cloth over the shelves inside Greg's wardrobe, finally emptied of clutter. Yesterday, she'd discovered a few bits of gold jewellery at the back: signet rings, cufflinks and a heavy chain with a tiger medallion. They'd fetched a useful sum at the jewellers in Clifton Village.

Next, she would sell the car. Living this close to the city centre, she didn't need one. Her stay in Cliftonwood had been extended now that fear no longer ruled her life. Not that she was completely free of it. On her release from hospital, she'd begun sleeping on the sofa. She still didn't venture into the bedroom at night. Rufus had died there. She'd nearly been killed. But she was determined to overcome the trauma. Rufus couldn't hurt her anymore.

Simon Heath wasn't buying the flat after all. He'd asked for another price reduction, and she'd told him where to go. Juliet was softening towards Bristol, and there were signs of Bristol softening towards her. Rufus's murderous attack had made the news in a big way. Shirley Wilks, now convinced Juliet was innocent, had done interviews to say so. Juliet should receive a medal for sending Rufus to hell, according to her.

That wasn't all. Strangers had brought flowers to the hospital. When she was discharged, Hugh Wimbush had taken her to lunch. He'd passed on two translation projects from clients. Later, she was meeting a training company he knew. With health and finances on the mend, she had much to be thankful for.

She switched on her laptop, found a radio station and sang along to eighties cheese while she did housework. A loud Chas and Dave song nearly drowned out the buzzer. Juliet jumped, heart racing. Then she remembered. There was nothing to be scared of.

"Yes?" she asked, expecting a delivery for one of the other flats.

"It's Penny. Can I come up?" She sounded self-assured. The old Penny would have giggled nervously, and said 'please'. A lot changed in thirty years.

Penny had stolen her life. Why speak to her at all? But perhaps it was time to leave resentment behind. Look what it had done to Rufus and Damien.

Juliet buzzed her old friend into the building. A soft tread grew louder as Penny ascended the stairs. Of course, Penny was as tall as a man; she'd never risk stilettos.

Opening the door revealed Penny in pristine white trainers, the sort paired with flowery dresses by ladies who lunched in Clifton Village. Penny had chosen a cream trouser suit to go with them.

The sun-kissed blonde hair, sweeping lashes and glossy pink nails must have cost time and money. Juliet stared at her. Penny had remodelled herself to be a wife George could show off. Who would believe the two women were the same age? Penny looked two decades younger.

Penny smiled warmly. Her teeth hadn't been so straight and white before.

"OMG, Jules. After all these years... You seemed to vanish off the face of the earth. I couldn't believe it when I heard Rufus tried to kill you. Are you okay?"

"Getting there." Juliet's voice faltered. With Rufus gone forever, she should be ecstatic. Somehow, life didn't feel peachy yet.

"And you're in Bristol. How come I didn't know?"

"Do you want to come in?" Juliet asked, because Penny showed every sign of staying for a long chat, and it was crazy to have it on a landing. Anyone who passed by would hear them. Not that she'd seen much of her neighbours, apart from Brooklyn and Vix. Even they weren't around anymore.

"I'd love a cup of tea," Penny said. She reached inside a chic ivory handbag with a double C logo. "I brought cookies."

"Hobnobs?" Juliet asked, clocking George's favourite brand.

"Chocolate ones." Penny marched in. "Point me at your kettle. What do you drink these days?"

It took her all of sixty seconds to find the kitchen, choose a mug and start making tea. The Hobnobs were arranged on a plate.

Nostalgia gripped Jules as soon as she bit into one. She recalled George in bed, crunching biscuits to cure a hangover. The crumbs went everywhere.

Hastily, she flicked the vision away. She didn't want to giggle and have to explain.

Penny ignored the plate and sipped from a mug of milkless Earl Grey, made with a teabag she'd brought with her. "Where have you been all this time?"

"Apart from prison, you mean?"

Penny picked up the sharp note. "I wrote to you there."

"I know. And I didn't reply. Sorry."

But she wasn't. Not after seeing George and Penny hold hands in court.

She hadn't blamed George. But Penny?

Juliet savoured her Hobnob, noting how Penny watched hungrily. There was a price to pay for being rich, thin and pretty. It took effort.

"I didn't return to Bristol when I left prison," she said. "I joined a commune. An organic farm."

"It sounds idyllic," Penny said, a dreamy expression on her face. "And what are your plans now? Staying in Bristol?"

"It's looking that way," Juliet said.

"George sends his regards."

Not his love, Juliet noted. Hardly surprising.

"We had a chat about you," Penny said. "He always thought you were good at paperwork—"

"No kidding." Juliet grinned. When they were a couple, she'd done all the administration for George's business. He had no patience for it. With worse problems to occupy her, she hadn't bothered to think how he'd manage once they split up. Presumably he'd paid someone, or maybe Penny had stepped in. She'd taken over everything else, hadn't she?

"I see you've got a laptop," Penny said. "Can you use Sage? Our bookkeeper just left, and I wondered if you might do a spot of temporary work."

Juliet stiffened. "Did you twist George's arm?"

"A bit," Penny admitted. "But he'd like to help you. The past is water under the bridge to him."

A tic played at the corner of Juliet's mouth. She imagined sitting in an office as her ex barked instructions, or greeted her with stony silence. He wasn't one to forgive or forget, whatever his wife said.

"Do you need time to think about it?" Penny pressed.

"Sorry." Juliet scrabbled for a convenient excuse. "I've no experience with Sage. Mainly, I work as a German translator."

"How about tutoring? One or two of my friends have asked me about language tuition."

Of course they would. Penny used to teach French. Not that she'd need the money anymore. George was doubtless pleased to keep her at home, under his thumb.

Penny stretched. "George has clout, Jules. If you need a favour, just ask."

"Thanks, but I'm okay."

Penny nodded, as if she'd expected Juliet's reaction. "Well, I must be off," she said. "James is expecting me round at his place. It's not far from here."

"So I understand." Juliet remembered the canvasser saying he lived around the corner. She sensed her heart thumping as suspicion swept over her. "Is that how you found me?"

"Yes." Penny winced. "It was awkward, I'm not going to lie. We hadn't told the children that George was married before. Then this dreadful business with Rufus was in the news, and James twigged. He said he'd met you through his politics."

If James had given Penny this address, he'd probably told Damien too. The two men were friends, weren't they, and why not? Damien was James's uncle.

And Damien had lured Rufus here. He'd used her.

Penny burbled on. "I can't see James getting anywhere with the Conservatives, whatever George says. One of these days, he'll switch to the Greens, I expect. Damien's been pestering him."

Talk of the devil.

Penny must have noticed the suppressed frown. "Damien bears you no ill will. It's a shame you won't get to see him. He's sailed off into the sunset. Did you know he had a boat?"

No, she didn't, and nor was she aware that Damien had let go of the past. He'd agreed to spare her only to save his own skin. That was what had happened, wasn't it? But she'd recounted a different version of events so often, she almost believed it.

Penny read Juliet's silence as interest. "Yes," she said, "one of those barges people live on. I pulled strings to get him a mooring in Bristol. George jibbed at it, but I'll drag him into the twenty-first century if it's the last thing I do. I mean, snubbing your own brother because he's gay – how mad is that? Damien is family, and that's everything. My children have a right to know him."

George's personality clearly hadn't improved. Perhaps it was a blessing their marriage had ended when it did. Penny was welcome to him. Kudos to her for working out how to manage her husband. The mouse had turned into a lioness.

Penny checked her watch, a fancy digital gadget. "I'd better go. But let's stay in touch. I'd love to catch up properly, find out more about organic farming."

That wouldn't take long. She hoped Penny was just being polite.

"Give me your number, then," Penny said. "And let me know if there's anything George and I can do for you."

"Okay." Juliet was polite too, because why spoil the moment? She wasn't ready to have Penny as a friend again, though. And while one day she might be, she'd definitely avoid George.

"Sure?" Penny asked.

"Absolutely." Juliet faked sincerity with a breezy smile. "Well, I have to dash to a meeting with my solicitor. I'll leave the building with you."

"Not bad news, I hope? I mean, you had witnesses, didn't you?"

Juliet gawped at her.

Penny's wide, long-lashed eyes indicated nothing worse than concern. She wasn't casting aspersions.

"Nothing to do with Rufus. And yes, there were witnesses." She shuddered, disquiet nagging her. The downstairs flat remained shuttered and mute. Brooklyn and Vix hadn't come back, and that could only mean one thing. "Penny – about them – the witnesses?"

Penny raised an eyebrow. "Yes?"

Juliet blurted out the words. "They're young people, and I think they're in some sort of trouble. But they don't deserve to be."

She tried to recall what the policeman had said to them, dredging up fragments of overheard conversation. He knew the boy, Brooklyn, and seemed to like him. She remembered that. So much had been blurred by her nightmarish, drugged state.

Penny's gaze flicked to her watch.

"They're good kids," Juliet said. "You said George had influence? Find out what's going on with them. Please. See if you can help. They saved my life."

"I'll do my best," Penny promised.

Chapter 55

November 2023

Brooklyn

"Cheer up, mate. It may never happen," Keith said.

Brooklyn glared at his balding, overweight cellmate. What did he know? "Worried about my sister," he said stiffly.

"She'll be all right," Keith said. He nodded for emphasis, chin wobbling. "The girls get looked after. Not like you and me, lad. It's the Wild West in 'ere."

"Yeah," Brooklyn said, although his memories of the movies were nothing like Bristol Prison. Cowboys didn't ride the range here, firing guns and retreating to smoky bars with beautiful women. There was no colour and life. He shared a tiny box with Keith, its white walls scuffed and faded to grey. The lino was a darker shade of it, while the sky, glimpsed through a barred window, was often the same.

They spent most of their time watching TV. After six days, Brooklyn was already bored. He wished he was back at work, using his skills and being busy. Simon Heath probably missed yelling at him too. To be fair to the gaffer, he'd offered to put up bail, but the magistrate wouldn't give it.

In the rest of the premises, doors slammed, keys rattled and men shouted. Often, they used the same meaningless words over and over again. Occasionally, you were allowed out for ten minutes. Brooklyn never had any trouble because, Keith said, Ricky Tamm had put the word out. That was just as well, because Brooklyn was involved in the death of an old lady, and most cons loved their grandmothers.

Ricky had a lot of friends inside, Keith being one of them. No doubt Ricky would expect a favour in return for his protection. Then again, he must be relieved that Brooklyn hadn't let him use the garage. There was no way the police wouldn't have searched it by now.

A key turned in the lock. The door swung open.

"Brooklyn? You've got a visitor." Tony, one of the guards, stood at the threshold.

"Who?"

"Solicitor."

"Dev Singh, yeah?" Keith said, not receiving a response.

He added, "Might be your lucky day. I've told you, he's all right as briefs go."

Brooklyn didn't share his optimism. He looked down at his feet, letting Tony escort him through landings, corridors and locked gates. They ended up in a room similar to his cell. The same chipped paintwork, barred window and gloomy atmosphere greeted him. Only the furniture was different: a plasticky table and two chairs.

Dev Singh stood up to shake Brooklyn's hand. His thin frame lengthened by a sharp suit, the young lawyer smelled of aftershave. Brooklyn was painfully aware that he hadn't showered since Sunday.

Dev nodded to Tony.

"I'll wait outside," the warder said.

"Going to sit down, Brooklyn?" Dev said, when Tony had left. "How are you?"

Brooklyn shrugged, slipping into the chair opposite his lawyer.

"Well, I've got good news." Dev smiled.

"Is it about Vix?"

"Not exactly. But your sister's being treated well, I believe. In a secure facility near Bristol."

At least it wasn't the other end of the country. It might as well have been, though. Banged up in jail, he couldn't visit her.

"I came to see you about something else," Dev said. "The police are dropping the murder charge. They've discovered your carer died from natural causes, as you said all along. They accept your account is truthful."

"Whoa." The heaviness in Brooklyn's limbs eased. Suddenly giddy, he took a deep breath.

"They're not dropping the other charge yet. Preventing a lawful burial. But I'm reapplying for bail, and they won't oppose it. Your employer is keen to see you back at work, I understand. We should be able to get you out tomorrow."

"Awesome." He'd better not tell Keith. It might upset him, as Keith was looking at a five-year stretch for possessing a gun.

He shuddered. That gun could have been in Nanna Lizzie's garage.

"Thought you'd be pleased," Dev said.

"What about Vix?" Brooklyn asked. "Now they know we didn't kill anyone, can she come back to stay with me?"

"I'm working on that. Your neighbour, Juliet Price, offered accommodation—"

"Um, her flat's too small," Brooklyn said.

"Victoria can't stay there anyway. Juliet Price is a sex offender in the eyes of the law, even though there's doubt about her conviction."

"I don't think she did it," Brooklyn said. He no longer believed she was mad either. Her paranoia had turned out to be entirely justified.

"Still. She wouldn't be allowed to look after your sister. It's likely Victoria could live with you if we can get all charges dropped. I'm working on that too."

Dev paused.

"No promises. But a little bird tells me it will happen."

Chapter 56

May 2024

Juliet

Juliet stepped off the bus beside a brown brick sixties building. The café's shutters were just coming down. Beside it, the phone repairers had already closed for the day. Only the off-licence boasted a neon OPEN sign. On the edge of Bristol, the suburban shopping parade didn't attract tourists like Clifton Village. There were no chic boutiques and bars here, but it was quiet and more affordable.

She walked at a brisk pace to the end of the row, feet swivelling around into an alleyway. Two doors, painted black and decorated with mouldings and brass letterboxes, sat side by side. She pressed a doorbell, the digital sort that sent images to the owner's phone. These days, she had one herself. Brooklyn had helped her install it.

She was buzzed in and ascended a steep, straight staircase covered in no-nonsense vinyl. Vix stood at the top.

"Cup of tea? I could use a break from homework." Vix was still short and fragile-looking in her school uniform.

Juliet nodded. "Tea would be nice. Don't let me stop you working, though. I expect Brooklyn is keen to get our lesson out of the way."

She followed Vix to the lounge, a dinky room cramped even more by the kitchen units along one wall.

"Brooks," Vix yelled, filling a kettle.

He emerged from his bedroom, which Juliet knew to be hardly bigger than the single mattress within it. "How's things, Jules?"

"Good. You?"

He smiled, joy crinkling his eyes. "My Universal Credit's all sorted out. I can pay you back."

"That's a relief."

She might even use the money to go on holiday abroad, her first for three decades. Best not to mention it to Brooklyn and Vix. They were bearing up, but although she'd helped Brooklyn apply for benefits, the pair weren't awash with cash. Brooklyn had been turned down for a foster care allowance. It seemed the state was keen to make savings now Elizabeth Novak was dead.

She'd died of natural causes – a massive stroke – but then they'd put her body in the freezer. It was the kind of scenario you read about in the

236

papers, a situation where your point of view depended entirely on what you were allowed to know. So it would be easy to infer a dark motive for Brooklyn to cover up Elizabeth Novak's death. For instance, suppose Brooklyn and his sister were murderers?

Suppose a promising teacher had pimped out her young brother-in-law to a paedophile?

A journalist, or a jury, or the proverbial man on the Clapham omnibus might believe it. That didn't make it true.

The policeman, Errol, had visited for a heart-to-heart. Bad things happened to good people, Errol told her. Good people sometimes did bad things. Brooklyn and Vix had panicked when Elizabeth Novak died. They were afraid the authorities would split them up. He, Errol, would do his utmost to bring them back together. Not only that, but in his opinion, the only offence they'd committed was preventing a lawful burial. He didn't believe it was in the public interest to pursue charges.

As a humble traffic cop, Errol couldn't make that call. Luckily, his superiors agreed in the end. The CPS decided not to prosecute. Juliet had no idea if George had used his influence. Probably not. Why would the CPS listen to him?

Their paths hadn't crossed. She liked it that way. Penny had agreed to go for coffee without telling him. The biggest change to Juliet's life, though, was seeing Brooklyn twice a week.

He and Vix had returned briefly to the flat in Aldworth Terrace. When Simon Heath's client sold it, they'd moved into this tiny, shabby apartment. It had one big advantage: Brooklyn could afford the rent.

Flush from selling Greg's car, Juliet had lent him the deposit. To her surprise, he'd agreed to meet regularly too.

Vix, having made the tea, took hers to a corner of the lounge. She sat on a floor cushion, balancing a laptop on her knees.

Juliet removed a comic book from her backpack. "'Watchmen'," she said to Brooklyn. "It's kind of science fiction. Want to give it a go?"

"Might be interesting." As usual, he unfolded a table, setting it in front of the two-seater sofa. She sat next to him, observing Brooklyn's concentration as he began to read aloud. His technique was improving; he no longer traced the words with his finger.

After ten minutes, she told him to take a break. His tea would get cold. They sipped their drinks together. Next time, she suggested, she would bring a story printed in a special font. It was called Lexend, and it had been designed for easy reading. What did he think of that?

"Yeah," Brooklyn said. "Try anything once. Guess what? The other day, I went to the library. They have these Quick Reads. I read a whole book and I enjoyed it."

"Well done. That's wonderful." Juliet recalled her teaching days, when it seemed extracting homework from pupils was harder than pulling teeth. If only her students had shown Brooklyn's enthusiasm.

"I like this story too. Let's start again." Although he hadn't used a bookmark, Brooklyn flicked quickly to the correct page. Maybe the illustrations helped him find it. "By the way, Jules, do you want to stay for a meal? It's my turn to cook."

"I'd love to. Are you a dab hand in the kitchen, then?"

Vix snorted. "He's not. We're having spag bol. Quorn mince from a packet. Sauce from a jar. His only challenge is not burning the pasta."

"Better than Pot Noodle," Brooklyn protested. "Yeah, I thought I'd better learn. Vix will be off to uni one day."

"Like your friend, Marley. She's going next year, isn't she?"

"Yeah." Brooklyn's mouth clamped shut. The sparkle in his eyes dimmed.

Of course, he expected everyone to leave him. It was all he'd ever known. Juliet flashed him a sympathetic smile.

"Cheer up," she said. "It's not for ages yet. Anyway, they'll both come home in the holidays."

Maybe they would, maybe they wouldn't. He was barely twenty; he had a whole life ahead in which to achieve his goals and fall in and out of love. She knew that even if Brooklyn didn't. But she'd say nothing, because when did the young ever listen?

"How about another cuppa?" she asked. "I'll be mother."

She stood up, stretched, and switched on the kettle. It was full of limescale. She'd have to show them how to get rid of it.

Brooklyn waited patiently, an expectant look on his face as he glanced at the comic book. Juliet turned away, making a show of dealing with the teabags as she blinked out an unwanted tear.

That was something else he didn't know. Whatever anyone else intended, she wouldn't desert Brooklyn or Vix. She'd be around for them as long as they wanted. Because Penny was right. Family meant everything. And they were family now.

ooo0ooo

He stole her childhood. Can she escape before he takes her life?

BRIGHT LIES is AA Abbott's darkest psychological thriller. Look inside to start reading:

https://mybook.to/BrightLiesPaperback

ooo0ooo

AA Abbott has also written other psychological thrillers and the **Trail series** of thrillers, a lighter read sizzling with suspense and family drama. Take a look at the first book in the series, **THE BRIDE'S TRAIL. Shady friends and sinister secrets. When a shy graduate finds herself framed, can she survive long enough to clear her name?**

https://mybook.to/TheBridesTrailPback

Visit AA Abbott's website to find out more, and sign up for her newsletter to receive a free ebook of short stories, news and offers.

https://aaabbott.co.uk

ooo0ooo

Did you enjoy **RUN FOR YOUR LIES?** Help other readers find their next psychological thriller – review this book on Amazon and Goodreads.

oooOooo

ABOUT THE AUTHOR

British author AA Abbott, also known as Helen, writes suspense thrillers about women who find strength when they're facing deadly danger. Like Jenna Wyatt, she lives in a 19th century house in Bristol. She's also lived and worked in London and Birmingham, so all three cities feature in her intelligent and pacy novels.

While Helen is not dyslexic, many of her family are, which is why she is especially keen to make her books accessible. All of them are available in dyslexia-friendly large print as well as standard ebook and paperback editions. BRIGHT LIES is also available as an audiobook, recorded by award-winning voice actor Eilidh Beaton.

Find out more on Helen's website **https://aaabbott.co.uk/,**
Facebook **https://www.facebook.com/AAAbbottStories/,**
Instagram **https://www.instagram.com/aaabbottstories/,**
Threads **https://www.threads.net/@aaabbottstories,**
and Twitter **https://www.twitter.com/AAAbbottStories.**

oooOooo

BOOKS BY A.A. ABBOTT

Up In Smoke

After The Interview

The Bride's Trail

The Vodka Trail

The Grass Trail

The Revenge Trail

The Final Trail

Bright Lies

Lies at Her Door

Flat White Lies

Run For Your Lies

All books are available in ebook, standard paperback and large print (super-easy to read). RUN FOR YOUR LIES and other books are also available in hardback and BRIGHT LIES is available in audiobook.

oooOooo

ABOUT BRIGHT LIES, AA ABBOTT'S DARKEST THRILLER

He stole her childhood. Can she escape before he takes her life?

Emily longs to be an artist. Her dream comes true when her new stepfather, a rich painter, begins mentoring her. But she's shocked to discover his dark side, and fear sends her fleeing his fancy home.

After facing further danger in a night on the streets, Emily accepts shelter in a squat. Building a future as an artist, she's terrified to learn her stepfather has turned to the media to hunt her down. Can she survive betrayal by her new friends and escape a killer's revenge?

If you enjoy nail-biting suspense, slow-burning secrets and dark domestic noir, you'll love AA Abbott's chilling psychological thriller.

Read BRIGHT LIES today and stay by Emily's side as she runs for her life!

https://mybook.to/BrightLiesPaperback

ooo0ooo

Printed in Great Britain
by Amazon